I0751145

Goose Island
CURE

Other Books By G.R.Kinra

Goose Island Chill
Goose Island Black Jack

≈≈≈≈≈≈

Goose Island Cure is the third book in the Goose Island series featuring Kate Houlihan's crime-solving skills, passion and love for the Texas Gulf Coast.

≈≈≈≈≈≈

Goose Island CURE

A Kate Houlihan Mystery

G.R.KINRA

GOOSE ISLAND CURE

ISBN: 978-0-9913213-1-5

∼∼∼∼∼∼

This is a work of fiction. All of the characters, organizations and events portrayed in this novel are either a product of the author's imagination or are used fictitiously. The characters and events described herein are imaginary and are not intended to refer to specific places or living persons.

∼∼∼∼∼∼

Published in the United States of America, May 2021.
G.R. Kinra, PO Box 863462, Plano TX 75086.

∼∼∼∼∼∼

∼∼∼∼∼∼

Goose Island Cure is dedicated to my spouse, the love of my life, the person I waited my whole life to meet. My inspiration, my muse, the perfect companion with whom I share every minute, every day, even when we are sometimes apart - chasing our demons and following our dreams.

~~~~~~
~~~~~~

When you sail alone on the ocean at night,
May a blanket of stars surround you.
May you always have the courage and will to fight,
Following seas and fair winds behind you.

≈≈≈≈≈≈

Contents

1. Splash

Kate Houlihan basked in a tropical dreamscape of golden, sand covered beaches with palm trees swaying in the breeze. She had a fruity rum infused concoction with a small, decorative paper umbrella in the glass next to her beach chair that sank a wee bit lower in the sand with each new wave that washed ashore. The ebb and flow of the water from the tide swirled lazily around her toes. The warmth of the sunshine on her skin felt wonderful.

A gorgeous hunk of a surfer floated effortlessly towards the shore, tumbled into the waves and then reappeared in the shallow water just in front of her chair. She had not recognized him at first because the sun was in her eyes. However, as he approached her pulse quickened and her knees grew weak as she fell sideways out of her beach chair. It was her friend Ray Looney, the only person in the world who could make her heart race just by the way he looked at her. She blew him a kiss as he walked up the beach towards her to help her up.

GOOSE ISLAND CURE

Kate's idyllic reverie was rudely interrupted by the sudden crash of thunder outside her window. The surfer with the body by Michelangelo, who had just started spreading sun tan lotion on her back, vanished in a wisp of smoke. She opened her eyes just in time to see a bolt of lightning arc through the sky. It was raining heavily, and she could hear a dog barking in the distance. The impressive display of lightning and thunder left no doubt as to who was in charge. She found herself counting the seconds between the flash of lightning and the sound of the thunder. One Mississippi, two Mississippi, three Mississippi, BOOM. That put her at a safe distance, at least a half mile from the lightning. Any closer and she might need to look for a new home at daybreak.

Kate slept fitfully for the next hour. The sound of the falling rain was interspersed with the sounds of all the other things that go bump in the night.

The rum infused drinks from her dreams had left her feeling as dry and parched as an armadillo who has travelled clear across the southern half of the State for a chance to swim in the cool, clear water of the Texas Gulf Coast. Hunkered down in the shade of a palm tree at Mustang Beach and waiting for the sun to go down before making one final dash across the sandy beach to the water.

Kate lay in bed and stared at the ceiling until her thirst got the better of her. She arose and walked down the stairs from her bedroom to the kitchen for a glass of water. She almost tripped on the last step to avoid a small child playing with a little yellow toy car in the hallway leading to the kitchen.

"Oops!" she said. "Sorry!" As she took a few more steps towards the kitchen it occurred to here that there were no children in her house, that she knew of. She turned around to look at the stairway behind her. There was nobody behind her. She opened her eyes wide and looked again. There was still no one there. No little boy. No matchbox-sized yellow car in the hallway. The hair on the nape of her neck stood upright all at once, to have a look at the stairs for themselves.

Of course, there was nothing in sight. Kate did not have any small children staying in her house. Rationale dictated that she had just imagined seeing a child on the stairway. However, she did have a vivid imagination, and it was a little unnerving each time she happened to see something that wasn't there.

Kate said a few "Hail Mary" prayers just in case. The fact was that her house on Marlin Street had been built more than a century earlier. It had been home for any number of previous owners and their families, and who knew what secrets lay hidden beneath its eaves.

She drank a few sips of water in the kitchen. Then she placed a small plate of cookies on a footstool next to the refrigerator for the little boy, or the leprechauns who may be hanging around inside her house. One of these days she would have to build a leprechaun trap. She could always use a pot of gold from a benevolent stranger.

She carried the glass of water carefully back to her room. She walked slowly down the hallway, half expecting to see a small child playing near the stairs. There was no one in sight. The stairs creaked as she went up to her room. Kate heard a small giggle behind her when she reached the last step at the top of the stairs. There was a Celtic Cross on the wall at the top of the stairs. Kate crossed her heart as she walked past it quietly over to her bedroom, without turning to look behind her.

She lit the candle with a picture of the Blessed Virgin Mary, 'Our Lady of Guadalupe', on the outside of a glass tumbler. She gazed at the picture of the Virgin Mary glowing on the candle and she felt an immense sense of peace permeating the room and casting its warm glow over the entire house.

Kate said another "Hail Mary" and lay down to go to sleep. She blew out the candle and closed her eyes. As her eyes adjusted to the darkness she felt the presence of an angelic figure float into the room and stand directly above her. Her heart began to race uncontrollably. She could sense the angel directly above her, looking at her sternly.

"He's only a little boy! He doesn't mean any harm," said the angel.

"I know," Kate said silently, never once opening her eyes. "I'm sorry," she said to the angel. She kept her eyes closed and felt an eerie quiet fill the room. At that moment, it would have been nice to have had her soul mate Ray Looney in bed next to her. Even though he would have been fast asleep, she could have held his hand and given him a hug and a kiss to make everything feel better for herself.

When they had first met, Kate and Ray would spend hours with each other, walking on the beach, watching the sunset, holding hands and talking about anything and everything. Hours that always ended with the most incredible kisses that she would remember vividly for the rest of her life.

The ocean breeze blew into her room through the open window. In the distance she could hear the relentless sound of the ocean and seagulls foraging for food.

Kate drifted off to sleep and imagined herself walking along the shore in the twilight just before dawn. She felt a pudgy little hand grasp hers as she walked along the beach, splashing through the surf at the edge of the water, looking for Michelangelo.

* * *

When she awoke it was light outside. The rain had stopped falling sometime during the night. It was time to attend to the joys of owning and operating the Goose Island Bed and Breakfast. She hurried downstairs to the kitchen to prepare some coffee for her guests, a couple of snowbirds who had just checked into the B&B earlier that week. When her B&B guests stumbled into the dining area of her establishment later that morning, they would be greeted with the welcoming aroma of freshly brewed coffee. The dining area would include fresh fruit, yogurt, orange juice, home-baked bread, blueberry muffins and other delectable food items to help them jump-start their day.

Kate's best friend, Shirley Winters owned the Goose Island Bakery, one of the oldest business establishments on the island. It was in the Goose Island Town Square about a mile from the B&B. The Bakery had been started by Shirley's parents, Bridget and Sean. They had retired a few years ago and left her in charge of the Bakery. She had perfected the recipes she had received from her mother and expanded the operation to include additional snacks and sandwiches. Shirley had shared her recipes with Kate to the benefit of everyone who stayed at the B&B.

Kate's B&B guests included the Caseys, from Minnesota. Kevin Casey, a retired accountant and his wife Karen were spending a month at Goose Island. For the first two days since they had arrived they had spent most of the day basking in the warmth of Kate's back porch. Karen liked to read and watch the steady flow of birds who frequented Kate's back-yard fountain for a quick sip of water before they continued their journey South. Kevin and Karen enjoyed the short walk to Shipwreck Beach, and the Goose Island Town Square, which met most of their needs with its corner grocery store, bakery, post office, bank, and restaurants.

* * *

Goose Island is a small, peaceful, coastal community on the Texas Gulf Coast. A place where you could not help knowing everyone you passed on the street during the daytime, or on Shipwreck Beach in the evening. The Goose Island Sherriff, Troy, made sure everyone always obeyed the law. Goose Island was the kind of place where nothing exciting ever happens. Unless you include all the times when Olga the County Clerk visited the Goose Island Beauty Parlor to dye her hair and paint her nails in a new color to match her latest outfit.

Kate had launched her fledgling B&B business from her home at 121 Marlin Ave. a few years ago. She had received an abundance of support from Ray, her friends Shirley and Troy, and neighbors Charlotte and Jerry.

The guys had helped transform her large four-bedroom home into the Goose Island B&B. They had helped to landscape the garden, remodel the patio, replace doors and windows, hang curtains, and install window air-conditioner units throughout the house.

Shirley and Charlotte had helped select the curtains, linens, towels and all the accessories that had helped to decorate the house. The girls had gone shopping to local Antique Malls, garage sales and found the nautical bric-a-brac that gave the Goose Island B&B its welcoming feel from the minute you stepped inside the front door.

Shirley had shared some of her baking secrets, and Charlotte had contributed some of her most treasured recipes that had been passed down to her from her grandmother.

Kate loved her job at the B&B despite the long hours and hard work that went into making sure everyone who stayed with her was well cared for, and everything always functioned as intended. Towels and linens were changed routinely, restrooms were cleaned, the floor was swept, the water in the pool was always crystal clear and free of leaves, the bird feeder always had birdseed in it, the flower beds were always free of weeds, telephone messages were answered quickly, breakfast was always served promptly at 7:00 am each morning, and a million other things were attended to each and every day.

The Goose Island B&B had succeeded thanks to Kate's attention to detail and because it provided an essential service in an area where there were virtually no other hotels or motels nearby. The closest hotels in the area were in Port Aransas, or Rockport. Excellent customer endorsements and repeat customer business was the key to the success of the B&B.

* * *

It rained intermittently all day. By late afternoon, the rain had dissipated into a fine mist as a cloudy, grey, humid day settled down upon Goose Island. Thanks to the ozone released during the storm, everything smelled clean, fresh and invigorating. A smidgeon of sunlight finally crept out from behind the clouds by mid-afternoon. Kate called her friend Shirley on her cell phone to ask if she wanted to go down to Shipwreck Beach to look for any sea glass that may have blown in during the storm.

Shirley was watching her favorite soap opera on TV when Kate had called. She had little or no interest in sea-glass. It took her an effort to tear herself away from her favorite show, get up from the chair, and answer the phone before it rolled over to voice mail. In retrospect, she would probably have preferred to let it roll over to voice mail.

"Are you out of your cotton-picking mind," Shirley remarked. "Isn't it raining?" she asked.

"Not anymore," Kate replied. "The sun's out," she added. "Good things come to those who sweat, remember?"

"I think you have that all wrong," Shirley said. "We should 'wait' for the weather to improve. There are a lot of dark clouds in the sky. It looks very gray and depressing to me."

However, Kate was relentless. She reminded Shirley that their New Year resolutions involved getting more exercise. The New Year resolutions they had set for themselves just a few short weeks ago were starting to become a bit of a nuisance. Shirley agreed reluctantly to Kate's request to go for a walk. That's what friends are for! She put on her sneakers and turned off the TV. As she stepped out to meet Kate she knew that she would be not be able to learn what the star of the TV series she was watching, was going to get his wife for her birthday.

* * *

Kate drove over to Shirley's apartment to pick her up. She waited in the parking lot beside a statue of a ginormous conch shell. Shirley hopped into the passenger seat beside her and they drove to Shipwreck Beach and parked at one of the beachfront entrances.

They could hear a low rumble of thunder in the distance as they made their way to the shore. The sunshine that Kate had seen earlier that afternoon had retreated behind a cloud. Last night's storm was threatening to return. However, the weather was decent and at least there was no rain at the moment.

Kate kept one eye over the water in the Gulf as she walked barefoot down a lonely stretch of Shipwreck Beach. Their footprints trailed fleetingly behind them in the sand until they were washed away by the incoming tide.

"Nice day for a walk," Kate said cheerfully. She paused to bend down and pick up a small object from the sand to see if it was made of glass. It wasn't glass. Just an odd colored shell. Kate picked it up and placed it in her pocket.

"Are you kidding me" Shirley said. "I'd much rather be home where it's nice and warm." Shirley replied. "And dry," she added. "It looks like it is going to rain again. Maybe we should go home and come back when the weather improves." She was still thinking about the soap opera that she had been watching when Kate had called. She wanted to find out how it ended.

"It's not raining Shirley," Kate replied. "It's just a small patch of fog. Put your big girl shorts on and deal with it. Besides we're not going to let a little rain stop us, are we?"

"Right," Shirley said. "I'm just not sure how I let myself get talked into this," Shirley muttered under her breath.

"Actually, it's pretty good to be here today," Kate replied, trying to put a positive spin on things. She had heard every word Shirley said and knew exactly what she was thinking. "It's nice and cool. It looks just like this in Ireland."

Kate had just returned to Goose Island from a short vacation to Galway with her 'fella' Ray. Her thoughts returned to the time they had spent together at a small private inn near the beach on Coral Strand. Everything had been so perfect. The week they had spent on vacation together had vanished far too quickly. She felt an emptiness in her heart whenever Ray was away.

The invisible thread that connected him to her was so strong that she could feel him beside her, even when he was not around. It made her smile just thinking about him making coffee in the morning, dressed in the super hero boxers she had given him for Christmas; mowing the lawn in the afternoon, shirtless of course; or doing the laundry just after he had finished mowing. He would have put his clothes into the washing machine before stepping into the shower wearing nothing but the ring she had placed on his finger.

"Send me the pillow that you dream on," Kate whispered to herself. She just had to close her eyes to picture him making the bed, ironing his shirts, taking out the trash; and doing a million mundane things that became exciting and amazing just because he was the one doing them.

Ray worked for an oil company in Odessa and was only able to visit on weekends. She would have to call him when she went back home to see if he needed a ride from the airport. She missed him and wanted very much for him to come over to visit her soon. She wished Ray could be there to make dinner plans with her, or any other plans for that matter. However, that would have to wait for just one more day. It was

Thursday and he would be in her arms by this time tomorrow.

"I've never been to Ireland," Shirley said. "I like it just fine when everything here looks like Texas. Let's just leave 'Danny Boy' out of this. If you start singing you might scare away the seagulls, Sis. It will sound as if someone just died. Let's just get this evening walk over with, shall we."

Kate laughed. The girls continued down the beach in silence. The only sound was the screech of an occasional seagull and the surf. The evening stroll provided Kate with a welcome break from the responsibilities and chores she had to finish before retiring for the night. When she returned home, she was scheduled to host a wine and cheese hour with her guests, a special time together for everyone staying at the Goose Island B&B. Later that evening she would have to clean-up and get ready for the next day's business. It would never do for her guests to find dirty dishes in the kitchen if they went in there for a midnight snack while she was asleep.

Kate had a full plate on her hands between keeping up with the operational aspects of her business and her volunteer work at the Goose Island Marine Rescue working with rescue seals and dolphins. Kate loved helping to feed and take care of the rescue dolphins and seals at the Goose Island Marine Rescue. She loved it when they leaped out of the water at feeding time. Dolphins and seals are very intelligent and friendly species who rely on the ocean and other marine ecosystems for their survival. They are mammals who breathe through their lungs, making frequent trips to the surface to catch a breath. The most rewarding part of the care that was provided by the Goose Island Marine Rescue Team was when they were finally able to release the animals back into their natural habitat.

* * *

Shirley Winters had been at work since five in the morning at the Goose Island Bakery. She had baked cookies, muffins, prepared wraps, sandwiches, served customers, cleaned tables, and washed dishes from early in the morning until she had closed for the day at 2:00 pm.

The high point of Shirley's day had come when she had sold out of her signature, blueberry lemon muffins before 10:30 am, which was a new record for the bakery. Her secret ingredient, Jamaican Rum, provided the special flavor that her customers tasted with every bite. The trick was in knowing how much rum to add to the recipe without ruining it.

GOOSE ISLAND CURE

It was just past low tide and Shirley's poor aching feet complained each time she stepped out of the way to dodge the incoming surf. She was tired and soldiered along desperately as she strove to keep up with Kate. Her hips swayed with each step so that she resembled alternately, the girl from Ipanema and GI-Jane. Shirley wanted nothing better than to go home, park her posterior in her favorite chair, sip on a cold bottle of Guinness Lager, put her feet up on the ottoman in her living room and watch her favorite TV show.

A nice foot massage from her fiancée, Troy, would be nice. However, she knew that Troy, the Goose Island Sherriff, did not get off duty until later that night and so she probably would not see him again that evening. It was nice to see him every day, but she was torn between being too easy and playing hard-to-get. They had not set a date for their wedding yet, but both Shirley and Troy had agreed that it would be sometime this year.

"I was just thinking," Kate said.

"About?" Shirley asked, after waiting for Kate to continue.

"Would you be interested in taking a class on kick boxing?" Kate said, finally.

"No!" Shirley replied vehemently. "Not a chance, Kate."

Shirley was tired of her New Year Resolutions and was getting ready to tell Kate that it was time to make a few adjustments. Walking on sand is not as simple as a walk in the park. You must take your time and allow the sand to squish up between your toes to enjoy the experience. Walking at the torrid pace Kate set, just to burn off calories, took all the fun out of being on the beach. In Shirley's opinion, it would be a good thing to skip the beach-walk altogether and turn it back into a recreational activity to be pursued at one's discretion.

However, Kate showed no sign of slowing down. She was a real drillmaster and there was always the risk that she might want to add a few more miles to their daily dose of sand torture. Shirley was starting to fall so far behind Kate that she did not have the energy to yell loud enough to get Kate's attention. Kate forged ahead, marching along like a woman on a mission. All she needed was a bone necklace, one-piece loincloth, a razor-sharp lance in her left hand, war-paint on her face and a full moon to go spear fishing for her evening meal on the Amazon river.

The girls hurried on along the beach. They had started from the rocky outgrowth at one end of the beach and were walking steadily towards the new fishing pier at the other end of the beach. The Copano Bay bridge was visible in the distance.

The girls turned around just before reaching the fishing pier. It was getting late and they wanted to return home before dark. As they turned, Kate heard a strange ghostly shriek behind her. She whirled around not sure what to expect, but there was no one in sight.

≈≈≈≈≈≈

2. Myrtle

The fishing pier was a blot on the landscape, stretching on and on for almost two football fields into the Gulf. The neon signs at the end of the pier shone garishly in the waning light of the day to advertise the availability of food, drink and good times for all who cared to dine there. It was a complete eyesore, but one had to admit that it had improved the local economy.

It did not seem to matter whether the fishing was good, bad, or indifferent. All the anglers stopped by the Goose Island Bakery in the morning for a fresh cup of Joe and a blueberry lemon muffin.

"Did you hear that?" Kate asked her friend.

"Hear what?" Shirley replied, stopping to look at Kate.

The girls paused to look around the beach could not see anyone nearby. The only sound was the waves lapping at the shore and the occasional seagull in the distance. The fog had turned into a fine mist. Shirley had been right. This was no day for a walk in the park.

"Never mind," Kate said. "I'm not sure what I heard. It was probably just a seagull."

However, there was another unmistakable shriek. It sounded strangely human. Both Kate and Shirley stopped dead in their tracks. They heard a loud splash in the water near them. As they turned toward the ocean, they saw a shadowy figure in the Gulf a short distance from the shore. The splashing continued, and Kate felt a cold chill course through her veins.

"I'm not sure what's going on," Kate said. "Something is churning up the water pretty fiercely."

"Oh dear," Shirley said. "It sounds as if someone getting attacked by a shark!"

The churning continued and then suddenly the splashing sound stopped and there were several more shrieks.

"Maybe we better leave," Shirley said. "I don't have a good feeling about this."

"Hold that thought," Kate said. She scanned the water in front of her quickly, trying to determine where the sound was coming from. There was a lot of activity in the water a short distance from the shoreline. "It looks like it's a school of dolphins!" Kate exclaimed.

"Oh Wow! Would you look at that?" Shirley exclaimed. There at least a dozen dolphins cavorting around in the water. Intermittently, one or two of the dolphins would rise out of the water, their shadowy figures barely visible in the fog. A couple of the dolphins blew a plume of water into the air with the blowholes.

"I don't think we need to worry about sharks," Kate said. "Sharks are rarely seen around dolphins."

"Why is that?" Shirley asked.

"Well for one thing sharks are solitary predators, whereas dolphins travel in pods," Kate said. "Hey, I think these dolphins are trying to tell us something,"

"Whatever are they doing?" Shirley wanted to know.

The dolphins cruised effortlessly in a rhythmic motion through the water. However, there was something else in the water with them. A couple of the dolphins were pushing a small object through the water with their noses. Kate waded gingerly into the water for a few feet to get a closer look.

"Do be careful, Kate!" Shirley admonished.

"I will," Kate said, as she continued into the surf. "Another reason sharks avoid dolphins is because dolphins are smarter and more flexible, and they can outmaneuver a shark in a dogfight."

By now, Kate was at least a dozen yards from the shore. She was waist deep in the water and the sand had started to drop away from the shore. She continued, for a few more yards and felt the water getting deeper around her. Then throwing caution to the winds she dove headlong into the water.

Kate was a good swimmer and she paddled over towards the dolphins. Perhaps there was an injured dolphin in the water, who needed assistance. One of the dolphins raised its head out of the water as she approached and made a trilling "ee ee ee" sound as she approached. Kate caught a glimpse of the object that the dolphins were nudging carefully in her direction. She wondered if one of the dolphins had gotten entangled in a discarded ghost fishing net. There were a lot of shrimp boats in the area near Copano Bay. The Gulf was full of fishing debris that was a constant hazard to the fish and sea creatures there. It would not surprise Kate to find a baby dolphin trapped in an old shrimp net.

Unlike other animals, a pod of dolphins works as a team. If one becomes injured or sick, the rest of the group will follow it and care for it, even though it could put their own lives at risk. The team focus shifts to saving the injured dolphin. Kate was sure that there was a baby dolphin who had gotten into trouble and the rest of the pack was looking for someone to help them.

There was a gurgling sound from the object floating in the water. Kate thought she saw something resembling a human form within the makeshift float that seemed to be covered with seaweed. She swam towards the object floating near the lead dolphin. The dolphin cow swam away leaving Kate alone. Kate placed a hand against the floating object and steered it carefully towards the shore.

It took forever to reach the shore, even though the tide was coming in. Kate was relieved when she could feel the sand underneath her feet once again. She waded slowly out of the water pushing the floating object to the shore in front of her. She lost her balance momentarily as one of the waves was a little larger than usual. As she stumbled to regain her footing, she had to let go of the object. It floated on up to the shore in front of her.

"Are you okay?" Shirley asked, as Kate got up and started walking up to the shore.

"Yes," Kate gasped, as the floating object drifted away from her. "Grab that float, Shirley. There is something in it. I think it needs help."

As Shirley reached for the float, her pulse quickened. There was a small creature gazing back at her. Shirley took a step back. She did not know what to make of the bright-eyed creature staring at her. It was covered with seaweed and slime.

"Ooo," Shirley said. "That looks nasty. Is it a seal? I'm not sure if I want to touch it."

"It might be a turtle," Kate said. "I think it needs help." Another large wave had knocked Kate down and she was having difficulty keeping her balance.

"Uhh", said the creature within the float, moving ever so slightly as the raft shifted within the surf.

"Good grief!" Shirley remarked. She almost lost her balance in the surf. She positioned the swath of seaweed between herself and the beach and slowly started pushing it towards the shore. Kate followed close behind her.

"I think it's a baby," Kate said. "It looks as though it might be a baby girl."

"My goodness!" Shirley exclaimed. "Oh, you poor, poor, poor thing! Are you okay?"

Shirley reached down into the float and grasped the baby by the waist. As she picked her up a swath of seaweed fell to the ground. The float disintegrated. The baby chortled and chuckled happily when Shirley picked her up.

"Mm mm," said the baby.

"Is this a baby mermaid?" Shirley asked.

"I doubt it," Kate replied. "I think her tail is just some more seaweed. However, I dare say that there could easily have been a mermaid in the water with the dolphins who brought this baby here. It's hard to tell what you are looking it in this fog."

The baby clung tightly to Shirley. It attached itself to Shirley like a magnet hanging from a refrigerator. Shirley ignored the seaweed that was now dripping through her T-shirt and shorts. The magnetic attraction between her and the baby was so strong that there was no force of nature that could separate the two of them at that moment.

"I think it's a girl," Shirley said.

"From the looks of it she's probably less than a year old. Poor thing!" Kate said.

"Let's take little Miss Myrtle home and get her out of these wet clothes," Shirley said.

The girls pulled the small raft out of the water and hastily dragged it into the grassy area away from the shore. Shirley cradled the child in her arms as they went up the boardwalk leading to the access area where they had parked their bicycles. There was a shower at the end of the boardwalk. Shirley stepped into the shower and washed off as much of the seaweed and slime from the baby as they could. The baby didn't seem to mind at all. She blinked her eyes and stuck her tongue out of her mouth as the water ran down her face. Shirley ran her fingers through the baby's hair and made sure that it was clear of all traces of sea-weed and slime.

Shirley used her cell phone to call Troy. He answered immediately.

"Hello Troy, do you have a minute?" she asked.

"For you? Always," he replied.

"Kate and I just found an abandoned child on Shipwreck Beach."

"Wow! How old is the kid?" Troy asked.

"About a year old. I don't think it's injured in any way. I was wondering if you could stop by and help us figure out what to do next."

"Are you still at the beach?" Troy asked.

"No, can you meet up with us at my apartment in a few minutes?" Shirley replied.

"Be there in a minute," Troy said.

Kate heard him switching on the sirens in his police cruiser over the phone line as she disconnected the phone. Then the girls headed towards her apartment that was located on Shore Line Road, across from Shipwreck Beach. They could hear Troy coming from a mile away. By the time they reached the parking lot he was just pulling in to greet them with his flashing red and blue lights ablaze.

* * *

The girls were soaked through and through from having rescued the baby.

"What's going on?" Troy asked. "Is that the baby?"

"Yes, I think she's okay. She's pretty cute.," Kate replied.

"She sure is!" Troy said.

"Kate had to swim out into the ocean to rescue the baby," Shirley said. "Who in their right mind would do such a thing?" Shirley said. "It's so unconscionable to throw an innocent defenseless baby off a fishing pier."

"How far did you have to go?" Troy asked.

"Not far. Maybe fifty or a hundred yards," Kate replied. "There was a school of dolphins near the baby," Kate added. "One of them shrieked and splashed to get our attention."

"That's pretty unusual," Troy said. Dolphins usually swim farther out from the fishing pier.

"I know," Kate said. "When I saw them, my first thought was that there might be a baby dolphin trapped in a fishing net or otherwise in need of assistance. It turned out to be Baby Myrtle. However, the dolphins are the ones who actually rescued the baby."

"They are amazing animals," Troy said. "I've heard that they can communicate with each other under water by blowing bubbles and whistling at each other. They have amazing sonar capabilities that allow them to detect objects under water more than one hundred feet away."

"We pulled the baby's raft out of the water. It was full of sea weed. The raft is probably still lying on the beach," Shirley said. The baby was nestling comfortably in her arms. She had closed her eyes."

"Is the baby okay?" Kate said.

"She's fine," Shirley said. "She's just trying to sleep."

"We're going to have to call CPS," Troy said.

"I'm so glad you're here," Shirley said. "I would not know what to do without you. What's CPS?"

"Child Protective Services," Troy said.

"No way," Shirley said.

Kate looked at Shirley with dismay. This was not going to be easy.

"Shirley, we are going to have the baby checked out to make sure she'd okay," Kate said.

Baby Myrtle like shiny objects and started tugging on the bright gold badge on Troy's shirt.

"Well the baby does not look as if she's in any immediate danger," Troy said. Baby Myrtle was making him uncomfortable. He had some difficulty prying her tiny fingers off his badge. "Can you girls take the baby to the ER at Goose Island General Hospital?" Troy asked. "I'll call ahead so that they know you are coming."

"Sure," Kate said, before Shirley had a chance to protest.

"You mean to say we don't get a police escort?" Shirley complained.

"No," Troy replied. "I need to take a quick look to see if I can find the baby's parents."

"Best of luck," Kate said.

"Call me if you need anything," Troy said.

Shirley pouted. She was not happy about having to take the baby to the hospital to be poked and prodded by a bunch of doctors with cold hands. Even though she did not have any children of her own, she instinctively knew that all that the baby wanted was to be left alone to get some much-needed sleep and rest. Baby Myrtle was her little turtle and she did not intend to give it up to someone from CPS.

"Are they going to take her away from me?" Shirley asked. "I'm not giving her up to just anyone who shows up. They'll have to prove they are family. You need to get them finger-printed and DNA-typed, and all of that sort of thing, right?"

"Yes, they will, Troy replied reassuringly." He loved it when Shirley got all bent out of shape over something important, such as making sure Baby Myrtle was well looked after.

"Let me clean her up first," Shirley said.

"Maybe just take her to the ER," Troy cautioned. "They'll want to take some swabs. It might help with the investigation."

"No, you listen here Troy, this here is a living, breathing, flesh-and blood baby, not an investigation," Shirley said shaking her finger in his face. "Why don't you just hop in that fancy car of yours and go find whoever threw the baby off the fishing pier and leave the baby care to me and Kate!"

"We'll take the baby to the ER," Kate said gently.

"OK," Troy said. "I'll go on over to the fishing pier and see what I can find out"

* * *

Troy went up to the fishing pier on Shipwreck Beach. It was dark by now and there were just a handful of people on the dimly lit pier. He wrote down the license plates of all the cars parked nearby before walking out onto the pier. Some of the people on the pier he recognized instantly and some he did not know at all. He made a quick list of the folks whom he knew. The figure leaning over the railing at the end of the pier was none other than Jerry Duncan, Kate's next-door neighbor. Jerry and Charlotte were retirees who had settled on Goose Island many years ago.

"Catch anything yet, Jerry?" Troy asked.

"Sure have," Jerry replied. "The fish are biting like crazy tonight. Especially the pompano."

"That's odd," Troy said, as he carefully surveyed the fishing pier. "All you fellows are fishing from the same side of the pier, the one facing Copano Bay."

"Maybe so," Jerry said. "But it sure seems like there are more fish on this side of the pier than on the Gulf side. Must be something to do with the tide."

It could also be something to do with the dolphins Kate had seen on the Gulf side of the pier. Dolphins tend to feed on a variety of fish including speckled trout, redfish and pompano. When the dolphins had appeared on the Gulf side of the pier, they must have driven all the other fish in the water over to the Copano Bay side of the pier.

"Did you see anything unusual on the pier tonight?" Troy asked.

"No sir," Jerry replied. 'I've just been busy catching fish."

Troy looked at the trout floating lazily in Jerry's bucket. "Good looking catch!" he remarked.

"It sure is," Jerry said. "Best day all year! What time do you get off work? Why don't you come down here for a bit? I haven't seen anything like this in a long time."

"Maybe I will," Troy said. "But don't count on it. Have you noticed anything unusual tonight? We just had a small emergency on the island and it's going to be a busy night." He proceeded to give Jerry a quick summary of what had happened.

"A baby floating on the water?" Jerry said. He was having trouble wrapping his mind around what had happened on the other side of the pier that evening. "Just a hundred yards from here? Wow! I don't know how I missed that," Jerry said, as he proceeded to reel in his line. "I was so busy catching fish that I didn't even think about anything else."

"I think Kate and Shirley have taken the baby to the hospital to make sure she is doing okay." Troy added.

"I'll go home and get Charlotte," Jerry said. We'll try to find Kate and see if we can give Kate and Shirley a hand with the baby."

"Thanks," Troy said. "Sorry to interrupt your fishing."

"Not at all," Jerry said. "Sorry I couldn't be of more help. I guess I was so busy reeling in redfish that I didn't pay any attention to what was taking place on the other side of the pier."

Troy didn't mention the dolphins. He was hoping that Jerry would corroborate the information Kate had provided. Unfortunately, Jerry had not noticed the dolphins or anything unusual. Neither had anyone else on the fishing pier.

* * *

Troy stayed on at the pier after Jerry left. He proceeded to stop by and talk to each of the anglers on the pier one by one. Surely, someone had to have seen or heard something having to do with the baby.

He jotted down their answers to his questions. Names, addresses, etc. How long they had been out on the pier. Whether they had seen anything unusual, whether they had noticed any dolphins, or anything out of the ordinary. The answers were very similar and consistent. Nobody had noticed anything unusual. They had not noticed any dolphins on the Copano side of the pier. Most of them had not taken the time to look at the Gulf side of the pier. It had just been a pleasant Friday evening. Nothing else, other than the fact that they had all caught several nice fish that evening.

Troy stopped by the front office at the entrance of the fishing pier. He made sure that the fellow working the office, selling ice, bait and other essentials understood that the video from the security camera at the entrance to the fishing pier would not be erased. After leaving the pier, he walked up and down the beach a couple of times until he found the small inflatable raft that Kate and Shirley had mentioned. He placed the raft carefully into the trunk of his vehicle. After that there was nothing left for him to do. Then he left Shipwreck Beach and drove to the hospital to make sure that the baby was alright.

≈≈≈≈≈≈

3. Emergency Visit

Shirley and Kate left Goose Island for the General Hospital located near Aransas Pass. There was a steady rain failing by now. Kate drove carefully down the slick road while Shirley cradled the baby in her arms. The baby had attached itself to her and there seemed to be no need to rush.

"How's the baby doing?" Kate asked Shirley.

"She's cute," Shirley remarked, gently stroking the baby's head.

"She's a doll," Kate replied. "We're going to have to get her a car seat pretty soon."

"I'm keeping her," Shirley said.

The baby chuckled as Shirley played peek-a-boo with her. The sound of her laughter had a musical quality that made Kate and Shirley fall in love with her immediately. However, after a few minutes the laughter dwindled down. The baby started to whimper and began clawing at Shirley's shirt.

"I think she's hungry," Shirley said.

Baby Myrtle had succeeded in opening the top button of Shirley's shirt.

"We need to get her something to eat," Shirley said. "Isn't there a Piggly Wiggly or some other grocery store nearby?"

"What about getting the kid to the hospital?" Kate asked.

"They're open all night," Shirley said. "The grocery store might be closed by the time we get out of the hospital. I don't think this kid is going to be able to wait that long."

Myrtle had managed to pry open a few more buttons. Shirley was doing her best to distract the baby. Kate pulled into the parking lot of a Randall's grocery store located along the highway. She ran inside and picked up some diapers, some formulated baby milk, a bottle to drink from and some baby food snacks. She walked to the checkout lane just as the store was closing. It was almost 10:00 PM. The woman behind the cash register gave her a nice friendly welcoming smile. She looked very familiar. It was someone whom she knew but Kate couldn't place her.

"Hi," Kate said. "Do you'll close at ten?"

"Hi Kate!" said the cashier. "We sure do. I've been here since two this afternoon. I can't wait to get home."

"I guess that makes for a pretty long day," Kate replied. She struggled to remember the cashier's name.

"Long time no see," said the cashier. "How the heck have you been?"

Kate looked at the name-tag pinned to the front of her shirt. Thank goodness for name-tags! It was Wanda Gleeson. Wanda was the catcher on the Goose Island All American Girls Softball Team. Kate had run into her a few times when she had gone to the softball field to cheer the star pitcher, Shirley, on the home team.

Wanda surveyed the baby food items as she totaled up Kate's purchases. "I don't know you had a little one. Congratulations! Good for you! Did you marry that cute fellow you were dating last year?"

"Hi Wanda," Kate replied. "Good seeing you. Thanks, but I'm not married yet. Maybe someday. I'm just baby-sitting a little girl for someone who had to go out of town for a few days."

Wanda raised her eyebrows. There was more to this than met the eye. Mothers don't leave their babies alone with friends for several days at that age. "Oh okay," Wanda said. "Call me if you need any help. I love kids!"

"Thanks," Kate said. She was eager to leave and get back on the road. However, it was clear that Wanda wanted to chat. "I really have to go. Do you want to meet sometime for a cup of coffee?"

"Sure, I'd love that," Wanda replied.

"Just stop by the house sometime. Give me a call to let me know you're coming over and we'll go get some coffee together," Kate replied.

Kate rushed back to her car and handed Shirley the grocery bag. Shirley rummaged through it and found the baby formula. She rinsed out the baby bottle with some clean water and poured the milk into it, squeezed the nipple a few times to make sure it was working, and handed it to Baby Myrtle.

Myrtle knew exactly what to do with the bottle. She leaned back against Shirley and settled down contentedly against her shoulder.

* * *

Troy had called ahead to the Emergency Room so there was only a short delay before the doctor on duty took Baby Myrtle back into one of the private rooms behind the admissions desk for an examination. Shirley carried Baby Myrtle into the examination room. However, the nurse stopped Kate and asked her to step aside to the admissions desk.

One thing about a hospital that that you can always be sure of. There are bound to be a million and one forms to fill out. Many of these ask for detailed personal information that have nothing to do with your personal condition or the reason why you are there in the first place. Kate had to fill out a detailed form that began with the patient's name and address and so shortly after they had found her, Myrtle Houlihan became an official resident of the Goose Island B&B at 121 Marlin Ave in Goose Island, Texas.

Shirley and Kate went in with the baby and tried to distract her while the doctor proceeded with his examination. Baby Myrtle was amazing. She smiled pleasantly at the doctor who made her sit on the edge of an examination table with her feet dangling helplessly over the edge of the table. Shirley and Kate took up positions on either side of the exam table. Myrtle nodded cooperatively despite being poked and prodded by the doctor. Kate winced when he proceeded to listen to her heartbeat with his stethoscope. "That's got to be cold," Kate thought to herself as she recollected her last physical. Myrtle stopped smiling and scrunched her face into a frown. For a moment it looked as if she was going to turn on the waterworks. However, she never uttered a sound and suffered silently through the exam until he accidentally touched her beneath her arms, an area where she was extremely ticklish.

The tension in the room disappeared as soon as she began laughing,

As the exam continued, Myrtle discovered that she liked kicking the Doctor with her tiny legs when the he tested her reflexes. She thought it was a game and she kicked him several times when he wasn't looking. The Doctor had to enlist Kates help to restrain the baby while he continued the exam. Baby Myrtle also liked the part where she got to stick her tongue out and say "Aah". She did it repeatedly and everyone smiled at her as if she was the smartest child they had ever seen.

"How old do you think she is?" Shirley asked the Doctor.

"Oh, I'd say she's more than a year. Based on her height and weight she's somewhere between fourteen and sixteen months.

Baby Myrtle smiled at the Doctor and yanked his stethoscope away from him. She put it into her mouth and started chewing on the rubber hose that connected the ear-piece to the measuring instrument.

Shirley promptly fished the stethoscope out of the baby's mouth. She didn't react when Myrtle bit her finger instead. "I think she's ready for a bottle," Shirley said.

And she was.

* * *

Charlotte and Jerry reached the ER while the baby's examination was taking place. Although there was no sign of Shirley and Kate, Jerry knew they were there because he had recognized Shirley's pick-up truck in the parking lot. They sat down to wait. There was a small group of people on one side of the waiting room. Charlotte and Jerry sat down and joined the group that was watching the evening news on the TV in the corner of the waiting room. Jerry told Charlotte everything he knew but it was simply not enough. Charlotte was very worked up about the fact that Jerry had been right there and did not have any idea what had just happened right in front of his eyes.

"You're clueless," Charlotte said to him under her breath. "That poor baby was right under your nose and you were too busy fishing to notice what was happening. Right under your nose! Huh! What do you have to say for yourself?"

"Honestly Charlotte, that's such an unfair accusation. How can I help it if some troubled woman walks up to the pier and tosses her baby into the ocean?" Jerry shifted his weight in the chair and looked stoically at the TV screen. He did not want to make eye contact with Charlotte, just then.

"You should have jumped in to rescue the baby. That's the very least you could have done," Charlotte added. "It could have died! If you weren't so clueless, maybe you could have prevented the baby's mother from doing what she did. I just hope the baby's okay. It's a good think Kate and Shirley happened to be there to save the baby."

Jerry's protests made no headway at all with Charlotte. She was getting increasingly more perturbed and upset by the minute. He walked over the vending area and came back with a peace offering consisting of some peanut M&Ms. Charlotte proceeded to munch on them immediately without bothering the share the snack with Jerry. Jerry hid between the pages of an old issue of Field and Stream. The whole incident with the baby was very disturbing. Babies don't just float up onto the shore by themselves. Where were the parents? There were so many unanswered questions. However, it was obvious that Charlotte was going to make sure the baby received the best possible care that they could provide.

Jerry was relieved when another elderly woman walked into the waiting area and sat down next to them. The woman, whose name was Gail, was obviously in considerable pain and discomfort. Charlotte's attention shifted to

Gail, giving him a brief respite from her criticism.

"Oh Charlie", Gail moaned. "Charlie, Charlie, Charlie!"

Charlotte looked around and saw a bearded gentleman filling out forms at the counter. It had to be Gail's Charlie. Charlotte smiled at him while Gail waited for the next available physician.

Gail moaned softly as she tried to cope with her condition. Charlotte proceeded to offer a sympathetic ear to listen to her litany of complaints. Charlie finished filling out the forms and sat down next to Charlotte.

Gail was not shy about sharing her medical history which included having an appendix removed while on vacation in Aruba.

"Do you think it might have been something you ate?" Charlotte inquired.

"No, it was not something I ate," Gail declared emphatically.

"Wow!" Charlotte said sympathetically. "I cannot imagine having to be treated for a medical emergency while on vacation."

Gail proceeded to describe her other personal health skirmishes. It included the time that she had slipped on the wooden floor while getting up in the middle of the night to turn off the lights in the dining room. She had split her lip on the floor and been unable to eat solid foods for a month.

"Imagine having to drink everything through a straw for weeks," Gail remarked.

"You poor dear," Charlotte agreed.

"You have no idea," Gail continued. "It was so hard to get any suction at all. I must have damaged a nerve because I had no feeling in my lower lips for months afterwards. My Charlie had to take care of me without getting any special favors or treats for weeks. I really owe him a huge thank-you," she added. Gail turned to look at Charlie.

Charlie smiled and nodded silently. He was not particularly communicative because Gail was doing most of the talking. She had stopped moaning, and starting to appear quite normal, by now.

Charlotte felt trapped. She was seated between Gail and Charlie and could not help wondering if they would prefer to be seated next to each other. She got up and walked over to the water dispenser. Charlotte didn't know another human being who had been through so many medical adventures as Gail.

It was a relief when the nurse called Gail back into one of the examination rooms. Charlie seemed content to sit in the waiting area and stare vacuously at the television screen located at the end of the room, about twenty feet away from him.

She went back to her seat and sat down next to Jerry. There was a lot of activity outside the ER and Charlotte and Jerry saw Troy's flashing police lights through the window of the waiting room when he pulled into in the parking lot of the ER. He had parked right next to another police car with flashing lights. It was a busy night for the island community.

* * *

The doctor concluded his examination and advised Shirley and Kate that there was no sign of physical trauma or molestation. Baby Myrtle was about as healthy as possible for a one-year-old child.

After the doctor left, Kate and Shirley waited patiently for the ER nurse to complete her checkout process and discharge them. For some reason, there were a lot of people rushing around the ER. Kate could hear doors open and close, and carts scurrying down the hallway. Since the doctor had concluded his examination of Baby Myrtle, the door to the exam room was open. Kate could see additional exam rooms across the hallway from theirs. She observed a woman on a cart being wheeled into the room directly across the hallway, followed by a retinue of nurses and orderlies. From the sound of it they were hooking her up to the machines in exam room, including one that measures heart rate and blood pressure, and emanates a short beep every few seconds. Kate observed a uniformed police officer walk into the room on the other side of the hallway. A few moments later she heard fragments of a conversation involving an automobile accident. She overheard the officer tell the patient in the other room that their driver's license had just been suspended.

Kate waited patiently for the nurse to return to her room so that they could check out and go home but it seemed that they had forgotten all about her and Baby Myrtle. Shirley was playing peek-a boo with Baby Myrtle and the baby was enjoying the attention immensely.

Across from her the patient's family appeared in their pajamas and it seemed that they had just woken up in the middle of the night and driven to the ER. There was a young woman and her husband and a toddler wearing Spiderman underpants. Kate smiled and gave the young man a friendly wave. He looked at her suspiciously from across the hallway and then dashed into the room to catch up with his parents.

"This is a busy place," Kate said when the nurse returned with their paperwork.

"Sorry to keep you waiting," the nurse apologized. "This is typical for a Friday night," she continued as she walked them over to the checkout area. "Just the usual case of domestic violence, traffic accidents, and what have you."

It was almost midnight by the time they walked out of the examination room. They met Charlotte and Jerry who were sitting patiently in the waiting room. There were several people in the waiting room by now. Kate was surprised at the fact that there were several additional uniformed police officers standing nearby.

"This has to be the safest place on the planet at this moment," she remarked to Shirley.

"I know," Shirley replied. It feels like we just dropped into a meeting of the 34th Precinct. Shirley was having some difficulty holding on the Baby Myrtle who kept turning her head first one way and then another as she checked out her surroundings.

They walked over to an area where Charlotte and Jerry were waiting patiently.

"What a doll!" Charlotte remarked as she expertly extricated Myrtle from Shirley's grasp and cradled her in her own arms.

"Aah," said Baby Myrtle sticking her tiny pink tongue out of her mouth as far as she could. She proceeded to stick her finger in Charlotte's mouth.

"Aah," said Charlotte and everybody had a good laugh. Babies have a way of taking the stress out of a difficult situation. Troy was waiting for them with another police office. He waved at Shirley and Kate to step aside into a small area, away from the other individuals in the waiting area. They took a brief statement from the girls. The second police officer standing next to Troy took pictures of Baby Myrtle. It was not easy. Baby Myrtle turned her face each time the camera flashed in her direction.

"Have you seen anyone from CPS?" Shirley inquired when they returned to the area where Charlotte and Jerry were seated.

"They probably don't work after hours, or on weekends," Charlotte replied.

"I don't know," Shirley said. "Let's just hurry up and get this baby home before they show up and take her away from me. She's plumb tuckered out and so am I."

Shirley left the ER with Charlotte and Jerry. Charlotte waved to Charlie as she was leaving. There was no sign of Gail. She must have gone back into one of the examination rooms to see the ER Doctor.

Kate drove home by herself so that she could pick up a few things for the baby on the way home. The rain seemed to have picked up and it was both rainy and windy by now. As she drove, Kate dialed her buddy Ray in Odessa on her hands-free telephone. She brought him up to date on the events of the evening.

"My Goodness," Ray said, when Kate finished. "That's one lucky baby."

"Sure is," Kare replied. "For a tiny little thing she sure has one keck of a strong grip.

Ray assured Kate he would stop by the first thing the next day.

Kate stopped at the Walmart Supermarket in Rockport on her way home from the hospital. She bought several baby outfits, diapers, blankets, some toys and food. The food was the hardest part. She really didn't know what to buy for the baby. Most everything in the store came in squeeze bottles. She did the best she could and decided that she would have to return to the store for anything she had missed the next day. Her last purchase was a large beach bag to hold everything for the baby.

Little did she know that she would be making several trips to the Supermarket every day for the rest of the week. Babies can be very demanding, and she was quite unprepared for what lay ahead. When she reached home, Kate parked her car and walked over to Charlotte's house to pick up the baby.

It's always a little uncomfortable to show up at someone's house after midnight. You never know how many times to ring the doorbell, or knock on the door, how long it will be before they open the door, or what state of undress they will be in. Kate tapped lightly on the back door leading to the kitchen. It was dark and very quiet. She waited for a minute and gave the door a second light tap. If there was no answer this time she would probably have to ring the doorbell.

The light in the kitchen came on and Charlotte opened the door wearing a peach colored nightgown and motioned for her to come in. The baby was fast asleep on the sofa in Charlotte's living room. Shirley was sleeping on the floor next to the baby. If the baby fell off the sofa in the middle of the night she would probably land on Shirley's stomach.

Kate offered to pick up the baby and take Myrtle home with her for the night. However, Charlotte insisted that Kate leave the baby with her for the night. There was no need to wake her up. The poor little girl had had a very rough day and she was sleeping so peacefully that it would be a shame to disturb her. Kate dropped off the baby things she had picked up at the store and left soon afterwards to get some shut-eye.

* * *

Troy left the ER and returned to his office despite the late hour. Time was of the essence and there was work to be done. He watched the security video from the fishing pier several times. He was half expecting someone to arrive with a small package that they were getting ready to toss into the water. This did not happen. Most of the people came with fishing poles, coolers full of ice and buckets of live bait. Baby Myrtle had been rescued completely unharmed. The baby's parents could not possibly have smuggled her on to the fishing pier hidden in a cooler or a bait bucket.

There was one elderly couple in the security video. They had driven up to the fishing pier in a van and placed their fishing gear in a small cart. It seemed to take them forever to get all their supplies out of the van. However, after watching the security video several times Troy was convinced that they were just using the cart to transport their gear. There was no sign of Baby Myrtle.

Troy concluded that the baby had not be tossed into the Gulf off the fishing pier. The camera angles of the security video from the fishing pier did not provide any evidence of someone arriving within the vicinity of the fishing pier with a package that resembled a baby. About the only things being tossed into the Gulf were fishing lines.

Baby Myrtle had appeared so suddenly on Shipwreck Beach that she could have been an astronaut returning from a trip to the moon. If the baby had fallen off a ship in the Gulf, then it was a miracle that she had been able to reach the shore unharmed. Just one day on the ocean would have caused severe dehydration and sunburn. Somehow, she had managed to reach the shore just as right as rain, without any effects of the harsh conditions she must have faced on her journey. The cloud cover and the rain from the storm had probably helped her stay hydrated. However, even so, she seemed to be no worse for the wear from whatever journey she had endured. Sometimes the Lord must improvise to display his magical power over Mother Nature to preserve and protect his flock from harm.

Even though it was late, Troy picked up the phone and called the Coast Guard office in Corpus Christi. He advised them of the events that had transpired at Goose Island and requested them to keep a look out for any distress signals or other requests for assistance from a family in the Gulf. They assured him that they would let him know immediately if they heard of any shipping incidents in the Gulf.

Troy turned the lights off in his office. There was nothing more to be done until the morning. It was time to go home. As he walked toward his car in the parking lot, he couldn't help thinking that the baby had to have floated in from somewhere out in the Gulf. Perhaps someone had placed her into the water at some other point on the beach. After floating around in Copano Bay for some time her raft could have ended up where Kate and Shirley had found it. It had been low tide and that may have helped the raft float into Shipwreck Beach.

There was really no way to tell what had happened without more information. At least the baby was safe and unharmed. However, Troy had to wonder about the baby's parents, and their state of mind. Particularly if the baby's mother had abandoned her little girl.

≈≈≈≈≈≈

4. Sea Weed

Kate went over to Charlotte's house shortly after breakfast the next morning. She walked across the stepping stones that led to Charlotte's back door. It had rained some more during the night and the ground was still wet.

Charlotte's dog Milo was the first one to hear Kate arrive and he barked joyfully as he saw her approaching the back door. Charlotte, Jerry, and baby Myrtle were in the kitchen when she arrived. Jerry saw her profile through the screen on the back door and opened it to let her in.

"How is she doing?" Kate asked.

"She's just as fine as can be," replied Charlotte.

"Uh, huh" said Baby Myrtle. She scrunched up her cheeks and gave Kate a stink-eye with a smile.

Everybody smiled. Baby Myrtle was adorable. Everything about her, from the unruly blonde hair on top of her head to the tiny little toes on her little baby feet was perfect. Kate had bought Baby Myrtle with a few toys the previous evening. Charlotte had opened the presents for the baby, and Kate noticed that Myrtle liked the small stuffed puppy dog that she had left at Charlotte's house the previous evening. Myrtle had tucked the toy puppy under her arm and figured out that it barked when you pressed its right paw. Myrtle loved the puppy. It looked very realistic and had nice soft fur. Myrtle put the puppy against her cheek.

"Do you like your puppy dog?" Charlotte asked as she opened the kitchen door to let them into her house.

"Gah!" Myrtle exclaimed. She like the sound of the word. "Gah, gah!", said Myrtle nodding her head and beaming.

"Oh, how cute. She's trying to say dog," said Charlotte.

"Gah," repeated Baby Myrtle softly. She pressed the red emblem on the toy puppy's right paw.

"Arf, arf arf!" said the toy puppy, nodding its head, and wagging its tail.

Charlotte's dog, Milo let out a soft growl.

"I think you are right", said Kate. "Gah does sounds a little like dog. She likes dogs."

As if on cue, Myrtle walked unsteadily over towards Milo, who was sitting by the fireplace, minding his own business.

"Gah," said Myrtle, as she introduced her stuffed dog to Milo.

"Arf, Arf, Arf!" said the stuffed dog when Myrtle pressed its paw. Baby Myrtle pressed the stuffed animal against Milo's cheek.

Milo wanted to have nothing to do with the puppy. He glanced suspiciously at the imposter and moved quickly out of the way. Milo moved out of Baby Myrtle's reach and hunkered down to hide behind the sofa. Baby Myrtle followed him. She wanted him to make friends with her new toy.

"Now, now, Myrtle. Leave Milo alone," said Charlotte gently.

Myrtle smiled. She beamed at Charlotte and proceeded to pounce on Milo. She grabbed a fistful of Milo's fur in her scrawny little hand and shoved the toy animal in his face again.

Milo squealed and freed himself from the baby's grasp. He scampered over into the kitchen and sat down, looking warily in the baby's direction.

Charlotte went over and picked up the baby. She did not want the baby to provoke Milo any further. Without any warning, Myrtle put her hands up in the air and wriggled out of Charlotte's grasp. She did not want to be held. She wanted Milo to adopt her puppy. Charlotte opened the kitchen door. Milo ran outside. He loved chasing the birds in the back yard.

"Gah," said Baby Myrtle looking in the direction that Milo had gone. She opened and closed her little hand as if to wave goodbye to Milo.

"Gah gone," said Charlotte. "This child is very wiry and agile. I bet that's how she survived her trip across the Gulf." Charlotte moved her chair next to the kitchen door in front of Myrtle, blocking her access to the door. She caught the baby in her arms and tickled her each time Myrtle tried to get past her. Myrtle giggled and chortled with laughter.

"Would you like some milk?" Charlotte asked, handing the baby a bottle of warm mile.

"Yes, Mama," said Baby Myrtle.

Everybody looked at each other in surprise. Charlotte beamed with pride. She leaned over and gave the baby a kiss on the forehead.

"Isn't she the most precious thing you have ever seen? Charlotte asked.

"She's beautiful," Kate replied.

Jerry nodded appreciatively as well. "She's like a breath of fresh air!" he remarked. "If anyone comes here to harm her in any way they will have to deal with me first!"

There was no sign of Shirley in the house, and Kate surmised that Shirley had woken up at the crack of dawn to get ready for her customers at the Goose Island Bakery.

"Did Shirley leave for work?" Kate inquired.

Charlotte nodded. "She did not get much rest last night. I think she slipped out around 4:00 am to bake up a fresh batch of her carrot raisin, and blueberry muffins. "I don't know how she does it."

"It makes me hungry just thinking about it. Let's go down to the Bakery this morning and visit Shirley," Kate suggested. "I could use a cup of coffee and a blueberry muffin. Might be good change for the baby too."

Charlotte agreed.

"Mi-lo," said Baby Myrtle in a sing-song voice. She opened and closed her fist several times to wave goodbye to Milo as they were leaving. Jerry and Milo waited until they had left before returning into the house.

"Bye Mi-lo," replied Kate echoing Baby Myrtle.

"Bye Mi-lo," said Kate, Charlotte, and Myrtle in unison as Kate backed her car out of the driveway a short time later. They all laughed together as Kate drove down to the Goose Island Bakery. With her hazel eyes and golden hair, Baby Myrtle was a charmer.

*   *   *

Shirley greeted Kate and Charlotte at the door as soon as they entered the door to the Goose Island Bakery. She promptly grabbed Myrtle away from Kate and gave her a kiss. She went bouncing off with the baby. Shirley wanted to show Baby Myrtle the assortment of baked goods that she had on display behind the counter.

"Well!" Kate remarked as she watched Myrtle and Shirley disappear behind the counter.

"That's how it goes, with little children," Charlotte replied. "They can be so very ungrateful. You can wear yourself out taking care of all their needs and they will still leave you in a heartbeat for a complete stranger who is willing to give them a chocolate cookie."

There was an empty table about half way down the left side of the bakery. Kate and Charlotte walked on over and sat down. Kate looked over the group of customers within Bakery and waved at Kenneth Porter, a familiar blot on the Goose Island landscape. Ken had positioned himself strategically at the end of the counter. His vantage point allowed him to observe Shirley as she served her customers. Kate shook her head disapprovingly as she observed his actions. His head moved forward and from side to side each time Shirley moved to get a better look at her posterior each time she bent over to reach for a muffin or one of the other baked goods on display at the counter.

"I told Shirley not to let Ken finance the loan on her bakery," Kate said to Charlotte in a whisper. "He is such a sleaze."

"I know what you mean," Charlotte replied. "That man is nothing but trouble."

"He is such a pervert," Kate said. "I used to rent a store front from him several years ago. It was a big mistake. If he ever gets close enough to give you a hug, you feel violated by the time you are able to get out of his grasp."

Shirley stopped by their table with Baby Myrtle attached to her hip. She placed a booster seat on the chair next to Kate. Myrtle sat down at the table without a fuss. She was beaming. She had a chocolate drop cookie in her tiny hand.

"I hope it's okay for her to eat a cookie," Shirley said.

"She'll be fine," Charlotte

Myrtle took a tiny bite from the cookie. She turned and offered Kate a bite from her cookie.

"How sweet. She loves you, Kate," Charlotte said.

Kate beamed. They could feel everyone in the room looking at Myrtle. Kenneth Porter could not resist the temptation to visit Kate and find out more about the baby.

"What have we here?" he said as he ambled his oversized figure over to their table. He sat down next to the baby and started to tickle the baby's toes. "Kootchie, kootchie, koo. What's your name?" he asked.

Myrtle screwed up her toes. She made a face and pushed him away with her tiny hand.

"Gah," said Myrtle firmly.

"Good Girl!" Kate applauded. "Tell Uncle Ken to go back to his own table. He's nothing but a big dog."

Myrtle continued to push Ken away with her hand. When he failed to get the message, she reached over and grabbed his cheek with her fist. The chocolate on her cookie found its way to Ken's nose.

"Ouch," Ken said earnestly. "That kid has a grip like a pit bull."

"Watch out," Charlotte said. "She'll bite your finger off if you let her."

"Gah," said Myrtle, thoroughly enjoying all the attention she was getting. She raised her hand in the air, opened and closed her tiny fist several times as if she was saying goodbye to Ken.

Everybody in the room laughed, including Ken. He liked babies. Before long, all the customers knew that Baby Myrtle had just arrived at Goose Island the previous day. The conversation quickly progressed to who she might be, how she could have been abandoned by her parents, and how she had found her way to Goose Island.

Jeremy Stapleton, the local reporter for the Goose Island News was sitting at one of the tables by the window. He had stopped by the bakery for a pick-me-up snack. As a small group congregated around Baby Myrtle's table, Jeremy's ears perked up. Before long, he joined the group and started jotting down notes in the black notebook that he carried with him everywhere he went. He followed Baby Myrtle around the main dining area of the Bakery and took several pictures of the customers fawning over the baby. Kate and Shirley never mentioned the dolphins, and certainly not the mermaid they had seen the previous evening. One word to Jeremy about a mermaid and Goose Island would probably attract hordes of crazy people as soon as the newspaper hit the stands the next day.

"She probably fell off a cruise ship," suggested Francesca Giordano. Francesca and Don Giordano owned the Italian restaurant across the street from the Goose Island Bakery. Francesca loved going on cruises. However, it bothered her that some of the children on the boat seemed to have no manners at all. Francesca had been swimming laps in the pool one morning on a cruise to the Caribbean when a group of teenagers had jumped into the pool without warning. They had proceeded to play an impromptu game of volleyball while she swam laps underneath an invisible net. It had not been a good experience for Francesca who decided to leave after getting bonked on the head after an errant serve.

"Yes, but the cruise ships leave from Galveston. It's a long way from Galveston to Goose Island," replied her husband Don. There's no way the baby could have travelled hundreds of miles to get here. If she did then it's a miracle that she didn't drown."

"She could if God was protecting her," said Francesca firmly. What if she had a life preserver around her waist," replied Francesca. A little thing like that could go a long with a life preserver around her waist."

"She's probably a princess. The sole heiress to a vast fortune. Someone must have tried to kill her by throwing her into the ocean," Don suggested. "Probably a wicked uncle who was trying to steal her inheritance," he added. "It happens all the time in Europe."

Kate and Shirley looked at each other. She did look like a princess. This was a scary thought. Neither of them remembered seeing a life preserver around the baby when they had rescued it from the sea. Kate had no idea whether the baby had been tossed into the ocean from the fishing pier by a mother who did not want the child, or if the baby had fallen off a cruise liner. The cruise liner seemed like a better alternative. Anything was better than being abandoned by your parents.

If someone was trying to kill Baby Myrtle they would probably try again. Kate knew that the news about the baby was all over town by now. The Goose Island News could be counted on publishing a story about Baby Myrtle by Saturday. Once the it was published it was only a matter of time before the killers descended upon Goose Island for a second attempt at taking baby Myrtle's life.

"There are also a lot of sharks in the water," continued Don. He had grown up in Italy and knew a thing or two about sharks. The Mediterranean Sea is home to almost fifty species of sharks.

"I will have to prepare some 'zuppa di squalo' for you some day," Don said. "A sharks is known as a 'squalo' in Italy. We were always afraid of the squalo when we went to the beach. Squalos are attracted to bright colors. If the baby was covered with seaweed as you described, then it may have helped to save her life."

"I think I'll pass on the shark soup," Kate said. She was not sure if she could swallow Don's 'zuppa di squalo', even though it was probably delicious.

"She's so tiny the sharks probably didn't want her for breakfast," said Olga, the county clerk. The Goose Island Court House was across the street from the bakery and Olga had dropped in for her mid-morning fix. A dark mocha cappuccino.

Myrtle smiled gratefully at Olga and clapped her hands. She looked over at Ken and waved bye-bye to him again.

"I think she needs another cookie," added Olga.

"She might be thirsty," said Charlotte. "Do you have any milk?" she asked Shirley.

Shirley went around behind the counter and returned with a bottle of milk for the baby. Myrtle tipped the bottle back and took a quick swig of milk. She was thirsty. Eating cookies is hard work for a baby.

"There's no doubt that Kate and Shirley saved this baby's life," Don continued. "We have had so much rain the last two nights. This baby would have drowned in the ocean if they had not pulled her out of the water before the downpour started."

The baby fell asleep in Kate's lap. Kate swaddled her in a blanket. "We should leave soon," she said as she handed the baby over to Charlotte.

They drank their coffee in silence. The crowd by the table thinned out as if to give the baby a chance to rest.

"We have to find who she belongs to," Kate said.

"I know," Charlotte replied.

"If no one shows up to claim her, she's mine!" Kate added.

"Sounds like a plan," Charlotte said. "You adopt the baby and I'll help you take care of her anytime you want. No charge." Charlotte wanted to keep the baby as much as Kate. She was a little doll. Charlotte cradled the little bundle that was Baby Myrtle sleeping peacefully against her breast. She could feel the warmth of the baby against her body. It was a feeling like no other. Both Kate and Charlotte knew that they would do everything in their power to make sure no one could ever harm the baby.

≈≈≈≈≈≈

5. PharmaSea

The Supervisory Officer at the Rockport Coast Guard station, Bill Griffin, contacted Troy early in the morning. There had indeed been a marine accident about twenty miles off shore. A small fishing trawler named the PharmaSea had crashed into an offshore drilling rig the El-Sombrero-III just ten miles off the Gulf Coast. The trawler was drifting helplessly at the time that it had bumped into the rig. The crew on the rig had received a scare, but there had been no harm done to the oil rig.

The Crew Chief at the El-Sombrero-III had contacted the coast guard immediately and secured the boat to the rig. The Crew Chief was pretty upset when he had spoken with the Coast Guard. The boat was severely burned and there had been an apparent homicide. They had found a dead body on board the PharmaSea. Bill's team had travelled out to the El-Sombrero-III immediately. They located the floating wreckage of the PharmaSea right away and secured the boat in the early hours of the morning. Bill had thanked Troy for contacting the Coast Guard the previous night and assured him that someone on his team would be in touch soon.

Troy was familiar with the rigs that comprised the El-Sombrero field. The platforms are all circular in shape with a railing that extends across the circumference of the rig. There is an elevated structure, rounded at the top, in the center of each rig. From a distance the rigs look like a collection of Mexican hats floating on the ocean. Some of the rigs in the El Sombrero field are unmanned. El-Sombrero was renowned in the area near Port Aransas for its good fishing, especially Red Snapper, Yellowfin Tuna, and Amberjack. The fish bite hard, and literally pounce on the bait in the area near El Sombrero. When the seas are calm, and the weather is nice there are any number of fishing charters trolling in the area near the oil field.

However, what had transpired on the PharmaSea was no accident. When the Coast Guard boarded the PharmaSea, they realized immediately that someone had attempted to scuttle the ship by starting a fire in the wheelhouse. It appeared to be an act of modern-day piracy. The boat was registered to Robert Rhodes, residing in Raleigh, North Carolina. They had found the charred remains of a man and a woman on board the vessel. The bodies were presumably what remained of Robert Rhodes and his wife. Bill did not know much about Robert's family. However, he assured Troy that he would make the necessary inquiries and for the moment it seemed safe to assume that the baby who just washed up on Shipwreck Beach was Robert's daughter.

The fire had been extinguished by the tropical storm that had swept through the Gulf on the night that the ship had been destroyed. The ship had stayed afloat thanks to the rain and because the PharmaSea had very little fuel in its tanks at the time of the blaze.

* * *

Later that morning Troy received another call from the Coast Guard. Troy was fortunate to speak in person with one of the Coast Guard officers who had personally boarded the vessel. Jesse Ward was a retired naval officer who now worked part-time for the Coast Guard. Jesse had just heard about Baby Myrtle's amazing adventure in the Gulf and wanted to get an update on Baby Myrtle and whether she was doing okay. Troy assured him she was doing remarkably well, given the circumstances surrounding her incredible journey from the PharmaSea to Goose Island.

"That's a relief," Jesse said.

"I know," Troy replied. "Her guardian angel sure came through for her in a big way."

"I'm so glad she's not hurt," Jesse said.

"Not even a scratch," Troy replied. "Just as bright-eyed and bushy-tailed as a bunny rabbit."

They spoke briefly about Baby Myrtle's trip to the Hospital and how she had been released with a clean bill of health. As they spoke about the events that had transpired, Troy realized that everyone was trying to compare notes and piece together exactly what had transpired the previous day.

"It was a bloody mess," said Jesse.

"I'm sorry," Troy replied. He was not sure what to say.

"You know how it goes," Jesse said. "Some days are diamonds, and some are coal. This was definitely something I never want to see again."

Jesse informed Troy that when the Coast Guard had contacted the owner of the vessel to inform them of what had happened, they learned that Robert and Brenda Rhodes were working on a cancer research study in Texas, collecting marine samples as part of the first phase of their research. Their study required marine samples of a certain species of bioluminescent shrimp. Robert and Brenda were attempting to evaluate whether this species contained some genetic material that had the potential to provide a miracle cure for cancer.

The Coast Guard had towed the trawler to their station in Corpus Christi. Robert and Brenda Rhodes had been shot at close range. Brenda had been shot in the back of the head. There was evidence of a fight for survival on board the ship with broken glass everywhere. There was a baby crib and some baby clothing and toys on board the ship but no sign of a baby.

"This should never have happened to Robert and Brenda," said Jesse. "They were a pair of medical researchers who were on staff at the Medical School in Raleigh, North Carolina. The two of them were a team who had been working together for several years. Robert and Brenda had published several articles dealing with the early detection of cancer in some of the leading medical journals in the country. They were two of America's finest, out to save humanity from the scourge that is cancer. They were out in the Gulf looking for some sea creatures that could someday provide a miracle cure for cancer."

"Wow!" Troy said. "That's so wrong! I am so sorry Jesse."

"I know. This is a real tragedy and we may need your help to bring the killers to justice."

"Sure," Troy said. "Just let me know if there is anything I can do to help."

Troy used the computer in the Sherriff's office to access Birth Certificate Records to ascertain whether Brenda Rhodes had given birth to a baby daughter within the past two years. She had. Eleanor Rhodes had been born in Cary, North Carolina, on November 28th, more than a year ago. Robert and Brenda were listed as the parents. That would make the baby almost fifteen months old within another week. Baby Myrtle, who was being cared for by Shirley and Kate was almost certainly Eleanor Rhodes. Troy knew that the coast guard would contact the baby's family soon to inform them that the child was safe. He could probably expect to receive a call from the Rhodes' family before long.

* * *

It was mid-morning by the time Troy drove around to the Goose Island Bakery to give Shirley a heads-up regarding what he had learned about Baby Myrtle's parents from the Coast Guard. She was not going to like it. Her maternal instincts had kicked into high gear ever since she had found the baby. He parked his car by the courthouse at the center of the Goose Island Town Square when he noticed the familiar figure of Ray Looney, Kate's boyfriend getting out of a red Jeep Wrangler in the parking lot.

"Well howdy, Ray. Did you just get into town?" Troy asked.

"Sure did," Ray replied.

"Nice car," Troy remarked.

"Thanks," Ray said. "It's just a rental. Kate was tied up when we spoke last night, and I didn't want to ask her to come out to the airport to meet me. I drove past the B&B, but Kate wasn't home.

"Well, they might be in the Bakery," Troy remarked.

"I hear that y'all rescued a baby girl on the beach last night," Ray said. "Is the baby okay?"

"News travels fast," Troy said with a laugh. "Yes, she's inside the Bakery right now, keeping Shirley company. It was a bit of a rough night," Troy said. "Let's go in and see how everyone is doing,"

They crossed the street from the parking lot to the Bakery. Troy found Shirley holding Myrtle against her waist. Shirley gave the boys a friendly wave when they walked into Bakery. She walked over and gave Troy a hug. Myrtle kicked him away with her tiny feet and waved good-bye. Her limited circle of huggable friends included Kate, Shirley and Charlotte.

Ray walked over to give Kate a friendly hug and a peck on the cheek. However, she was having none of the 'happily married for fifty years' routine. She reached into his waistband with her right hand. Making a fist around his belt buckle she pulled him towards herself. Then she proceeded to plant a big, wet, slobbery kiss on his lips. Ray blushed. He was not used to being treated in this manner in public. Kate didn't care. Ray closed his eyes, not wanting to make eye contact with anyone he knew. Kate's lips were delicious.

"Cute kid", Ray said.

"Don't let her size fool you," Kate replied. "She is a tough little cookie."

"Missed you," Ray said. His eyes were still closed.

"You better have," Kate replied. She loved that Ray had travelled down to see her from Odessa at such short notice. He was always there when she needed him. Her right hand wrapped itself around the topmost button of his shirt. She reached over and pulled him towards her and give him a long, lingering kiss.

"Alright you two," Francesca said, with a wink. "Keep it clean. There are little children over here watching everything you say and do."

Troy and Ray sat down at the table. It was obvious the group had just been discussing the baby's plight. Troy proceeded to describe about what he had learned from the Coast Guard about the accident near the El Sombrero field.

"El Sombrero is a good ten miles from the shore, isn't it?" Jerry said. "Due east from Port Aransas. I hear there is some good fishing out there."

"That's right," Troy replied. "The fishing is great at El Sombrero. I think the reason the baby floated here is because the tide was coming in at the time."

"It's pretty deep over by the El Sombrero field," Jerry continued. "It's got to be at a depth of a few hundred feet of water."

"The first oil rig in the Gulf was built about a mile offshore in just 13 feet of water by Superior Oil in 1937," Ray added. "Since then they have just been moving further out and building in deeper water. There are several wells in more than a thousand feet of water now."

"Yeah," Troy said. "That Deepwater Horizon disaster was for a well in more than four thousand feet of water.

"Took almost three months to plug DH," Jerry said. "You would think that they would slow things down after an accident like that, but if you look around, it seems to be business as usual once again."

"It's big business," Ray replied. "The Gulf of Mexico produces more than a million barrels of oil a day. Most of the rigs are on the western side of the Gulf, just off the Texas-Louisiana coast. The eastern side of the Gulf is still largely protected from oil exploration."

"Can you imagine a baby floating almost ten miles by herself in a storm?" Jerry asked rhetorically. "I just cannot believe it. There are so many things that could have happened to her on the way here."

"What this baby accomplished is absolutely incredible!" Troy said. "She travelled across almost ten miles of open sea all by herself in less than 24 hours." He proceeded to fill the others in on what he had heard about the events at PharmaSea until it drifted into the El-Sombrero-III.

Ray turned towards Kate and Shirley. "What time did you find the baby?" he asked.

"It was just getting dark," Shirley replied.

"That means it would have been around high tide. If you had not happened to find her when you did, the tide that helped to bring the baby to shore, would have carried her out to sea again."

"I guess you are right," Kate said. "The murders occurred in the middle of the night and the PharmaSea drifted into the El-Sombrero-III.

Meanwhile the baby floated to Goose Island because the tide was coming in."

"The dolphins helped too," Shirley added.

"They probably knew the tide was going back out again," Kate said. "That was why they were trying to get our attention."

"There are two high tides each day," Ray said. "If you hadn't rescued Baby Myrtle when you did, no doubt the tide would have carried her back out to sea. I doubt the baby would have survived another day on the open water."

"Two high tides!" Shirley remarked. "I didn't know that. I thought there was just one each day."

"That depends on where you are. Texas has two," Ray replied. "The first is when the earth is closest to the moon as it goes around the earth. The second is when it is furthest from the moon. The second one has to do with the earth's rotational spin. The centrifugal force from the earth's rotation causes the water from the high tide that occurs when the earth is closest to the moon to slosh back again just when the earth is farthest from the moon."

"I see," Shirley said, even though she didn't see how this was possible at all. "And it was a full moon on the day that we found Baby Myrtle," she added.

Ray described how the earth and the moon rotate in the same direction around the sun. How it takes an additional fifty minutes each day for the moon to rotate once around the earth. Additional minutes that cause high and low tides to occur at different times throughout the year. "This leads to lunar cycle that is approximately 28 days", Ray said.

"I know," Kate replied. "Call me crazy, but that is exactly the same as a woman's menstrual cycle."

"Now that, I did not know," Ray said.

"That's why we girls always meet up on the beach and howl at the moon once every 28 days." Kate said.

"It's a miracle that this baby is alive," said Don Giordino. "Something bad always happens whenever there are drugs and narcotics. Do you know if the Coast Guard found any drugs on that pharmacy boat? That's big business too you know. Probably more money in it than the oil business. Was it opioids? I have heard that more people are dying of opioids in America than were killed in the Vietnam War."

"I don't think there were any narcotics on board the PharmaSea," Troy said. However, there's no way of knowing what was on board the ship that attacked the PharmaSea."

"With a name like that it sounds like a floating drug factory," Ray said. "Might not have happened if they had just called it the 'Loose Goose' or something.

"Well I'd never get on board a boat called the 'Loose Goose'," Kate said. "That is so insulting. You have no idea how to name a boat."

"What would you call it?" Ray inquired.

"I'd call it the 'Miss Steak'" Kate said with a wink at Shirley.

"I think it's time to feed the baby," Shirley said as Baby Myrtle was starting to get restless.

"You poor thing," said Francesca. She held the baby's hand and pressed it against her cheek.

"We'll just have to pitch in and look after you," said Olga. She took the baby from Shirley and did her best to rock her back and forth until Shirley returned with a bottle of milk.

They all agreed that the miracle baby who had just arrived on Goose Island would get the best care they could provide until Baby Myrtle's family came to her rescue.

The baby was getting restless and had started to fuss. Charlotte and Jerry picked up Baby Myrtle and left to go home. The group at the Goose Island Bakery left to go about their daily business. Kate and Ray decided to take a walk on Shipwreck Beach and look at the spot where Baby Myrtle had been found the night before. Troy returned to work. He was going to drive by the Copano Bay Marina to talk to the Harbor Master and some of the shrimpers about the PharmaSea.

* * *

Later that afternoon the group gathered at Charlotte's house. Shirley was the first to arrive. She came as soon as she had closed the Goose Island Bakery for the day. Kate and Ray were the next ones to arrive. They had stopped by the Supermarket and picked up a few more things for the baby. Baby Myrtle entertained everyone with her antics. She was fun to watch even when all she did was lie on a blanket and suck on a bottle of milk. The girls took turns holding her and caring for her.

Troy came at the end of his shift. Kate and Ray left for a short time to make sure the Caseys who were staying at the Goose Island B&B were taken care of. They returned with some pizza and beer to share with the group. Shirley brought a salad and red wine and the close-knit group enjoyed a pot-luck supper together.

It wasn't long before the topic of conversation evolved into a discussion surrounding the motives of the 'Drilling Rig Pirates' who had murdered Robert and Brenda.

There was not much by way of additional information. Robert and Brenda Rhodes had been so committed to their research that they had used their personal funds from a family inheritance to purchase an old fishing trawler. The University had subsequently assisted Robert in converting the boat into a research vessel. All the equipment on board the vessel belonged to the University. Robert and Brenda were living on the boat. They came to port a couple of times each month to ship their samples to the research lab in North Carolina for analysis.

The motive for such a vicious homicidal attack on the PharmaSea was not clear. Why would someone want to murder a pair of marine researchers who were trying to help humanity in such a noble cause? It could not be attributed to anything quite so simple as a fishing rivalry with the local shrimpers. Robert and Brenda had never attempted to sell their shrimp on the shrimp market or otherwise infringe on the territory of the shrimpers in the area.

Fifty years ago, there were thousands of Shrimp boats fishing in the Gulf every day. Shrimp were plentiful and there was enough to go around for all the shrimpers who took to the seas every day. Anyone willing to roll up their sleeves and put in a hard days' work could do quite well for themselves. When they were not out in the Gulf catching shrimp, shrimpers could often be seen repairing their nets near the marina.

However, several changes had occurred in recent years. Over fishing had resulted in smaller shrimp catches over time. So much so that more than half the bycatch within a shrimp boat's nets was comprised of other species such as Atlantic Croaker fish which are often used as bait and has no commercial value to a shrimper. In addition, the Gulf shrimp market had been flooded with foreign, farm-raised shrimp the Shrimp Industry had suffered severe economic hardships. It was much cheaper and easier to grow shrimp in captivity than it was to go out in all types of weather to harvest them from nature's bounty. Their numbers dwindled and only the ones who loved going out on the ocean, to feel the wind at their back made the effort to continue doing what they had been doing for generations.

Shrimp boats often operate on a very narrow margin. Perhaps another shrimp boat had viewed Brenda and Roberts activities as an encroachment of their territory and decided to eliminate the competition. However, just a cursory background check would have made it clear that they were no threat to the other shrimp boats in the area. A rival shrimper just had to ask his shrimper buddies what the Rhodes family was doing out on the Gulf to know enough to leave them alone. Was it even remotely conceivable that a shrimper would murder the Rhodes family just to keep them from harvesting a few specialized shrimps for medicinal purposes?

So, if it wasn't a rival shrimper then Troy reasoned that there had to be some other reason why Robert and Brenda had been killed. In recent years, the Gulf Coast had been overrun by drug smugglers and their ilk. The narcotics industry did not hesitate to serve out its brand of justice as violently as possible. How had the Rhodes family run afoul of the narco-traffickers?

Was this an attempt to steal intellectual capital? The financial rewards of a miracle cure for cancer could be huge. What if a single drug company could control the miracle cure for cancer. Was there something of value on board the ship that the attackers had been after? If so what could it have been? Had they stolen something of such tremendous value that it justified the double homicide?

Why not wait? In due course, the results of their studies would have been had been published by the University. Whatever they had learned about the cancer prevention properties of shrimp would be available at little or no cost within the public domain.

Another reason for the attack could have been an attempt to prevent the disclosure of any type of miracle cure for cancer. The pharmaceutical industry made enormous sums of money through conventional cancer treatments that would dry up if there were to be a miracle cure for cancer. A clinic or hospital facility who depended on treating patients with vast amounts of radiation therapy was unlikely to welcome a miracle drug based on shrimp oil with special chemical cancer preventive properties. Could it be the result of a slash and burn approach to eliminate the researchers who were on the cusp of developing this cure? Doing so could delay progress for years, if not forever.

* * *

As she walked across the path that led to the B&B from Charlotte's house at the end of the day, Kate pondered Baby Myrtle's fate. Without her parents to look after her, Baby Myrtle at the mercy of her extended family to provide for her. Troy had mentioned that the PharmaSea was owned by Robert Rhodes. It seemed reasonable to assume that any family that could afford to buy a sea-worthy, ocean going boat had enough resources to provide for a small child.

There was also the possibility that the Rhodes family might put Baby Myrtle up for adoption. She wondered if she could step up to the challenge and adopt Baby Myrtle. Kate looked at Ray quizzically and gave him her 'Mona Lisa' smile. She gave him a friendly bump as they reached the back door to the B&B. Ray turned around just in time to be welcomed with a hug from Kate that quickly developed into something a little more special. The full moon had a little something to do with it. As they entered the B&B as she wondered if he was up to the task of being a parent? She had always thought that he would make a fine Dad, and she had even secretly dreamed about having his children. She would like nothing better than a miniature version of Ray walking around in her kitchen in his Spiderman boxers, rummaging around for cookies in her cookie jar. Boy that would be sweet! Yes, if the opportunity to adopt Baby Myrtle presented itself there was no doubt in Kate's mind that she would be first in line for the chance to be her surrogate Mom.

The walked up the stairs to her bedroom. Past the step where Kate had seen a small boy playing with his yellow toy car. The one who had held her hand as she walked along the beach looking for Ray. No sign of him tonight. Kate lit a candle on the table beside her bed while Ray opened a bottle of red wine.

Kate turned out the lights in the room. They took a few sips of wine just as they undressed hastily between hugs and embraces, and the same long lingering kisses that they just shared at the back-door of the B&B. Ray never got tired of the warmth of Kate's body against his. Only Kate had ever felt so wonderful, so soft, so warm, so fragrant and so beautiful. Only Kate knew how to get his attention with just a single look, or the touch of her hand. She knew exactly how to get his motor started and shift all his senses from zero to sixty in a matter of a few milliseconds.

The storm that raged deep within Ray's heart had the force of a hurricane, growing ever stronger as it raced across the Gulf toward the Texas coastline. Never hesitating for a moment until it made landfall on a deserted stretch of coastline surrounded by towering waves that washed ashore on a moonless night. Waves of passion that reached out with the arms of an insatiable lover, pulling him relentlessly towards her, holding him tightly against her bosom. Kate pushed him down beneath the waves, starving him for air, holding his hands with a fierceness that surprised him. Promising never to let her go, Ray sank lower and lower, gasping for air until she pulled him back up towards her. She kissed him tenderly and began to rock him as gently as a leaf floating upon the water. The storm surge passed, and then time stood still and the only sound in the room was the measured sound of their breathing.

"I love you, Kate," whispered Ray. "You are so very beautiful! I think you must be the most beautiful girl in the whole world!"

"Je t'aime, mon amour," Kate said, as she nibbled hungrily on his shoulder and held him close to her, against her body. She smiled. "I love you too!" she said.

"Are you doing okay?" he asked.

"Have you been listening to me?" Kate asked. "Would I be screaming my head off and telling you how much I love you if I was anything but okay?" She replied.

"Thanks," Ray said tenderly. "I was just checking-in with you. I am so lucky to have you beside me." He had felt the earthquake too.

Ray fell asleep listening to the gentle rhythm of Kate's heartbeat, completely spent and more than completely satisfied. Kate ran her fingers through his hair and blew out the pink candle on the table beside her.

≈≈≈≈≈≈

6. Grilling

Myrtle slept fitfully through the night in a small makeshift crib just a few feet away from Charlotte's bed. Charlotte surrounded the baby with several pillows and cushions to keep her snug while she slept. Myrtle kept waking up and making the sweetest, most amazing little baby grunts and groans throughout the night. Charlotte woke up each time they heard the baby. She leaned over and checked the baby each time to make sure that the little princess was okay.

Jerry didn't mind. Not even when Charlotte reached over and picked up the baby and brought Myrtle into their bed just before dawn. It was time for him to get up in any case. He got up, put on his slippers and went to the kitchen to make some coffee, while Charlotte comforted the baby.

Jerry knew that Charlotte was just filling in for Kate and Shirley until they were ready to take on the responsibilities that come with taking care of a baby; keeping it safe, warm, happy, loved, and always fed. Changing diapers, changing clothes, bath time, play time, story time and nap time. Breakfast, lunch, and dinner time, and each little thing that must be done every day of every year, until it is no longer necessary to do it at all because they are all grown up and ready to face the world on their own. All the many, many things that conspire to make the day disappear in a flash. Where the hours of the day dwindle down like magic. When it is already night time before one realizes it is over, even though you know exactly where the time went and what was done throughout the day before it came to an end.

Jerry warmed up a bottle of milk for the baby. He took it to the bedroom and handed it to Charlotte. Then he returned to the kitchen to drink his coffee, read the news, and looked out the kitchen window as dawn gave way to the morning sun that quickly filled the sky.

* * *

Kate awoke to the sound of seagulls squawking in the distance and foraging for food. She went downstairs to the kitchen and got ready to prepare for the day. It was only a matter of time before the house guests at the Goose Island B&B materialized in her kitchen for a warm cup of coffee and some fresh fruit, an English Muffin, or one of the house favorites, a carrot raisin muffin from the Goose Island Bakery.

When breakfast was served, Kate surveyed the food counter and double check if everything was in place, creamer for the coffee, sugar packets, butter, jelly, plates, silverware, a small refrigerator full of yogurt, etc.

Kevin and Karen Casey generally got off to a slow start each day. They pretty much rolled into the kitchen whenever they wanted to. Kate and Ray were generally out of the house by the time Kevin and Karen were ready for breakfast. Kate covered up the food when she left the kitchen and Karen was more than capable of heating up whatever she wanted and making sure that Kevin was well looked after.

Ray came down to the kitchen for breakfast about the time that Kate had just finished getting the breakfast buffet ready. Kate and Ray got a plate of food from the breakfast buffet and settled back comfortably in their chairs to watch the news on TV while they were eating. Ray went back and got them each a cup of coffee. Black with sugar for himself, and extra cream for Kate.

There was a knock on the door to the patio and Shirley appeared with a dozen blueberry, and carrot raisin muffins from the

Goose Island Bakery. Close behind her were Charlotte and Jerry, and of course the baby, Myrtle.

Jerry had a copy of the Goose Island News with him. It contained Jeremy Stapleton's article and pictures from the gathering at the Goose Island Bakery the previous day. The front-page headline read "Miracle Baby Survives Tropical Storm. Makes Landfall on Goose Island."

Ray read the article intently. Even though he had not been there when the girls had discovered Baby Myrtle on Shipwreck Beach, the news story contained a pretty good synopsis of the situation. Since no one knew who had attacked the PharmaSea on the day of the storm, the newspaper referred to the attackers as the Drilling Rig Pirates.

"I wonder why the Drilling Rig Pirates decided to attack the PharmaSea" Ray said.

"No idea," Jerry replied. "It doesn't make any sense."

"I hope they don't come after my baby," Charlotte said. "I could never forgive myself if anything bad happens to her. After what she has been through it's our responsibility to make sure she is cared for and protected."

"I agree," Kate said.

Ray looked at Kate's expression and knew exactly what she had in mind. She was going to leave no stone unturned in her search for the Drilling Rig Pirates.

* * *

Shirley closed the Goose Island Bakery promptly at 2:00 pm. She called Troy and they both converged at the Goose Island B&B at about the same time. Kate and Charlotte were hanging out by the swimming pool with Baby Myrtle. Ray and Jerry had fired up the BBQ grill in the back yard.

Kate and Charlotte were playing Marco-Polo in the pool and Baby Myrtle was loving every minute of it. Charlotte was doing her best to hold on to the Baby, but she kept wriggling away from Charlotte as soon as Kate appeared to be within reach of catching them. Charlotte simply could not hold on to Baby Myrtle who would simply put her hand up in the air and slip through Charlottes fingers. Baby Myrtle kept disappearing under the water and reappearing a few seconds later, several feet away from everyone.

"Oh look!" Shirley remarked. "The baby knows how to swim."

"Wow!" Troy replied. "That's probably how she survived through the storm the other day.

"That's probably how she did it," Ray said. He served up some freshly grilled hot dogs and Jerry passed out some cold beer.

They sat underneath the shade of some mature live oak trees.

"Any news on how the Baby's parents were killed?" Ray inquired.

"They were shot at close range," Troy replied, repeating what he had learned from the Coast Guard. He was not supposed to share privileged information, but what the heck. Everyone around him was a friend whom he would trust with his life. If anyone was going to help him figure out who had killed Myrtle's parents, it was going to be Kate. She had an extremely resourceful gumshoe gene and an unparalleled tenacity that had helped him solve more than one cold case in the past. "Robert Rhodes was shot in the forehead. His body was found near the wheelhouse of his fishing vessel. Brenda was shot in the back of the head. Her body was found near the railing of the boat. Perhaps the pirates shot her as she was attempting to leave."

"It must have happened just after she had thrown Myrtle overboard," Shirley remarked. "I bet she was getting ready to jump in the water when they got to her. They probably did not know that she had a baby when they shot her."

"Yes, that would seem to be what happened," Ray remarked.

"What kind of person would shoot a poor defenseless family?" Kate asked rhetorically. "What could they possibly gain."

"Well, a cure for cancer could be worth a small fortune," Jerry said. "Maybe they were out to steal their research.

"Why steal their research when it would be published in some research journal in due course?" Charlotte asked.

"Well someone either wanted the research all to themselves, or they wanted to prevent the research from being conducted," Troy replied. Either way it would seem to appear that the murders were motivated by 'Big Pharma'.

"Do the fishing charters go anywhere near the Oil Rigs in the Gulf?" Kate inquired.

"Sure," Jerry said. "Some of the best fishing is in the vicinity of the drilling rigs."

"What do you say you and I go out to sea on a fishing charter sometime soon, Sis?" Kate said turning to Shirley. "I think it will help if we get a close up look at the area where the crime occurred."

"Sure, that sounds like fun," Shirley replied.

"What about us?" Ray said. "Do we get to go fishing too?"

"Sure, you do," Kate replied. "We have to have you come along so we can use you for bait." She smiled cheerfully in a manner that left Ray wondering if she was serious or if she was just having a little fun at his expense.

* * *

Kate had just finished placing some cheese and crackers, a bowl of fresh fruit, and a bottle of wine on the kitchen table when the doorbell rang. It was Francesca and Don Giordano.

"We won't stay long, dear," Francesca said. "We just stopped by with a few things for the baby."

Kate poured them a glass of wine and they shared a few pleasantries. Kate told them that the baby was next door, and they soon left to visit Charlotte and Jerry. They had brought a stuffed animal for the baby and wanted to drop if off with Charlotte before going home.

The evening social at the Goose Island B&B got underway before long, and a few of the Islanders dropped in bringing their own bottle of wine to share with everyone. They were always welcome at the Goose Island B&B, even Kenneth Porter!

"Where's Myrtle?" Ken asked. He had picked up some children's books with hard pages that did not tear easily. They were a gift for the Baby.

"She's hanging out with Charlotte and Jerry, next door," Kate replied. "Charlotte is keeping an eye on her, and Jerry is making sure no strangers and get past him to get to the little girl."

"Surely you are not worried about her?" Ken inquired.

"Well we really don't know why her parents were killed," Kate replied. "I am not sure if they had stumbled onto something in their research that could lead to someone wanting to prevent them from continuing with whatever they were working on. Bioluminescent shrimp, or something." Kate could see Ken's ears perk up at the thought that there may be a financial aspect to the murders. Whenever there was money to be made Ken could be counted on to sniff his was to get a piece of the pie.

"I've eaten a few of those shrimps in the past," Ken replied. His other weakness was food. "They taste just like the other kind of shrimp. Personally, I prefer the jumbo shrimp."

"I bet you do," Kate replied. Ken had a large frame and looked like he had been eating jumbo shrimp all his life.

Ken left shortly thereafter to drop of his present at Charlotte and Jerry's house.

Wanda Gleeson stopped by just as Ken was leaving. She had brought a baby blanket with her for the baby. Wanda had a nice figure and Kate could see Ken lurking around by the entrance to the B&B waiting to put a move on her. She wanted to warn Wanda about Ken, but never had a chance to speak with her alone. "Wanda's a big girl," Kate thought to herself as she saw her disappear down the path to Charlotte's house with Ken. "She can take care of herself."

Kevin and Karen Casey, the house guests at the Goose Island B&B, had taken a brief excursion to ride the ferry across Aransas Pass earlier in the day. They had spent the afternoon watching ships sail past the channel on the north end of the dolphin docks at Port Aransas. Karen Casey had heard a rumor at Port Aransas that a mermaid-like Wonder Baby with her golden lasso could be seen riding a pair of dolphins in the moonlight. She wanted to know where they could go to see the Wonder Baby.

Kate and Ray exchanged glances. Clearly, this was how urban legends get started. Baby Myrtle had only been on the island for a day, and she had already made her mark on the island.

"Why sure," Kate said. "We have heard about the Wonder Baby. She hangs around Goose Island a lot. However, she can be awfully hard to spot. I think she only comes out when there is a storm and then only to help lead sailors to safety. Her lasso has a phosphorescent glow to it and it shines with an electric glow whenever there is lightning in the air."

"Goodness!" Mr. Casey remarked. "That's really something else."

"She sure is," Kate continued. "She looks like a moonbeam gliding slowly across the water. You might be able to catch a glimpse of her if you stand at the very end of the fishing pier the next time there is a storm."

"That's good to know," said Mr. Casey.

"You have to keep your eyes peeled," Jerry said. "Even when you see her, you have to pinch yourself and ask if you really saw what you think you saw, or whether it was just your imagination."

"Be sure to take your rain coats and rubber boots, when you go," Kate added. "I can loan you a pair, if you need. It can get pretty wet when the rain starts coming down sideways."

"Yes. Be careful not to get blown off the pier," Ray added.

Kate noticed Mrs. Casey raise her eyebrows. "Good Girl," Kate thought to herself. She didn't think the Casey's were going to risk standing at the end of the fishing pier in a storm anytime soon. Little did they know that Wonder

Baby was right next door at Charlotte's house that very minute.

* * *

Kate glanced through the window and noticed a large white van pull up into her driveway. She didn't recognize the driver. However, it looked like a commercial taxi service.

The door to the van opened, and Kate could see the profile of an elderly woman inside the van. Kate watched her through the living room window of the B&B. The lady in the van waited in the patiently inside the car until her chauffer retrieved her walker from the rear of the van and helped her out of the car. She transitioned from the van to the walker with some difficulty. Then she proceeded to walk carefully up to the front door. Jeeves followed close behind with her suitcase. Kate watched her taking one unsteady step after the other as she approached the front door.

"Hello everyone, I hope I'm not interrupting anything," said the old lady as she walked through the front door and looked around the room. "This sure is a nice place you have," she said to Kate who greeted her as she entered.

"Thanks," Kate replied. "Welcome to the Goose Island B&B."

"I'm Delores Rhodes," she announced. "The baby's grandmother. You can call me Lola. I was told you might be able to help me find a place to stay for a few days.

"Why sure," Kate replied. Troy had given her a head's-up to expect a call from the baby's family. She did not know it would come so soon. So this elderly woman was no other than Baby Myrtle's grandmother, Lola Rhodes. "Just let me know what you need, and I'll be glad to help."

"Thank you so much," said Lola.

"Make yourself at home," Kate said. "We have red wine and cucumber sandwiches in the kitchen if you would like a snack before dinner."

"That sounds wonderful," Lola replied.

It had been less than twenty-four hours since Baby Myrtle had been found on Shipwreck Beach. Lola must have left Raleigh to travel to Goose Island almost immediately upon hearing the news. Kate marveled at Grandma Rhodes for making the journey to Goose Island all the way from Raleigh, North Carolina by herself at short notice.

Grandma Rhodes teeter-tottered her way to a comfortable chair in the corner of the living room. She sat down and closed her eyes for several moments while she paused to catch her breath. The driver appeared at the door with Lola's suitcase. Kate led him down the hallway to Lola's room. It was clear at a glance that the check-in process that was reserved for most guests at the Goose Island B&B where billing and payment information was exchanged with the establishment at check-in would have to wait for a more opportune moment where Grandma Lola was concerned. Kate wondered how she was going to take care of Baby Myrtle.

"How was your journey, Mrs. Rhodes?" Kate asked as she returned with a glass of wine and some sandwiches for Lola.

"Just fine Kate. I heard that you were the one who rescued my grandson, Allen, the other day."

"That's no problem at all, Mrs. Rhodes," Kate replied. She was quite sure that she had just misunderstood what Grandma Rhodes had said. "I had lots of help from my friend Shirley Winters, and Charlotte Duncan who lives next door. However, there must be some mistake. The infant we rescued is a baby girl. She must be your granddaughter, not your grandson, right?"

"Oh!" Grandma Rhodes replied. "What about Allen? Didn't Robert and Brenda have a son called Allen? This is so confusing."

Grandma Rhodes paused to catch her breath and regain her composure.

"You mean Eleanor, or should I say Ellen?" Kate said. "Ellen if a girl, not a boy." They looked at each other in silence. Troy had informed Kate that Baby Myrtle's real name was Eleanor. She wondered if Grandma Rhodes had had a touch of Alzheimer's. She looked very disoriented as she blinked at Kate without speaking. She must have confused herself into thinking the baby was a boy called Allen, instead of her granddaughter Ellen.

"Thanks so much for taking care of the baby," Lola added finally. "Thanks also, for letting me stay at your B&B at such short notice.""

"I am more than happy to have you stay here with us, Kate said. "Please accept my deepest sympathy and condolences for what happened to your son and his wife."

"Yes, Robert had such an amazing future in front of him. It's a loss for humanity, you know. Robert was determined to find a cure for cancer. His father, my late husband, Jim, died of pancreatic cancer about ten years ago, and I think that is why Robert has dedicated his life to finding a cure for this disease."

"Robert must have been very close to his father," Kate said.

"Oh yes. Jim was an amazing man. He flew gliders into France several times during World War-II. Can you imagine landing a sheet of plywood in a meadow in France behind enemy lines, and then making your way home over land until someone can smuggle you across the channel just so that you can do it again? Jim flew more than a dozen missions into France. We were high school sweethearts, and when he returned, we started a restaurant on the coast. I think that's where Robert fell in love with the sea. Anyway, after Jim passed away I decided to move to Raleigh."

"Goodness, that sounds terribly dangerous," Charlotte said. "We owe so much to the boys who helped to carry us on to victory in Europe."

"Yes, we do," Lola said. There was a long pause. "So where is my darling granddaughter?" she asked.

"My neighbor Charlotte is taking care of your granddaughter." Kate said. "I'll go over next door and let her know you are here."

Kat walked slowly to the house next door. She began to wonder if Grandma Rhodes was simply being delusional, or was it possible that Robert and Brenda had another child? A baby boy called Allen?

Myrtle the turtle had a beautiful name, Eleanor. Phonetically speaking, it was easy to confuse Ellen with Allen. However, a grandmother like Delores would have noticed the difference between a grandson and a granddaughter the first time she changed the baby's diapers. Kate would have to let Troy know about the possibility that the Rhodes family may have had a son in addition to their daughter.

* * *

Kate entered Charlotte's kitchen and walked in expecting to see Baby Myrtle entertaining Charlotte with her antics, but she was nowhere in sight. Instead, she found the house deserted and Milo asleep in her favorite chair in the living room. He got up reluctantly when Kate entered the room. Kate panicked. Any responsible adult knows that you cannot leave a baby unattended for even a single minute.

"Charlotte!" Kate said. "Where's Myrtle?"

There was no response. Charlotte turned sideways on the sofa, away from Kate.

Kate went through the house as quickly as possible. There was no sign of Baby Myrtle. Kate opened all the bedrooms and closets. It would not surprise her if Baby Myrtle was hiding somewhere waiting to jump out from behind the clothes hanging in the closet and yell "Boo". At this moment Kate would have welcomed a little surprise to come darting out of her secret hiding place.

"Oh no," Kate thought to herself. Myrtle had either been kidnapped, or she had disappeared by herself. Neither one of these scenarios was going to be good.

It had not escaped Kate's attention that Robert and Brenda Rhodes must have had a significant family fortune. One that allowed them to operate a Shrimp Boat in the Gulf for an extended period. As frugal as they may have been, it was not cheap to pay for fuel and other essentials. Operational expenses would have made a significant dent in anybody else's budget, and if Robert could afford the expense then he clearly came from a wealthy family. His University Grant was unlikely to support such an extravagant lifestyle. His family would surely pay a handsome reward if they were blackmailed into doing so. And what better blackmail than to take Baby Myrtle captive.

Charlotte had often mentioned that Baby Myrtle was a handful. What if she had learned to open doors and had gone exploring on Goose Island while Charlotte was taking a nap? Whatever was she going to do if Baby Myrtle had escaped while Charlotte was asleep?

"Charlotte!" Kate said. "Wake up." She gave Charlotte's shoulder a gentle shake.

Charlotte grunted.

Kate was relentless. She gave Charlotte a healthy shove.

Charlotte opened her eyes and looked at Kate sleepily. "Well Hello, Kate," Charlotte replied. "Is everything okay? I just lay down to take a nap. How's everything getting along over at the B&B? I was about to come over for a glass of wine. Would that be okay?"

"Of course, Charlotte," Kate replied. "But where is Baby Myrtle?" she asked in a rush.

"Shirley came over and picked her up about an hour ago," Charlotte said. "That baby is like a wind-up bunny. She is so full of sparkle and energy. I think she just wore me out. I suspect they will be back soon. When Shirley came over I was so happy to get a break that I didn't ask Shirley where she was going or what time she would be back home."

"Oh, I'm so relieved," Kate replied. Thank goodness, the baby was safe. Kids are such a huge responsibility. "For a minute I thought something terrible had happened to her," Kate continued. "Myrtle's Grandmother Lola just arrived from North Carolina. Come on over and meet her."

"Well, she's going to have her hands full with Baby Myrtle," Charlotte said. "I'll be over soon."

Kate walked slowly back to her house. She did not feel good about having to go back home and let Grandma Lola know that the baby was nowhere to be found.

* * *

Fortunately, Kate did not need to offer any excuses or explanations. Shirley and Baby Myrtle appeared in the living room of the B&B at about the moment that Kate was getting ready to let Grandma Lola know that Baby Myrtle was missing. She was not looking forward to the questions and recriminations that were sure to follow.

Baby Myrtle tumbled out of Shirley's arms and ran across the room to give Kate a hug. Oh boy, oh boy, oh boy! There is nothing quite like getting attacked by a flying baby! Kate scooped her up into her arms and gave her a kiss.

"Where have you been, little girl?" Kate asked her.

Baby Myrtle nodded. "Uh huh," she said.

"Did you have fun?" Kate asked.

Baby Myrtle nodded again. "Uh huh! she said.

GOOSE ISLAND CURE

Shirley had just taken Baby Myrtle to the Goose Island Aquarium. Baby Myrtle had the most adorable expressions and every eye in the room was upon her. She had really taken a liking to the dolphins and was making shrill dolphin-speak sounds when she returned.

"Do you think the baby is okay?" Grandma Lola asked. "She seems to be traumatized. Perhaps we should take her to see a doctor."

"That's the first thing we did after we found her," Kate explained.

"She thinks she is a dolphin," Shirley added helpfully.

"Gah," said Baby Myrtle between shrieks. "Gah."

"That's what she calls Milo, my neighbor's dog," Kate said, also trying to be helpful. There would be nothing more traumatizing that having to take Baby Myrtle back to the doctor for Grandma Lola's peace of mind. "She calls Milo, Gah."

"Why doesn't she just call him Milo?" Grandma Lola asked.

"We're working on it," Shirley said. She did not like Grandma Lola very much.

"Did you see a doggy?" Kate asked the baby.

Myrtle nodded vigorously.

"She got really excited when she saw the dolphins. I think she was calling them dogs," Shirley said helpfully. "The dolphins came over to the edge of the water and shrieked at her when they saw her. She's practically speaking dolphin now."

Myrtle nodded again. She seemed to sense they were talking about her and she enjoyed all the attention she was getting.

"That must have been what saved her life," Shirley said.

Lola smiled politely, as if to say, "That's nice dear but I have no idea what you are talking about."

* * *

A short while later, Troy and Jesse Ward from the Coast Guard knocked on the door. They were both in full uniform and had clearly stopped by to visit in an official capacity. Troy asked if Grandma Rhodes was available. Both Troy and Jesse had a solemn look on their faces which made it clear that they had stopped by to give Grandma Rhodes an update on her son and daughter-in-law.

Kate stepped outside the house and steered them away for the door. She asked to speak with them in private before they met Grandma Rhodes. As the group huddled together for an impromptu meeting outside the front door, Kate explained how Grandma Rhodes had initially asked for her grandson, Allen Rhodes.

"It just seemed so strange to hear her ask for a grandson and not her granddaughter Ellen," Kate said.

"I agree," Troy said. "We'll have to look into it further and see if there is another missing child involved."

"Oh boy!" Jesse exclaimed. "This doesn't get any easier, does it?"

Kate nodded. They went inside the house and Kate introduced them to Grandma Rhodes. Troy and Jesse took Grandma Lola aside. A few minutes later, they were huddled over the coffee table with Grandma Lola deep in conversation. They looked as if they needed to be left alone and Kate gave them plenty of room. Grandma Jean was probably getting an update on her son and daughter. She would need to plan for some funeral arrangements before long.

Troy, Jesse, and Grandma Lola conversed for a good half an hour. At the end of their conversation, Kate noticed Grandma Lola signing several documents. When the officers had concluded their business and departed, Grandma Lola settled back into one of the chairs in the living room.

"Would you like another glass of wine?" Kate inquired.

"Why thank you, dear," Lola replied. "A glass of red wine would be wonderful."

Kate brought over a small bowl of fruit, some crackers and cheese, and a glass of red wine. The Caseys joined the group that was forming in the living room and they proceeded with brief introductions.

"The funeral is tomorrow," Lola said. "It will be three days since they passed away and it's time to put their bodies to rest. I have just made the arrangements to have Robert and Brenda cremated. If you can join us, I'd like to scatter their ashes into the Gulf tomorrow evening."

≈≈≈≈≈≈

7. Funeral Services

The caskets containing the bodies of Robert and Brenda Rhodes remained closed throughout a brief funeral service. Many of the Islanders, and several local fishermen attended the funeral to pay their respects to the couple who had been brutally removed from this world. By now, almost everyone on Goose Island had heard the news about the baby. They were shocked by the tragedy and the funeral became a show of solidarity for the Islanders.

The Giordano's, Don and Francesca, brought a beautiful bouquet of flowers as did Kenneth Porter, and many of the Islanders. All the Islanders huddled together in a group on one side of the chapel. There was whispered talk about making sure that "this sort of thing never happens again". Kenneth Porter was seated next to a chunky fellow with a beard. Kate did not recognize him, but she assumed he was one of his business associates. Kenneth was all business, all the time. The only thing that pre-empted his hound dog sense of sniffing out a good deal was the sight of a pretty girl in a miniskirt.

The turnout for the service at the funeral home exceeded all expectations, considering that no one there had known Robert or Brenda personally. In addition to the Islanders, there were a few people from out of town. The Coast Guard officer, Jesse, who had found the bodies of Robert and Brenda on the PharmaSea attended the funeral with his wife Danette. Seated next to Jesse and Danette, was another couple, Cindy, who worked for the DEA, and her husband Tommy. Everyone brought flowers and cards, and these were displayed beside the pulpit in a brilliant display of color.

One of Robert's high school friends, David Sullivan, better known as Sully to his friends, had flown down from North Carolina for the funereal with his wife Sheila. They knew Grandma Lola and sat next to her throughout the service.

Shirley held Baby Myrtle on her lap. She sat quietly throughout the entire ceremony. Shirley was wearing a necklace made of garnets and Myrtle seemed content to play with it. However, when she started pulling on it, Shirley had to take it off and put it away in her purse. Myrtle did not like that and she made a face to let Shirley know how she felt. Shirley had a small plastic figurine in her purse. She took it out and gave it to Myrtle who brightened up and began playing with it immediately.

Grandma Lola had prepared a short video presentation consisting mostly of pictures of Robert and Brenda. Baby Myrtle watched the presentation carefully. She pointed a pudgy little finger at the screen and turned to Shirley and nodded her head vigorously. Sully gave a small heart-warming speech about his childhood friend, Robert, the good times they had had together, and Robert's many medical accomplishments.

Sully recalled childhood memories chasing fireflies with Robert on Grandma Lola's front porch, and how Robert had gone on to help pioneer the use of bioluminescence in various cancer treatment programs. This included bioluminescence imaging as a strategy for monitoring the spread of the cancer cells within the body, as well as providing the ability to measure tumor response to various treatments. Sully also explained some of Robert's pioneering work in bioluminescence activated destruction where cancer cells are altered to make them luciferous so that they glow just like a firefly. This makes it possible to detect and destroy the cancerous cells without affecting normal cells with a photosensitizing agent.

The priest in attendance was the final speaker. He read several passages from the

Bible. Kate liked the quote from Proverbs which stated very simply that "In the path of righteousness is life, and in its pathway, there is no death." Roberts pioneering cancer research would surely take on a life of its own, helping to keep his memory alive for a long time, and Myrtle would make sure that her mother, Brenda's memory would live on inside her.

After the service the caskets were removed from the room and everyone filed into a small reception area for some sandwiches and drinks. Everybody stopped by Grandma Lola and offered their condolences. The fishermen removed their hats when they stopped by to speak with her. Some of the had beards and a definite nautical appearance to their attire and their appearance. However, many of them looked no different from the Islanders whom Kate knew.

Kate saw Kenneth Porter talking to some of the fishermen and tried to memorize the faces of the people he was talking with. It's too bad that you cannot take photographs of people attending a funeral the same way that you can at a wedding.

Charlotte stopped to talk with the bearded fellow who had been seated next to Kenneth Porter during the memorial service. It was Charlie. The fellow who Charlotte had met at the Emergency Room.

"How's Gail," Charlotte asked. There was no sign of her in the room. "Is she with you today?"

"No," Charlie replied. "I haven't seen Gail today."

"Do give her my regards when you see her. I hope she is doing okay."

"I sure will," Charlie replied.

Jesse Ward and Cindy met up with Troy in the reception area and they both stepped outside the room to talk privately about the tragedy. Kate chatted with Danette and Tommy. Danette and Tommy were the nicest people Kate had ever met. They both loved R&B music from the sixties and when they left Kate found herself promising to meet up with them again in the future.

The Director of the funeral service took charge of the caskets containing Robert and Brenda's bodies. Robert and Brenda were cremated while the reception was taking place. Their remains were placed in two large urns. About half way through the reception their remains were carried into the reception room and placed behind a photograph of the couple.

"We could probably scatter their ashes from the fishing pier at Shipwreck Beach," Kate said.

"No thank you, dear," Lola replied. I have made some arrangements for a tour boat to take us out to sea when we leave the reception. I planned this before I left North Carolina. I had plenty of time to make a few phone calls before leaving home. I think it is what Robert and Brenda would have wanted. I don't believe they would want to be buried next to an Oak or a Maple tree in North Carolina. They would much rather be out in the ocean collecting marine samples. Perhaps their spirits will help protect other innocent people who are out on the ocean from being attacked in such a terrible manner.

* * *

As per the tradition in Texas, the cars who were going to attend the burial ceremony left the parking lot of the funeral home one by one with their lights on. The procession of cars drove to the marina after the service. Troy and Shirley drove Grandma Lola and Myrtle in the lead car with their hazard lights flashing. Kate and Ray brought up the rear of the procession with hazard lights, and a pair of white funeral flags.

There were about fifty people in attendance. They gathered silently in a small outdoor patio at the marina where the charter boat was located. When the captain was ready he gave them the signal to begin boarding. They came on board quickly and sat down either in the main center section of the boat or upstairs in a raised, open air deck area. It was a sunny day and there was a cool breeze in the air that wafted across the marina.

Grandma Lola stayed downstairs with Troy to keep her company. Shirley and Myrtle went on upstairs. Baby Myrtle sat next to Shirley with her feet dangling happily in the air. Kate and Ray went upstairs as well. Baby Myrtle gave Kate a big welcoming smile when she sat down next to her.

The chairs on the deck faced backwards and they watched the marina disappear and fall into the distance. The travelled slowly down a narrow channel that led to the Gulf. The girls, Myrtle was now one of them, watched the waves that that boat left in its wake.

Once they were in the Gulf they heard a distinct change in the sound of the engines as they began moving more rapidly through the water. It did not take them long to travel about ten miles off-shore, close to the drilling rigs where the tragedy had occurred. When they reached the designated area the sound of the engines changed again to a slow steady sound. The captain gave two long blasts with his horn to let the other fishermen know what he was doing. Waves lapped alongside the boat.

There were several fishing vessels in the area and from all appearances, everyone seemed to be minding their own business. No one paid them any attention when their charter boat came to a halt about a half mile from the nearest drilling rig.

The priest who had performed the service at the funeral home said a small prayer just before Robert and Brenda's ashes were disbursed into the ocean. "We commend unto thy hands, most merciful Father, the souls of the departed, and we commit their bodies to you, ashes to ashes, dust to dust. Grant this, O merciful Father, that they may be found acceptable in thy sight for the sake of our Lord and Savior, Jesus Christ." His final words were still swirling through the Kate's mind when Robert and Brenda's ashes were scattered into the ocean.

No one spoke for several minutes. Shirley and Baby Myrtle blew a goodbye kiss into the wind just before Robert and Brenda's remains were carried away by the ocean currents. Baby Myrtle kept opening and closing her little fist as she said goodbye. Shirley could feel her eyes well up with tears as she hugged Baby Myrtle and wrapped her arms protectively around the baby.

The captain gave two short blasts once again and the sound of the engine changed to a higher pitch as they turned the boat around and made their way back to the marina. A half hour later they were back on dry land.

* * *

Kate opened a bottle of Cabernet when they returned to the Goose Island B&B. Shirley poured the wine into small disposable glasses and passed these out to the guests. She followed with cheese and crackers. Myrtle got some milk.

Grandma Lola was worn out from the events of the day and left shortly afterwards to rest up and get some shut-eye.

"Well, what's next?" Shirley asked Kate. Baby Myrtle nibbled on a cracker. She took a slice of cheese but instead of eating it she crumbled it into tiny pieces that fell on the floor. "I guess Grandma Lola will be heading back to North Carolina soon with Baby Myrtle.

"Twelve more days," Kate replied. "She reserved a room for two weeks when she arrived. I suppose she could leave any time, but the plan was for her to stay for two weeks.

"Maybe we can talk her into staying on a little longer," Shirley said. "Just so I can keep this little munchkin here on Goose Island. I'm getting very attached to her. I have really no idea what plans Grandma Lola has for Myrtle, but I am almost sure I am not going to like them."

"I hate funerals," Charlotte said. "They make me so sad."

"What a way to go!" Jerry remarked.

"I know," Ray said. "Brenda must have tossed her baby overboard after the Drilling Rig Pirates had shot her husband."

"It's too bad that it came down to this," Shirley said.

"What did you and Jesse and Cindy talk about at the funeral?" Kate asked Troy.

"Well first we talked about the baby," Troy said. Eleanor Rhodes' DNA matched Robert and Brenda with a 99% probability. There is no doubt that she was on the PharmaSea when it was attacked by the Drilling Rig Pirates. Next, we talked about Allen Rhodes. Robert and Brenda did indeed have a second child. The only problem is that he wasn't discovered on the boat and he still hasn't washed up anywhere along the coast. So officially, he's listed as a missing person."

"Have you told Grandma Rhodes about this?" Kate wanted to know. "She was pretty sure that she had a grandson called Allen when she reached Goose Island. She did not seem to know much about her granddaughter Ellen."

"We haven't discussed Allen with Grandma Rhodes so far," Troy said. "She's had a lot to deal with and we did not want to push her over the edge until we gather some additional information, if you know what I mean."

"Who's Allen?" Charlotte inquired.

"Yeah, what's going on here, Troy?" Shirley demanded.

"There was another child on the boat," Troy said hesitantly. "He seems to have been lost at sea."

"Oh!" Jerry said. "That does not sound good."

"I know," Troy said. "The boy's name was Allen which does sound a lot like Ellen. Its confusing, and for some time we thought that Allen and Ellen were one and the same person. However, clearly that is not the case. Jesse assured me that they are still looking into it. The Coast Guard just opened a missing persons investigation for Allen Rhodes along the entire Gulf Coast. However, it's akin to looking for a needle in a haystack. If someone found Allen and decided to keep him it could be years until he was tracked down via a DNA match in some other routine investigation."

Troy paused and looked at Kate. Neither one of them knew what to say next. Everybody in the room looked at each other in stunned silence. Kate and Troy waited for the rest of the group to soak in the fact that there was a missing child called Allen, who may not have survived the attack on the PharmaSea.

"Anything else?" Ray inquired.

"We talked about drug smuggling," Troy replied. "This has all the signs of a premeditated, gang-land killing. Someone chose to go aboard the PharmaSea in the dead of the night. They made a conscious decision to kill Robert and Brenda. These were no rival shrimpers. They were hardened criminals who were just carrying out the orders they were given."

"Yes, that makes sense," Kate replied.

Baby Myrtle had finished her cracker and she walked unsteadily over to the coffee table in the center of the room. She teeter-tottered across the room like a sailor and smiled impishly at everyone in the room. Kate gave her another cracker and she took a bite and then turned to Shirley and offered to share the rest of the cracker with her.

"How do the drugs get into this country?" Ray asked. He had a fair idea, but just wanted to hear Troy's thoughts on the matter.

"Any one of a number of ways", Troy said. "Over land, sea, and air." They still use mules to bring drugs across the border. Over land they smuggle them in cars coming across the border using hidden compartments, spare tires, and just about anything else that you can think of. However, now they have expanded to using tunnels, catapults, small airplanes, and boats. Hell, it even enters this country through shipments that are sent via U.S. Mail. Jesse and Cindy asked me to look at the marine vessels coming and going through the bay. I've been asked to call them if I see bales of marijuana floating ashore on the beach, or anything else that looks suspicious."

"Let me get this straight," Ray said. "Smugglers use the US Postal Service to ship illegal drugs into the US!"

"Yes," Troy nodded.

"And we deliver it for them!" Kate exclaimed. "That's unbelievable".

"Aren't these shipments traceable?" Shirley asked. She was holding Baby Myrtle in her arms.

Baby Myrtle was getting a little restless and she raised her arms above her head and slipped easily down to the floor. She ran across the room and then into the hallway that led to the kitchen. There was a lot of giggling in the hallway. Kate was about to go look for Baby Myrtle when she returned to the living room.

The baby had a small yellow toy car in her hand when she returned. Kate recognized the toy car from the one she thought she had seen in the hallway a few times. She raised her eyebrows but did not say anything. As far as she could recall the car had not been in the hallway when she had swept it earlier that morning.

Kate was about to ask the baby where she had found the yellow toy car but decided not to do so at the last minute. Some things are better left alone.

"Yes, but all the addresses are fake," Troy replied.

"Do you think the smugglers are located near Goose Island?" Charlotte asked. "I mean, couldn't they be anywhere on the Gulf coast? What about Galveston, Freeport or Port Lavaca? What about Port Mansfield and Port Isabel?"

"Cindy said they could be anywhere on the Gulf Coast," Troy replied. "They probably are smugglers in all the cities that you mentioned. However, they tend to travel short distances to avoid detection. The Coast Guard can easily track a vessel going from Mexico to Galveston. However, if the same vessel goes just fifty to a hundred miles from Mexico, unloads its cargo to a floating barge, and then returns home it draws little or no attention to itself. Later another vessel from Port Mansfield will pick up the barge and bring it on into port. Sometimes they will pick up the barge and drop it off elsewhere in the Gulf to move it closer to Corpus Christi or Galveston. The process is repeated until it gets to its intended destination and all without any unnecessary risks to the smugglers who never have to go through a DEA checkpoint."

"Yes, I see", Jerry replied. "Well I do a fair amount of fishing from the pier and I'll keep watch on the ships coming and going through the harbor.

"Thanks. Just let me know if you see anything unusual," Troy said.

"Thanks Troy," Kate replied. "Shirley and I will keep watch on the beach. We'll let you know in case one of the floating barges gets lost and comes on into Goose Island. I'd like nothing better than to help you catch these evil people."

"I know you will, Kate," Troy said. "Thanks for your help. Please keep your eyes open, and please do not take any unnecessary risks. We need to do this for ourselves, not just for Baby Myrtle."

"Do you think they are going to come after Baby Myrtle?" Shirley asked.

"No, I don't think Baby Myrtle has anything to do with this," Troy replied.

"Thanks," Kate said. "I feel a lot better."

However, Shirley was not reassured and simply held Myrtle more tightly

"My guess is that they were killed because they saw the smugglers bringing contraband across the border," Troy said. Shrimpers are very hard-working, simple, God-fearing people. Some have been doing it for generations. Others are refugees from Vietnam who settled here after the fall of Saigon in 1975.

The fellows who have been shrimping for generations and the newcomers don't always get along. I'm not saying that there isn't a bad egg in the bunch, but my instinct tells me that they are unlikely to hijack a research vessel on the open sea and murder everyone on board. They are far more likely to get into conflicts with each other than with Robert and Brenda. Besides the State of Texas mandates the hours that commercial Shrimp boats can operate and in Spring it is from 30 minutes before sunrise until 2:00 pm. This is to restrict shrimpers from overfishing the depleted resources in the Gulf. I seriously doubt there were any shrimp boats on the water when Robert and Brenda were murdered.

"That makes sense," Kate said. "Thanks for the heads-up. We will just have to keep our ears open and eyes peeled at all times, won't we Troy!"

"That we will," he replied. "Do be careful. I don't want anybody getting hurt. Let me know immediately if you see something unusual. These people are ruthless and more dangerous than you can imagine.

* * *

Ray was planning to return to work in Odessa the following morning. As usual the weekend had gone by all too fast and Kate was not ready to see his bony rear end leaving her behind at Goose Island by herself. She did not handle all his comings and goings well. It was an emotional roller-coaster ride for her.

They drove down to the Swamp Shack, a bluesy Seafood restaurant at the end of Copano Bay for dinner together. Ray had a lot on his mind and it was starting to get under Kate's skin. Even though he was seated next to her she knew that he had already hopped on the return flight to Odessa.

She tried to pay attention to him as he described his work as an Engineer for an Oil-Field Drilling company in Odessa. He was obviously very committed to the work he had been doing for the better part of his life. She admired his zeal and dedication to a career where she knew he would not be missed for more than twenty-four hours after he decided to hang up his hard-hat. The way 'Corporate America' worked, someone else would step up and take his place the very next day.

Kate's frustration stemmed from the fact that she simply could not get through to him that the life and death issues that she was dealing with on Goose Island were far more important than the mundane aspects of his day to day work schedule in Odessa. When she asked if he really had to leave the next day Ray voiced some of his usual excuses about having some important business meetings to attend to. Something about having to do a presentation for some auditors. Kate had tried to persuade him several times to move to Goose Island but there was always some urgent reason why he had to return to work. Sometimes she wondered whether he was married to her or to his work.

"Are you trying to cook the books before the auditors find all your malfeasance? All the money laundering and thievery and whatever it is that you do for a living?" Kate asked him as they sat down for dinner at the Swamp Shack, a cozy Seafood restaurant at the end of the Copano Bay bridge.

"I'm just an Engineer," Ray had replied. Kate was given to making wild unfounded accusations that were always right on target.

"I don't trust you," She said. "You're nothing but a liar, and a pretty bad one at that. I'm sure if there was a real oil field disaster everything would just blow sky high and a lot of innocent people would lose their lives."

"No dear," Ray protested weakly. She knew him so well that she could read him like a book! How did she know? He had to update his documentation of Disaster Recovery procedures to see what additional safeguards and precautions could be implemented before the audit commenced. The key was in having continuous automated monitoring and instrumentation in place, so that shut-down sequences could begin to engage without human intervention. To try to explain this to Kate over dinner was a recipe for a different kind of disaster. All Ray said was, "Sorry, Kate. I'm just trying to do my job to the best of my ability."

Life is all about choices, and Kate wasn't sure how to break it to Ray that just because he was good at something, that wasn't a compelling reason to continue doing it with complete disregard for his family.

"You're a good man, Ray," Kate remarked as they waited for the main course to be served. "You have your whole life in front of you and I want you to be happy with whatever it is you do at work. Just don't let your boss down in Odessa blindfold you, throw you in the back of the car and take you for a ride and sell you some ocean-front property in Arizona.

"Oh, I'll never fall for that," Ray protested.

"Ray, you helped me create the Goose Island B&B a few years age when you remodeled the patio, installed doors, windows, expanded the driveway and completed any number of improvements to make it what it is. This is your home Ray. You are welcome to stay here with me any time."

"Thanks Kate," Ray said. He made a mental note to write his resignation letter as soon as he reached the office the next day. Disaster Recovery Audits were not his idea of a good time. "I'd like nothing better than to be here with you all the time. I'll be here before you know it."

They finished dinner and drove back to Kate's home on Marlin St. Kate was right. It had really come a long way from the time they had started. The landscaping, the lighting in the yard, the driveway, plantation shutters all looked very warm and welcoming.

"Are you ready for dessert?" Kate asked.

"Anything you say, dear" Ray replied. "You look better than two scoops of Chocolate ice-cream topped with a maraschino cherry. Drizzled with honey."

"Would you settle for some Tullamore Dew and home-made peanut butter crunch?" Kate asked.

"Sure," Ray said. That sounds delicious. Anything you make has got to be good."

"Do you want me to fly down to Odessa with you tomorrow morning and let your project manager know who your real boss is?" she asked him, the night before he left. She had him at a serious disadvantage since they were just getting ready for bed, and the wrong answer would almost certainly end with him sleeping on the sofa downstairs, or in his rental car in the parking lot of Corpus Christi International Airport.

"I would love that, dear" he had replied as she proceeded to undress with her back towards him. He looked at her backside and wondered what to make of the situation. On the one hand here was a naked girl who was at this very moment in the process of getting completely naked right before his very eyes. On the other hand, he was getting some mixed signals from her. His mind was going through a sensory overload much like a circuit breaker that was just about to blow a fuse.

It seemed to take forever, but Ray had waited patiently until she turned around before reaching out to put his arms around her and give her a kiss. It was their last night together until he returned to her at the end of the week. They fell on the bed and devoured each other hungrily.

"Slow down, Ray," Kate whispered. This isn't the Olympics, you know."

"Uh huh," Ray replied. He proceeded to cover her with kisses, driving her out of control.

"Do you love me, Ray? Kate asked.

"Of course, I do!" Ray exclaimed without hesitation. "You're beautiful, smart, kind, considerate, caring, and the most thoughtful person I know. I love everything about you.

Your eyes, your face, your smile, your sense of humor, the way you lick your lips after a sip of coffee, the way you hold my hand when we are together, the warmth you exude when you put your arms around me. I love watching you sleep. I love the shape of your breasts and the curve of your belly. Everything about you never ceases to amaze me. I love when you bump into me when we are standing in the line for ice-cream at the Soda Shoppe."

"I do like going to the Soda Shoppe," Kate said. "They have the best peanut-butter-crunch ice-cream in the world."

However, Ray was not done yet. "I love you more than you can ever imagine, Kate. When I'm with you I'm so happy that I feel as if I'm floating in air. I worship the ground you walk on! I love the breath of fresh air that follows you like a halo wherever you go. I love remembering the past and dreaming about our future together."

"Oh really," she said with a twinkle in her eye. "You're nothing but a silver-tongued liar! Liar, liar pants on fire!"

"Well, yes," Ray said. "They are. However, that's for a completely different reason."

"We'll just have to do something about that," Kate replied. "Won't we?".

She reached towards him and undid the buttons on his shirt. She slipped her arms around him inside his shirt and gave him three short kisses. He kissed her neck and nibbled on her ear. Kate leaned forward and pushed him ever so gently backwards towards the bed. She held him up momentarily as he started to lose his balance and undid the top-most button of his jeans. He was still talking about the exquisite curvature of her spine when she let go and he fell on the covers. It was a struggle for control and Kate responded with a passion that took his breath away. Kate matched his every move with one of her own that demanded every ounce of his attention.

Kate's bedroom opened to a small patio that overlooked the entrance to Copano Bay. The French doors to the patio had been left open and the sea breeze from the ocean wafted past the curtains that billowed and flapped noiselessly, letting in an occasional moonbeam. In the near darkness, Kate could see the expression on Ray's face, mirror her own, ever increasing feeling of excitement.

"How is it that whenever we are having a serious conversation, I'm always flat on my back without any clothes on?" Kate asked.

"I love you so much, Kate. I couldn't bear to think of my life without you. You are my muse, my anchor, my soulmate. The one thing that is right with my life. I exist only for you. I am nothing without you, Kate. Life without you wouldn't be worth living."

Outside her window Kate could hear the chuga-chug-chug of a diesel engine on board a ship slowly making its way across the bay. It blended in with sounds of frogs chirping, and the buzzing hum of cicadas. In the distance a ship's fog-horn sounded out a warning to travelers sailing through the ocean.

Kate smiled, and then she proceeded to give Ray a million good reasons to come back to see her again at the end of the week.

≈≈≈≈≈≈

8. Federal Support

Some of the people who had attended Robert and Brenda's funeral stayed on in the area Goose Island for a few days after the funeral. The experience of losing someone you are really closing to can be very traumatic and it is sometimes necessary to stay close to other people for a few days to help recover from your loss. Sully, Robert's high school buddy stayed at a hotel in Port Aransas. He stopped by to take Grandma Lola out for lunch the next day before leaving town. Cindy the DEA Agent stayed at the Goose Island B&B.

Kate could not help wondering if Cindy was staying at the Goose Island B&B in a personal or a professional capacity. Cindy was very well informed, respectful, and likeable. She could carry on a conversation on just about anything at all. Her knowledge of historical facts and figures was impressive. She could reach into the vast recesses of her steel-trap mind to rattle off figures and statistics to bolster her comments and arguments. Cindy showed a lot of interest in everything Kate did and ingratiated herself into the inner circle of Kate's friends Shirley and Charlotte in less time than it takes to bake a fresh batch of blueberry muffins.

Kate was never able to ascertain her motives. Cindy's questions were very personal, but never prying. She did not offend Kate or any of her friends, but there was no denying that she was very different from anyone they had ever met before. Kate was glad to have her company and the chance to speak with someone her own age. Among the many things they discussed was Kate and Shirley's experience in finding Baby Myrtle on Shipwreck Beach.

"You were amazing," Cindy said, when she heard how they had found Baby Myrtle. "Weren't you afraid?"

"I'm not sure," Kate said. "It happened very quickly. I keep returning to that evening and ask myself if there was another child in the water near Baby Myrtle. However, I just don't recall anything else in the water."

"Same here," Shirley said. "I'm pretty sure there was no sign of Allen Rhodes in the water when we found Myrtle."

"Don't beat yourself up over it," Cindy said. "You did the best you could. If there had been anything else in the water, then I'm sure you would have noticed something."

Cindy had a pleasant, easy smile and a twinkle in her eyes at all times. If you did not know any better, you might assume that she was up to her eyeballs in some top-secret project that would cost you your life if she let you in on it. Once you got to know her a little better, you came to realize that most of her projects involved wine. She was the most likeable person in the world. Her job with the DEA was rather stressful and she had just decided to take a small vacation following her visit to Goose Island.

By the end of her first day in Cindy's company Kate was convinced that Cindy used wine as a truth serum to get people to open up and share their most private innermost secrets. Charlotte, Kate, Shirley and Cindy spent most of the afternoon hanging out on the patio by the pool at the Goose Island B&B. They were on their second bottle of Merlot when Kate found herself telling Cindy what a wonderful lover Ray was. It occurred to Kate that the information might encourage Cindy to attempt to steal Ray from her. It was a good thing Ray had returned to Odessa. She made a mental note not to mention him again in front of Cindy.

"You're fortunate to have a such good man," Cindy said. "Some women go through their entire lives without finding a lover who is patient enough to wait for them before they get their rocks off and leave you hanging."

"Thanks," Kate replied. "Ray's all right. He's never in a hurry."

The girls laughed. More secrets spilled out into the open. They talked about the people in town. Kenneth Porter's uncanny tendency to brush up against women whenever he was close to them. His ability to stand exactly where you were sure to bump into him when you least expected it. They drank more wine. Before long Cindy knew just about everybody in town.

"I dated a telephone repair man once," Cindy said. She proceeded to share some ribald details and lurid descriptions of her lover and their exploits. The girls doubled up with laughter with each embarrassing detail that was revealed in the unstated knowledge that it was being shared in complete confidence.

Myrtle laughed along with them. She enjoyed playing peek-a-boo with them and her imaginary friend. Ray had bought her a few more toys and she now had a nice new sleek-looking black Mama car to go with the little yellow Baby car that she liked to roll down the hallway. Myrtle's fascination with cars was a clear indication that she had once had an older brother who had influenced her recreational preferences.

Shirley shared her blueberry muffin recipe with Cindy. Kate and Charlotte gasped when they learned that Shirley routinely added amaretto liquor to her muffins. Charlotte shared personal details of growing up in Philadelphia and living in a row house on a street that was so narrow that you had to park your car with two wheels on the sidewalk. There was a lot of snow during winter and the streets would become impassable. To keep the streets clear, everyone would to fill up garbage cans with snow and empty them near a city park at the end of the street.

Kate described her near-rape experience with her uncle Walter, her mother's boyfriend. Walter had moved in after Kate's Dad had passed away. Kate despised Walter and the fact that he had groped her and put his hands up her dress had not endeared him to her, not one bit.

"I was visiting my mom Cathleen and uncle Walter in Colorado one summer," Kate said. "Uncle Walter drove us out to Creekside Park to watch the fireworks on July 4th. Mom and Walter were sitting on some folding chairs and I was lying on a blanket inside the station wagon waiting for the fireworks to start with the tailgate open. There was a lot of loud music and everybody was drinking beer and having a grand time. However, when the show started, Walter crawled into the station wagon next to me. I could smell his cigar breath everywhere. It was his car and I guess at first, I thought he was just looking for something in the car. But when he lay down next to me and put his hand under my dress I knew exactly what he was after. "

"Oh my," Charlotte said. She had met Cathleen and Walter on one of their most infrequent visits to see their daughter at Goose Island. Walter had struck her as a real wheeler-dealer. He wanted to know how much everything, and everybody was worth. Kenneth Porter was a perfect angel compared to Walter.

"It was disgusting," Kate said. "He had me trapped against the side of the car. He pulled down my tank top and started squeezing me in a completely inappropriate manner. I yelled at him, but no one could hear us due to the fireworks. I literally had to climb over him to get out. He kept pulling me back into the station wagon and ripping my clothes off. I have never been so scared in my life. I finally had to punch him between his legs to get away."

"Goodness," Cindy said. "Did you ever tell anyone what had happened?"

"I told my mother," Kate replied. "She asked if he had done anything else?"

"Did he?" Kate asked. "Did he rape you?"

"No, I escaped before he could do anything else," Kate said. "Mom said that it was my fault for going out in public with a tank top. After we returned home, I packed my suitcase and walked to the Greyhound bus station and took the next bus home. The bus station wasn't far – it was just a convenience store that doubled as a bus stop. I think they were worried about me because I didn't reach home until the next afternoon."

"Mother told me never to be alone with him again. I think she gave him a piece of her mind, because he never did anything like that again. But she is still with him after all these years. I don't understand it because she's financially independent and does not need to wait on him as if she was a maid. He's a bully, and never carries his share of the load. She pays for all his expenses and I do think he should treat her better."

Shirley kept quiet. She had lost her virginity on a beach in Alabama under similar circumstances. It had happened on a high school trip the year she had graduated. She didn't want to talk about it or relive the experience. She had been in love with the fellow who had forced himself upon her and had planned to spend the rest of her life with him. It was one reason why she had waited so long to marry Troy.

* * *

Cindy was a breast cancer survivor. She had taken it as a personal affront to humanity when Robert and Brenda had been murdered. What kind of maniac kills someone who has dedicated his or her life to finding a cure for cancer. In her book this was an unforgiveable act of madness and she planned to do everything in her power to bring the killers to justice.

Cindy describer her unfortunate experience beginning with the day that she had received the results after a routine annual physical. "Everything changed in an instant. My whole life flashed past me and everything was turned upside down. The routine physical turned into an endless series of visits to the doctor to get more and more tests. Less than six weeks later I had to have a mastectomy and had one of my beautiful breasts removed. I had just turned fifty."

"That must have been a horrible experience," Kate said.

"It was," Cindy replied. "I thought I was going to die. In many ways part of me did die. I look at life and people in a completely different way now. I feel like a completely different person. I have little or no patience with people who fail to realize what a gift it is to wake up each day for another chance to contribute towards making the world a better place."

"But your figure looks so good Cindy. I don't understand. Are you wearing a prosthetic device underneath your shirt?" Shirley said.

"Oh these?" Cindy said as she pulled her T-shirt up to show off her breasts. "These are brand new. After my mastectomy I went through reconstruction surgery and got myself a brand-new pair of twins. I think they turned out pretty good, don't you?"

"They look great," Charlotte said. "I've been thinking of getting a new pair, myself. Mine are just old and flabby."

"Yeah, but I would give anything to have a nice large natural pair of twins like yours. Before I had a mastectomy, my boyfriend used to love having me ride him like I was a bronco buster."

"Amen," Kate said. "Been there, done that!"

"Don't let these fool you sister," Cindy said. "The reconstruction process is every bit as painful as the mastectomy. I had to go around wearing bandages over half my body for months!"

"I've heard that the risk of getting cancer goes up with age," Kate replied.

"It's part of the aging process," Cindy explained. "Your immune system becomes less responsive. It's a process called DNA methylation where your body's DNA changes ever so slowly over time."

"Methylation sounds like a fermentation process. Is it similar to the process that is used to make wine?" Shirley asked.

"Pour me another glass, dear," Charlotte said. "I need to get methylated."

The girls laughed. There were having a good old time.

"Your immune system provides your body with natural defenses against infection," Cindy explained. "This includes T-cells which are part of your immune system that first identifies a new infection. The research that Robert and Brenda were doing with bioluminescent shrimp helps with early detection before the infection takes a firm foothold in your body"

"I'm a little confused about bioluminescent imaging," Charlotte said.

"It's really the holy grail of imaging, Cindy replied. "It's the ability to see through the body without the harmful effects of radiation."

"But what causes cancer," Kate asked?

"So many, many things," Cindy replied. 'The air we breathe, the food we eat. The surfaces we touch. All these exposures are opportunities for cancer cells to attach themselves to your body. The sooner you can detect it the sooner you can fight the disease and the higher the chance of survival."

"That's almost like a bad boyfriend," Shirley said. "Like your uncle Spencer."

The girls laughed.

"I was lucky," Charlotte replied. "He was trouble with a capital T"

"I guess your T-cells kicked in the minute he first stepped out of line," Kate said.

Cindy poured them all another glass of wine. It was time to open another bottle.

* * *

"What's the chance that Robert and Brenda were killed to prevent them from continuing their research?" Kate asked.

"That's a distinct possibility," Cindy replied. "Cancer treatment is a multi-billion-dollar industry. Early detection could eliminate the need for some of the expensive radiation treatments that are used to shrink tumors before they are removed from the body with surgical procedures. However, there are so many players in this area, so many clinics, doctors, hospitals, and insurance companies involved that there would not be any one group that would benefit more than others from a reduction in radiation therapy."

Kate wasn't convinced. Robert and Brenda were no threat to the shrimpers. From all appearances they were not involved in

Narcotics or Drug Trafficking. Whoever killed them had to have a motive, and in her simple mind the large pharmaceutical companies in Switzerland, Japan, and the USA had plenty of motive for the killing.

"I know what you're thinking, Kate," Cindy said. "Consider for a moment that someone has to pay a lot of money for cancer treatments. Insurance companies are not happy to have to shell out millions of dollars each year for these treatments. So, the medical industry has a built-in system of checks and balances to help keep everybody honest. Besides, what better way to hasten a cure involving bioluminescent shrimp than to publicize this treatment alternative by killing a prominent research such as Robert Rhodes. With all the recent publicity I assure you there will be renewed interest in bioluminescent shrimp until we find a cure for cancer."

* * *

Like Cindy, Jesse had stuck around for a few days after the funeral and Cindy, Jesse, and Troy could often be seen talking endlessly to each other before the visitors left town. Life returned to 'normal' after that. Grandma Lola was content to let Charlotte, Kate, and Shirley take care of Baby Myrtle. Myrtle spent the night with Charlotte, and then Kate and Shirley chipped in each day as part of Myrtle's extended family.

The day Cindy left started out just like any other day. Kate had finished her chores at the Goose Island B&B for the day. She stopped off at Charlottes house and picked up Baby Myrtle. Myrtle ran to Kate and gave her a hug. Kate bundled her up and drove down to the Goose Island Bakery.

"What do you suppose Cindy, Jesse, and Troy are planning?" Kate asked Shirley. "They sure have been spending a lot of time together."

"I think they expect the killer to strike again, Shirley replied.

"Oh," Kate said, surprised. "I was not expecting that."

"I guess anything is possible," Shirley replied. "From what I have been able to gather they think it was a case of mistaken identity. Nothing about the murders makes any sense. Robert and Brenda were a pair of peaceful, law-abiding citizens, minding their own business. They may not have been the persons whom the killer intended to attack."

"So, then the real targets are still alive," Kate said.

"Exactly," Shirley said. "From what I can tell, Jesse, Cindy, and Troy were trying to set up a collaborative task force so that the next time this occurs they can bring all their forces to bear quickly and catch up with the killer before he or she has time to get away."

"Makes sense," Kate said. She wondered who the real targets had been. Also, if there had been any other incidents in the past that might provide some bearing on the case. Then again, what if Robert and Brenda were indeed the intended targets. Was it possible that Myrtle's life was in danger because she had survived the attack where her parents had been murdered?

≈≈≈≈≈≈

9. Disaster Recovery

The next few days went by in a flash. Everyone fell into a steady routine. Jerry started spending more time fishing. He monitored the boats coming and going into Copano Bay using a pair of long-range field glasses with a built-in camera. This allowed him to take pictures of the vessels that he deemed to be suspicious from a distance.

Jerry took several pictures of boats of all shapes and sizes coming into and leaving Copano Bay. Pretty soon he had a picture of virtually every boat in the area. It was not exactly clear how these pictures were ever going to be of use. Jerry downloaded the latest photographs from the camera to his computer periodically. The computer was connected via a cable to the TV in the living room and it allowed him to review the photographs on a large screen. However, it interfered with Charlotte's movie time after supper. She viewed the photo collection dis-interestedly, often falling asleep in the middle of a presentation only to wake up to admire a sunset, or a picture of a bird, or other animal in the background when she should have been looking at the tattooed sailor, or the cargo on the deck instead.

Grandma Lola put out a reward of $25,000 for any information that helped solve the crime. The reward posters were displayed throughout the area, particularly near the Goose Island Fishing Pier and the Copano Bay Marina.

Shirley and Kate started taking long walks on the beach looking for any contraband that may have floated ashore by accident. The girls followed Jerry's lead and bought their own pair of similarly equipped binoculars. They had taken lots of photographs with their new toys in recent days, but none that met the bar for being overtly suspicions. Truth be told, it was very difficult to detect suspicious activity of any kind when it happened on a boat that whizzed by your eyes in a few seconds.

Cindy and Jesse checked in with Troy from time to time. Each time Troy got a little more information about their progress in the case. The authorities had interviewed several shrimpers in the area and had drawn a blank with regards to the murders near the El-Sombrero. To be sure, there were several groups of rival shrimper communities in the area, who did not always get along well with each other.

There was a simmering rivalry between the shrimpers who had lived on the Gulf Coast for generations, and the ones who had settled into the area from Vietnam. These differences had more to do with communication than with cultural differences. Differences between groups were typically settled privately amongst themselves in the local 'Shrimpers Court', a group of seasoned representatives from each group of shrimpers that met regularly to adjudicate on torn nets, damaged equipment and any other random act of kindness between group.

The authorities had found no evidence to link the shrimpers with the crime. In fact, they were convinced that physical violence of any kind, particularly to a woman would not be tolerated by the shrimpers. They were all aware of the tragedy on the PharmaSea and would have come forward on their own accord if there was anything that they could do to help solve the case. Add Grandma Lola's reward to the request for information and they would gladly have turned in any information that they might have had. As with any other cold case, if there is no break in the case within the first 72 hours then it seemed unlikely that they would ever find the killers.

* * *

Charlotte and Kate had stopped by the Goose Island Bakery. Baby-sitting is hard work, and they needed a create a diversion to keep Baby Myrtle occupied. Myrtle was anything but the adorable, sweet, charming young girl that everyone took her to be. She could turn on a dime and throw a tantrum to rival the Queen of England emptying a pot of ink on her head to express her disdain for having to learn the French language.

Troy stopped by to say hello to Shirley in-between chasing hardened criminals and keeping the peace at Goose Island. He stopped by Kate's table.

"How's the baby girl today," he asked.

Myrtle smiled sweetly and blew him a kiss. No one who saw her would believe that this was the same little girl who had dumped her cereal bowl over Charlotte's dog Milo just a few hours earlier that day.

Milo followed the baby everywhere. He would sidle up to Myrtle and look for an opportunity to take a bite of her sandwich, or cookie, or whatever she happened to have in her hand at the time. For her part, Myrtle like to crawl up to Milo and use him as a cushion to lean on. Milo didn't seem to mind at all. He had a goofy happy smile on his face and wagged his tail incessantly when he was around the baby.

"Any update on the shrimpers?" Kate asked. "Any idea if any of the other shrimpers was in the El Sombrero area when the Drilling Rig Pirates attacked the PharmaSea?"

"No, not really. None of them have stepped forward with any information relating to the night of the murders."

"Oh Well," Kate said. "Maybe something will turn up."

"Well there is a cold case dealing with one of the shrimpers that I found going back through the County records," Troy said. "About two decades ago there was a shrimper called Elliott Bradenton whose wife disappeared under suspicious circumstances."

"Oh," said Charlotte. "I do seem to remember something about that. There was a huge to-do when it happened. His wife was a beauty queen, wasn't she?"

"Yes," Troy continued. "Virginia Bradenton was Miss Shrimp, Texas about twenty years ago. She married Elliott, but shortly afterwards she just vanished without a trace. Just plain disappeared. Elliott was a prime suspect, but no charges were ever filed because they could never find Virginia's body. She was last seen getting on Elliot's Shrimp Boat, but none of the shrimpers who worked on Elliott's boat had anything to say about her disappearance. When I started interviewing the shrimpers in this area about Robert and Brenda they had little or nothing to say about the Rhodes family. I also inquired about Virginia because it is still tagged as a cold case. The interesting thing is that none of the shrimpers had anything to say about her either."

"You don't think they are related, do you?" Kate asked.

"Well there are some major differences," Troy replied. "We did find the bodies of Robert and Brenda.

"That's only because of the storm the night they were killed," Charlotte noted. If the rain had not doused the fire on the PharmaSea they would have disappeared without a trace.

"True," Troy said pensively.

"What happened to Elliott?" Kate asked. "Did you talk to him?"

"Well that's just it, Kate", Troy replied. "Elliott seems to have vanished from the area also. The shrimpers acted as if they had no knowledge of either Virginia or Elliott. However, he was one of them, and she was their Queen. There should be someone who remembers one of them, don't you think?"

"Sure," Kate replied. "That would just make too much sense, wouldn't it?"

*   *   *

Charlotte brought Baby Myrtle over to Kate's every day. It had warmed up considerably and Kate had opened the swimming at the pool adjacent to the Goose Island B&B. The leaves that had blown into the pool in Winter had been removed, the filters had been cleaned, the water was clean and clear blue. The girls started spending several hours each day enjoying the sunshine and the water. In fact, they were spending so much time hanging out by the pool that there was some talk of putting up a small cabana beside the pool.

Grandma Lola spent most of her time reading books and magazines in the shelter of the covered porch beside the pool. She did not like to be out much in the sun. Summer in Texas can be uncomfortably hot, and she was starting to wonder if it was almost time for her to return to North Carolina.

Charlotte had grown very attached to Baby Myrtle. More so than Kate and Shirley. It was not going to be easy for her to give up Baby Myrtle when Grandma Lola decided to return to North Carolina. She simply could not imagine not having Baby Myrtle in her life. Charlotte kept her opinions to herself but there was no doubt in her mind that she could do a better job of raising Baby Myrtle than Grandma Lola.

Grandma Lola had a lot of things on her mind. In addition to grieving for the loss of her son and his wife, Lola had to figure out what to do with the remains of the PharmaSea. The Coast Guard had towed it into a Marine Storage facility nearby. There was a daily storage charge that was starting to add up each day. Fortunately, she could afford the storage expense without difficulty.

There were just a couple more days remaining before Grandma Lola's departure when she took Kate aside and asked if she could have a word with her.

"I really don't know what to do about Eleanor," Lola said. "On the one hand I would love to take her back to North Carolina. However, the best I could do for her there is to hire a Nanny to take care of her and to help raise her. On the other hand, I cannot help noticing what a wonderful job Charlotte, and you and Shirley are doing. There is no denying that Eleanor is happy and loved by you all. I really must return home in a few days to attend to some personal matters. Would it be okay if I leave Eleanor with you for a week until I return?"

"Sure, I'd like nothing better," Kate replied. This was a surprise for Kate. She had just assumed that Grandma Lola and Baby Myrtle were going to leave Goose Island forever in just a couple of days.

"Thanks," Lola said. "I'd also like to stay with you at the Goose Island B&B for a few weeks when I return?"

"Why, sure. You are always welcome."

"It's so much warmer in Texas when compared to North Carolina," Lola observed. "Everyone on the island has been so hospitable since I arrived, that I think I'm going to try to move here for a few years. At least, until the baby is old enough to go to school."

"That makes sense," Kate replied. However, in the back of her mind she had to wonder why Lola was having this conversation with her instead of with Charlotte who had quickly become Myrtle's primary care giver. "Is it okay if she continues to sleep over at Charlotte's house?"

"Why of course it is," said Grandma Lola. "Charlotte is an amazing person. I am very fortunate that she was there to lend a helping hand when we lost Brenda and Robert. She is so kind-hearted and caring."

"I agree," Kate replied. "Charlotte has a really big heart. I'm very fortunate she lives next door. It's a big responsibility and I cannot speak for her, one way or another. But I can tell you this. Charlotte loves that baby more than anything else right now."

"I'm going to have to speak with Charlotte soon and help to pay for Myrtle's expenses," Lola added. "This all happened so suddenly that I really didn't have time to think it through before leaving home. Thank you so much for the kindness you have shown, Kate."

"You're welcome," Kate replied.

"I'm just an old woman without very much longer to live," Lola said. "I wish I had not had to see Robert come to this unfortunate end. For many years, the one thing that kept me going was the hope that he would one day find the elusive cure for cancer. That he would get the recognition from his peers that he so richly deserved. He could have gone to work for any of several large pharmaceutical companies and made a very comfortable life for himself and his family. However, he chose the road less travelled. It's too bad it had to end like this."

"I know," Kate replied. "It's a shocking tragedy to lose someone so bright. Someone who had so much to offer the world."

* * *

Ray did not return to Goose Island at the end of the week as planned. He had a wicked busy week at work after he returned to Odessa. He could have been a beaver building a dam with his bare hands and by the skin of his teeth before the commencement of Spring rains.

His manager made it clear that he would not hesitate to throw him under the bus if the Disaster Recovery Audit resulted in an unsatisfactory review. There were several veiled references to dire consequences for the project if the DR Audit was found to be lacking in a key metric called the DRT or Disaster Recovery Time.

Ray had to smile each time he thought of Kate's offer to come down to his office and let his manager know who Ray's real boss was. The one who would never allow him to work nights and weekends for free, to be on call twenty-four hours each day, or to have his cell phone be used as a de-facto paging device at his own expense.

It was Ray's job to persuade the auditors that his business unit could recover from an oil field disaster within an hour. Detailed plans for recovery had to be developed and records maintained through all reported component outages to allow the auditors to conclude that the DRT was achievable.

Oil wells had to be capped and uncapped routinely as part of these tests with someone standing by with a stopwatch in their hands to measure how long it took to perform each operation. DR testing was a bottomless pit because of the myriad number of DR scenarios that could occur. The more Ray thought about it, the more he realized that the auditors had no clue that the amount it took to deal with a real disaster depending on who happened to be on duty at the time. If you had the right people then the person on call at the time of the disaster would have the skills, the fortitude, and the presence of mind to deal with the situation while everything around him or her was blowing sky high with each passing minute. If you had Chance Buckman from the Hellfighters on your team everything would turn out sunny-side up. If not, then you better hope you have enough insurance to cover the casualty losses.

The audit had gone off remarkably well. The external auditor, Kevin, had like his documentation and the traceability between the component test results and the comprehensive DR plan. Kevin made some positive comments about Ray's work and his attention to detail. Rays manager sent him a very nice "Thank You" note with the comment that he thought Ray was the smartest person he knew and that he was so happy to have him on the Team.

With the audit behind him Ray had returned to his house after work on Friday with a satisfied bounce in his step. He had a few more tasks to complete the paperwork and so he called Kate to let her know he would be tied up over the weekend. Saturday and Sunday went by in a flash. Each new task that he completed spawned three new ones that he had not realized were needed when he started.

When he finally finished the last little detail on Sunday night he stepped out of his house for the first time that weekend to pick up something to eat for dinner. It felt good to get all the Oil Field Disaster Recovery documents filed away according to the guidelines that he had been asked to meet. Ray felt good about getting his assignments completed even though he had had to give up his nights and weekends to get them completed on time. It was late, and Ray realized he had not eaten all day. However, there was still time to pick up some Chinese takeout before all the restaurants closed for the evening.

* * *

As he waited in line at the take-out counter at the restaurant Ray checked his telephone messages and voicemail. He quickly realized, much to his chagrin, that he had received two missed calls from Kate more than a week ago. Ray tended to zone-out when he was working. and he had just not paid any attention to the fact that Kate had tried to reach him the previous week.

After that there was not a single message or missed phone call from Kate. Not one! Not a single message the entire time since he had last seen her after leaving Goose Island. This was very uncharacteristic. What happened? Was she okay? Was the Baby okay? Was she upset that he hadn't answered the phone when she had called more than a week ago?

The more he thought about it the worse he felt. He really should have checked his phone and called her back sooner. Kate had probably surmised that he placed a higher priority on his work than he did on his relationship to her, and nothing could be farther from the truth. Ray walked slowly back home with a four-pack of Guinness and Chinese take-out food for dinner.

He had completely lost the bounce in his step as he walked up to his house with a devastating realization. The real disaster that had just occurred was that he had not taken the time to call Kate a single time, not once, the entire week. He dialed her number pensively, wondering what excuse to make for his forgetfulness. He was really hoping to speak to her but there was no answer. The same thing happened when he tried to call Shirley and Charlotte. Ray was not feeling particularly bright as he sat down at the table in his house nibbling on Kung Pao Noodles and watching the late-night news on TV.

It was just not like Kate to go for an entire week without getting in touch with him. He sent

Kate another text. He waited and waited to hear from her but there was nothing. With each passing hour, his messages to her un-answered and un-acknowledged.

Ray could feel the walls closing in and his world reduced to nothing. He was trapped in his skin and couldn't escape his own shadow. He should never have left Kate alone on Goose Island. In retrospect, it was one of the most thoughtless things he had done. Ray made up his mind that he had to return to Goose Island immediately to make amends for his narcissistic behavior.

On Monday morning Ray packed his travel bag and drove down to the airport instead of going to work. As he paused in the line of people waiting to go through security he sent Kate a text to let her know he was planning to visit Goose Island that afternoon. There was no response. No playful text message from Kate telling him that she couldn't wait for him to arrive. No string of X's and O's at the end of the message that never materialized on his phone.

Ray became convinced that something terrible had happened to Kate. He submitted a request for a personal leave of absence from work while waiting to board the next flight from Odessa to Corpus Christi. Ray promised himself that he was never going to let his work get between himself and Kate ever again! Her love meant more to him than anything else in the world and he did not want to ever forget that for the rest of his life.

When he landed at Corpus Christi International there were still no messages from Kate. He priced up a rental car and drove the long lonely drive back to Goose Island. His heart was filled with anticipation when he crossed the Copano Bay Bridge, drove past the Goose Island Town Square, turned on Marlin Ave and pulled into Kate's driveway. He couldn't wait to see Kate again. However, there was just one minor detail, there was no sign of Kate. The house next door was also deserted. There was no sign of Charlotte and Jerry next door, either.

≈≈≈≈≈≈

10. Sea Goose

Kate, Charlotte and Lola had just left the house to visit the Goose Island Bakery with Baby Myrtle. Myrtle like the treats at the Bakery and Shirley loved for Myrtle to visit her there. Myrtle's favorite treat was the dark chocolate drop cookies. They were seated at the table by the window with ruffled curtains. It looked out on the cars coming and going to the Goose Island Town Square. Myrtle was helping Shirley find the best chocolate drop cookie on a sheet of about a hundred cookies.

Thanks for taking care of Myrtle, Charlotte," Lola said.

"Of course. You're welcome," Charlotte said. "That child is a blessing. I'm happy to be of help. But I honestly couldn't do it without the help I'm getting from Kate and Shirley."

"Thanks Charlotte," Kate said.

"There is one other thing," Lola said to Kate as they sat at the table by the window with their coffee. "How would you like to buy the PharmaSea?"

Kate sputtered. This had caught her completely by surprise. Lola repeated her question.

"But Lola," Kate protested. "I could never afford a boat like that."

"Well I know it's expensive to operate, dear," started Lola. "However, if you are interested I will let you have it for a dollar."

"Are you serious?" Kate exclaimed. "A dollar?"

"You'll be doing me a favor, Kate," Lola said. "The boat is useless to me. After what happened to my son and his wife I have no desire to set foot on board the PharmaSea. In its present condition, it is a burned-out shell of a vessel that needs a major overhaul. I couldn't help noticing that your friend Ray is very good at working on projects and I just thought this might be something fun for you to do together."

"That's a very generous offer Lola. I'm not sure what Ray will think about it," Kate replied. In her mind she couldn't help thinking that there's a big difference in laying tile in the bathroom and repairing a boat. "Let me talk it over with Ray. If he's up to it, we'll go for it."

"I was hoping you would, dear. I think it might be fun to use now and then."

"That it might," Kate said. Her mind was already evaluating the possibilities. Shirley and herself had often joked about owning a boat together. There were several small islands and sand-bars in the Gulf that were accessible only by sea. Shirley and Kate had even purchased some canoes and paddled to some of the islands near the Aransas Bird Sanctuary in Matagorda Bay. However, the PharmaSea was no canoe and it would require a lot more care and maintenance than she could manage on her own.

Kate had considered owning a boat as a means of providing sunset cruises for her guests at the Goose Island B&B. Kate and Ray liked to drive by the Copano Bay Marina every now and then and watch the sun go down over the water. Even though she had never owned a boat, Kate had always had a feeling of excitement that stemmed from hanging around the Marina. Kate and Ray enjoyed walking past the boats at the dock and pretending to be on a journey across the ocean. She wanted to accept Grandma Lola's offer, but wanted to discuss it with her friends before doing so.

* * *

Later that day Charlotte and Lola took Myrtle to the pool at the YMCA for swimming lessons. Myrtle was happy. She could not stop bouncing around and jumping up and down when she got close to the water. She wore a brand-new swimsuit with red and white polka dots. She also has a nice pair of child-sized swimming goggles. She looked adorable! Charlotte adjusted the goggles for Baby Myrtle and she joined a small group of older children who had enrolled in the Pre-Kindergarten 'Learn to Swim' class.

Charlotte and Lola kept an eye on Lola's recalcitrant granddaughter who had already convinced her swimming instructor that she had no need for any swimming lessons. Myrtle was swimming like a little fish around the group. Lola talked to Charlotte about Myrtle's future and how she intended to set up a trust fund for Eleanor. Charlotte agreed to take care of Myrtle until she turned eighteen.

"What about Brenda's family?" Charlotte asked. "I know Robert has no brothers or sisters, but I couldn't help wondering about Brenda."

"Brenda's Australian," Lola replied. "I've only met her parents once and neither one of them is in very good health. I doubt that they could take care of Myrtle for long. Her brother is rather wild and seldom stays sober for very long. I simply cannot see him as a very responsible parent."

Charlotte stopped to think about the options. She would be almost as old as Grandma Rhodes by the time Baby Myrtle would be getting ready to graduate from high school.

"I'm probably going to need help taking care of the baby," Charlotte said. "I think I could do it with Kate's help. However, I doubt if I can do it all by myself."

"That's more than I could ever ask," Lola remarked. "I'm almost ninety years old now, and it feels good to know that the child will be taken care of if I'm not here to watch over her. Let's plan to make sure that Kate and you have joint custody of Eleanor so that she would continue to be cared for even if something should happen to one of you."

"It's no problem at all, Lola," Charlotte protested. "I'd like very much to be her guardian. She is an amazing child. I'm sure Kate would welcome a change to help care for Eleanor."

The swimming instructor came by at the end of the class and suggested that they enroll Myrtle in a swim meet in Rockport at the end of the month.

"That little girl is amazing," said the instructor. "She's completely water-safe and has no fear of the water at all. She knows how to paddle and can hold her breath under water for almost half a minute. She can swim better than most children who are two of three times her age."

"I know," said Charlotte and Grandma Lola at the same time.

"I can see her in the Olympics in about fifteen years", said the instructor. "She's a natural. The think I like most about her is how happy she is in the water. I hope you will let me help groom her for the next swim meet."

"Sure," said Charlotte.

When they returned home from the YMCA Kate stopped by and picked up Myrtle for a walk along Shipwreck beach. The baby loved splashing through the waves. The only thing better was to hold the baby's hand and splash through the waves with her and to hear the silvery sound of the baby's laughter each time she dodged a big wave.

* * *

Ray walked quickly down to Shipwreck Beach to look for Kate. He saw her station wagon at the Beach Access Parking Area. She had to be nearby. Her car looked dusty and unwashed as if it had been parked there for days. Was she okay? He picked up his pace and walked rapidly past the sea grass alongside the path that led to the beach.

There were some fresh footprints in the path, but it was hard to tell whom they belonged to. He said a silent prayer and walked out onto the wide expanse of beach to look for Kate's familiar figure. She was nowhere in sight.

Ray walked down to the water and looked both up and down both sides of the beach. He walked part-way down to the rocky outgrowth at one end of the beach, and then turned and walked the other way. The tide was starting to recede, and it would be dark within another hour. Ray turned and walked towards the fishing pier. He scanned the water for any sign of activity and all he could see were the waves and the ebb and flow of the tide. As he walked towards the fishing pier, he noticed someone in the distance and his heart quickened.

Ray's heart was filled with joy when he saw Kate sitting half buried in the sand, sitting in the shallow water on the beach with Baby Myrtle. The girls had their toes in the surf and were staring up at the clouds in the sky. Kate was telling Baby Myrtle a story about Pete the Pelican who had been caught in a hurricane before he could seek shelter. Pete had survived by flying in circles in the eye of the storm until it made landfall and he was able to seek shelter under the eaves of a covered boat slip.

It was obvious at a glance that both Kate and Myrtle were fine. All that what had happened in Goose Island since he had been away was that Baby Myrtle had taken up all of Kates time and attention. Kate seemed genuinely pleased to see him. She looked beautiful, with a nice tan all over her face, neck and arms. Her toe-nails were a bright red color, and so were Baby Myrtle's. They looked like two peas in a pod.

"How are you?" Kate asked him when he sat down on the sand next to her.

"All good," Ray replied. "No issues." He took off his shoes and turned up the bottom of his jeans.

"It's good to see you," Kate said. "I missed you."

"I missed you too, Kate. More than you know," Ray said. "You are my only ray of sunshine in this world and I love you more than anything else in the world." Some things are better left unsaid. Ray did not mention how worried he had been when the entire week had gone by without being able to speak to her.

"That's nice, Ray," Kate replied. "I love you too."

He sat down on the wet sand next to her. It was good to hold her hand again. The water soaked through his jeans.

"How was work?" Kate asked.

"All good," Ray said. "We passed the audit with flying colors." He described the work he had done for the DR audit as concisely as possible. He knew that Kate had little or no interest in the details.

"I hope you're ready for the disaster audit scenarios that I have planned for you tonight. Such as how to free yourself after I flip you over, bend you backwards, and pin you down in a leg lock."

Ray laughed. Kate always had a way with words. He loved it when she talked 'smack' with him like a pair of boxers before a fight. As far as Ray was concerned she could 'float like a butterfly and sting like a bee'.

"You're not taking my audit requirements seriously enough," she said with a stern expression on her face and a twinkle in her eyes. "I assure this will be very thorough, and we will check and double check everything more than once to make sure you are following a repeatable process. Your response time to each event will be measured down to the nearest micro-second to how well equipped you are to deal with unforeseen contingencies." Kate's eyes lit up when she knew she had him at a serious disadvantage. She had the half Mona Lisa smile on her face that Ray loved so much.

"Yes Kate," Ray replied.

"Yes indeed," Kate replied. "And there will be plenty of oil involved," she added. "Baby oil!"

Ray put his arm around Kate and gave her a kiss. And suddenly, in a single 'Zippity-

Doo-Dah' instant, everything was right with the world.

* * *

Kate and Myrtle got up to go swimming in the shallow water near the beach. Ray sat on the sand watching them have a grand old time together. Kate held Myrtle's hand as the ran into the waves, and back again as the waves retreated from the shore. Sea shells tumbled through the ocean and fell in the surf on the sand. The baby chased after them as they fell on the shore. She had to hurry to pick them up before the next wave carried the seashells back into the ocean. Before long Myrtle had a small collection of seashells that she used to decorate the sandcastle that they had built a short distance up the shore out of reach of the waves.

As they danced through the waves Kate held the baby's hands and allowed the waves to pull Myrtle towards the shore. When the water retreated Myrtle ended up in Kates arms and she gave the baby a hug and they laughed with each other with a feeling of sheer joy, enjoying every moment in each other's presence.

As the day ended Kate and Myrtle watched the sunset as it descended behind the Copano Bay Bridge. A small sliver of sunlight was still visible underneath the bridge.

However soon, that too vanished behind the fishing pier on Shipwreck Beach. Kate and Myrtle dusted off the sand and folded up their beach towels. They packed up their things and put on their flip-flops. Kate allowed Myrtle to keep one small seashell in her tiny fist as they left the beach and returned home to Charlotte's house. She held on to it tightly.

"Mama, mama, you got something from me," Myrtle said excitedly as Charlotte greeted them at the door. She opened her fist and gave Charlotte the seashell. Charlotte smiled and gave the baby a kiss.

Charlotte was delighted that Kate was there to help her with the baby. With all the exercise Myrtle was getting she was not going to have any trouble getting the baby to bed that evening. Kate and Ray retired to the Goose Island B&B. They went upstairs and sat on the balcony catching up on the events that had transpired during the week that they had been apart.

* * *

Kate, Ray, Shirley, Troy; Charlotte and Jerry met for dinner at Giordano's the next day. Kate had invited everyone to help evaluate the opportunity to purchase the PharmaSea from Mrs. Rhodes. She had given everyone the gist of

Grandma Lola's suggestion and they had all had plenty of time to mull things over in their minds. She had made it clear that they would be joint owners of the PharmaSea if they decided to go forward with the purchase.

Jerry and Ray had gone down to the Coast Guard storage facility in Fulton to survey the damage to the PharmaSea. They had taken along a marine engineer from Goose Island with them to help develop an estimate of the repairs required to make the ship sea-worthy once again. Most of the damage from the fire was to the wheel-house, the cabin, and to the ships electrical system. The engine and pumps were as good as new. There was little or no damage to the hull. If it wasn't for the loss of its ability to steer, the PharmaSea would not even have needed a tow to return home. A rough estimate for the repairs was about 50,000 dollars.

"The damage to the ship is not as bad is it looks," Jerry said. "It can be repaired. We will need some help, but a lot of the work can be done on our own."

"On the surface, it seems like a sweetheart of a deal," Ray said. "However, owning a boat is a huge responsibility and I just want us to go into this deal with our eyes wide open."

"It's also pretty expensive to own and operate a boat," Jerry said.

"Don't they always say that the two best days of owning a boat are the day you buy it and the day that you sell it to someone else?" Charlotte asked.

"One thing in favor of fixing up the PharmaSea is her physical size," Jerry said. "She is about fifty feet long, and about 18 feet across. By any criteria, she's a large boat, making her inherently more sea-worthy than something smaller. If we can get her all fixed up and ready to roll, then I'd rather go out to sea in her than in something smaller. The down-side, of course, is that she could be a little harder to handle and to dock in close quarters."

"We need to make sure we always have the ability to get out there, catch some fish or do some sight-seeing and get back home in one piece," Ray added. "If she was fixed up, there's no doubt in my mind she could take us out and bring us back safely."

"When you look at buying a boat, the main expenses are the cost of purchase, insurance, mooring and maintenance," Troy said.

"Fifty thousand for repairs sounds like a bargain," Kate remarked when she heard the initial estimate for repairs. "Even if it is twice that amount it's a bargain. Once it is sea worthy again we could easily re-sell it for more than a hundred thousand dollars."

"How long would it take to make it sea-worthy?" Shirley wondered.

"She could probably be out on the water again in a few months. Maybe sometime this Summer. With a new radar, navigational equipment, and re-wiring to hook it up to all the motors, sump pumps, bilges and all, we could take her out for a test drive by July 4th," Jerry said.

"I can help out a bit," Jerry said. "I'm retired, so I have all the time in the world.

"I'm off from work for the next three months," Ray said. "I can handle the carpentry and rebuilding of the cabin. I can help with re-wiring, but we might need a qualified marine engineer to take care of some of the finer details," Ray said.

"Three months?" Kate asked. Ray's announcement caught Kate by surprise. She had been trying to get him to quit his job in Odessa and move to Goose Island for years. Perhaps this might be the thing that helped get him over the edge. Three months with him in her house every night was going to be wonderful. It would be delightful to see him lounging around her upstairs bedroom in his boxer shorts. It would be as though they were a family, not just ships that passed each other in the night.

"I might never go back," Ray said. "It's just not that important to me."

"Well good!" Kate said. "If you're going to be here that long, maybe we have separate boy and girl bathrooms. Because no one ever taught you the proper etiquette for raising the toilet seat and putting it back down again when you are done."

Charlotte and Shirley exchanged glances and smiled. When Kate started talking smack they both knew that she had already made up her mind.

* * *

"Don't we have to find a place to park our new boat after we go to pick it up?" Kate inquired.

"That should not be a problem. We can rent a mooring space at the marina on Copano Bay," Jerry replied. "I've seen some pretty large boats parked beside the dock there.

"We'll have to rename the boat. PharmaSea sounds very clinical," Charlotte suggested.

"I agree," Kate said. "We need something with a much happier sound to it."

"How about naming it after a fish? Do you like 'Blue Marlin', or 'Tarpon'?" Troy suggested.

"Sure," Jerry replied. "I think those are both excellent choices."

"Since Boaty McBoat is already taken, we could call it the 'Loose Goose'," Ray said, with a sideways glance at Kate.

"No thanks," Kate replied. "Let's go with something else. Something Texan."

"How about Sea La Belle?" suggested Shirley.

"I love that. It's so much better than PharmaSea," said Charlotte. "Who's La Belle?"

Shirley did a little curtsy for Charlotte. "Moi," she replied.

"That sounds pretty good," said Kate. "Let's add that to the short-list of names."

Jerry, Troy and Ray stayed out of the discussion. Naming a ship could be hard work. Besides it was not something they cared deeply about. BlueSea sounded just fine. It would be less work to just paint the letters Blue over Pharm.

"Do you like the 'Sea Goose' dear?" Charlotte inquired.

"Sure," said Kate.

Shirley nodded in affirmation. "That's a great name," she replied.

"You do know that it is considered bad luck to change a ship's name, don't you?" Jerry asked the others. "A common belief among sailors is that if you change the name you must have a re-christening ceremony to make sure that it does not offend Neptune, the lord of the sea."

"It's either that or ride around in a floating drug factory all day," replied Charlotte. "I think we are going to have to take our chances with Mr. Neptune.

"The rechristening sounds like an excuse for a party," Kate said. "It might be fun."

"Okay then," Jerry said. "Just don't bring any bananas or suitcases on board the ship. Those are bad luck too."

"Aye, aye Captain," said Charlotte.

Everyone agreed that their boat would henceforth be called the 'Sea Goose' and they would give her the best re-christening party that Goose Island had ever seen.

Ray motioned for Don, the proprietor of Giordano's to bring a bottle of champagne from the bar. Don eased the cork out of the bottle, capping it with this thumb as soon as the cork flew across the room with a loud popping sound. The group cheered. They raised their glasses in a toast to the Sea Goose, their ticket to great fishing on the high seas.

≈≈≈≈≈≈

11. Repairs

The Sea Goose was now parked safely in slot #514 at the Copano Bay marina. It had been towed to the marina from the Coast Guard storage facility in Fulton. Jerry and Ray travelled with the tug boat to the marina. They were waiting for Kate to meet up with them at the marina. Kate was hurrying and scurrying to get to the marina. It was her first visit to the marina and she was having a little difficulty with the directions.

The road to the marina was an unmarked turnoff immediately prior to the 'Marina Mart convenience store located on the other side of the Copano Bay Bridge from Goose Island. Marina Mart offered regular gasoline at premium prices, beer, wine, cigarettes, extra greasy brisket tacos and other essential items. Folks who were willing to fork over the twenty percent surcharge to get out on the water sooner rather than return to town to purchase the same items at a lower price. Kate stepped into Marina Mart for a Diet Coke, got the directions she needed and was back on track a few minutes later.

She drove slowly down the bumpy, pothole ridden road to the marina. It snaked for a mile past several weathered looking homes, many with small boats parked beside them. The road ended abruptly at the parking lot outside the marina. There was a large steel metal building at one end of the parking lot. The sign outside the building indicating that it sold boat motors and performed engine repairs. Boats of various shapes and sizes were strewn willy-nilly outside the building, waiting to be serviced.

Kate could hear the boat riggings slapping against their masts in the wind from the moment she stepped out of her car. She walked over to the wooden walkway leading to the marina office. The walkway continued over a small bridge that spanned a narrow strip of water. A group of ducks swam up to her as she crossed the bridge looking eagerly at her to part with a sandwich or something they could snack on. As she leaned over the railing to feed the ducks she heard the unmistakable sound of a loud wolf whistle from the direction of the marine. Kate straightened up immediately, but there was no one in sight.

"Hello!" exclaimed a shrill voice as she reached the office. "Hello, hello, hello."

"Hello," Kate said to no one in particular. There was still no one in sight. Kate walked past the marina office and noticed a large bird-cage off to one side. There was a colorful, long tailed, blue and gold macaw parrot looking directly at her from his perch next to the cage. "Well, hello Mr. Parrot," Kate said with relief.

"Hello, hello, hello," said the parrot nodding his head and moving excitedly from side to side on his perch.

"Hello Sweetie," Kate replied with a smile. "Are you the bad boy who just whistled at me? Aren't you something else?"

There was a sign on the cage that read 'Beware of Parrot'. The small dish of birdseed in the cage said "Ralph" on the side and Kate surmised that Ralph was indeed the guilty party. She would have to bring him some snacks the next time she visited the marina.

"Bye, bye, Ralph," Kate said, as she continued on down the walkway to locate the Sea Goose.

"Hello!" Ralph said as she was leaving.

Kate found Jerry and Ray standing next to the Sea Goose a few minutes later. The new owners of the PharmaSea had been lucky. They had procured the last space at the end of the fifth row of parking spaces. Each row of spaces in the marina was basically a U-shaped channel with boats parked on either side. There was a narrow boardwalk that snaked around the marina providing access to the boats that were parked there. The slots at the end had better access to the bay. It was also a great place to sit back and relax with a Guinness and watch the sunset at the end of the day.

Jerry and Ray saw Kate as she approached them at the end of the wooden walkway. They looked pleased as punch and welcomed her excitedly aboard her new boat. However, Kate had a sinking feeling in the pit of her stomach as she stepped on the deck of the Sea Goose. The boat was severely charred. She walked gingerly along the edges of the deck, afraid that she would fall through into whatever lay beneath. It was going take more than a little elbow grease to get it all fixed up. In addition, she could not help thinking about the fact that this was where Robert and Brenda Rhodes had lost their lives. It was a very sobering thought.

* * *

Several days later, Kate and Shirley had made several trips to the marina. Ralph had been treated to an assortment of apple slices, grapes, and different types of nuts. Everything except peanuts. Peanut shells contain harmful aflatoxins that are not good for parrots. The girls loved visiting Ralph, even though he stubbornly refused to repeat any of the words that they tried to teach him.

"He must not be very old," Kate said. "All he seems to know is Hello!"

"He does have a pretty cool wolf whistle," Shirley said.

"We'll have to smarten you up when we have more time," Kate said.

"Bye Sweetie," Shirley said.

"Hello," said Ralph as the girls continued with the immediate task of cleaning up the Sea Goose.

The girls had gone through the boat and cleaned up any remaining personal effects that had belonged to Robert and Brenda. Charlotte stayed home with Baby Myrtle. It was hard to tell if Baby Myrtle would be traumatized if she was re-introduced to the boat, or to things that connected her to that past. Kate did not like bringing Myrtle with her to the dock. There were abandoned boats and boat parts strewn about the parking lot. Kate had almost stepped on a rattlesnake on one occasion and it had scared the bejesus out of her.

When Kate and Shirley started tidying up the boat there were several toys strewn about the cabin. Kate and Shirley picked up everything in sight and put it away into a carboard box. Kate spotted a small piece of aluminum foil wadded up into a ball underneath the bed. At first glance it looked like a piece of trash. However, there was something unusual about the shape of the object within the aluminum foil. Kate's curiosity got the better of her. She unwrapped the foil and found a small hand carved toy duck underneath. It would have burned up when the boat had been set aflame, except the foil probably helped protect it from the fire.

Kate wondered if Robert had made them for his daughter. The picture of Robert sitting down on the deck of his boat and turning a piece of driftwood into a small wooden duck for his little baby girl to play with was heart-breaking. The duck had also been carefully stained and varnished. There was a crossbones shaped 'X' followed by a date etched underneath the hand-crafted duck. Kate and Shirley glanced at it and then put it away. They would have to decide what to do with the toys later. For the moment, the girls picked up the toys and stowed them away in a box.

After several days of repairs, the decks had been washed clean, the windjammers that held the fishing nets had been removed, and all the charred wooden structures had been removed and replaced with Yellow Cedar. The Sea Goose was beginning to transition from a fishing vessel to a sunset cruiser.

On most days, Jerry and Ray drove out to the marina in Jerry's white Ford pickup truck. They made a pit stop at the local hardware and lumber store for any supplies that they might need. Once they reached the marina all the supplies were loaded on to a small wagon which they pulled along to the Sea Goose. It was a short walk down the boardwalk to the Sea Goose.

Jerry and Ray decided that the first order of business was to make a break with the past and change the lettering on the boat. Within a few days Ray had repainted the sign on the back of the vessel. The PharmaSea had now transmogrified into the Sea Goose. Going the extra mile, Ray painted a small picture of a bird in flight on either side of the boat. With the stereo playing his favorite songs by the Doors, Ray proceeded to build out the cabin and the wheelhouse to the steady rhythmic beat of "Don't You Love Her Madly" and "L.A. Woman".

Jerry spent the day reading magazines and making spreadsheets to compare the available navigational systems alternatives. At some point in the project they would have to invest several thousand dollars on a new navigational system. Jerry wanted to make sure they made the right selection for this critical system component. Ease of installation was a key consideration. Between the two of them, they would either have to learn how to install it themselves or hire someone to do the installation.

Jerry musical preferences were quite different from Ray's. He would much rather listen to Benny Goodman or some Ray Price than the Doors.

"Don't you want to listen to Benny Goodman at least once to see what you're missing?" Jerry asked.

"Not really," Ray said.

However, Jerry was very persuasive. In the end Ray did not have a good answer to Jerry's question. On the one hand Ray was just fine with going through life never knowing who Benny Goodman was. On the other hand, it would not hurt to listen to Benny Goodman at least once.

Kate often showed up after wrapping up breakfast at the Goose Island B&B with an assortment of brownies, cookies, or banana bread.

"What's that music you have on," Kate asked when she stepped on board.

"Oh, just some old Benny Goodman," Ray said, feeling very proud of his recently acquired, vastly superior, musical knowledge. "I think it's called 'In the Mood," he added with a wink.

"I see," Kate said. She could tell exactly what was going through Ray's mind by the way he was looking at her and undressing her in his mind. "You'll have to tell me all about that when we get home tonight," she added without batting an eyelid. She liked to see the boys getting along so well. Jerry was like a surrogate Dad to her. Having lived next door to Charlotte and Jerry for years she was quite familiar with the music Benny Goodman.

"Yeah," Ray said. "It's one of Jerry's songs. You have to stick around for a bit and listen to this song by Ray Price called 'Deep Water'. It's pretty cool."

"I'm really impressed," Kate said. "I'm starting to fall for you," she added, echoing one of the lyrics in the song. You are so big and strong, Ray." Her eyes flashed briefly as she winked conspiratorially.

"Hard as steel," Ray replied as he held up his left elbow to flex his muscles. He knew Kate was just messing with him now. He looked over his shoulder to see if she was watching him as he disappeared into the engine room of the Sea Goose.

She blew him a kiss and silently whispered "I love you." Ray could feel his heart race as he made his way to the engine room. Kate was the one person in the world who get jump-start his motor with a single look.

Kate was an amazing cook and before long she was the Queen of the marina. She would put out the snacks at a small table next to the See Goose and all regulars at the marina would stop by for a cup of coffee and one of he treats. Some of the guys worked at the Harbor Master's office at the entrance to the marina. They called her "La Reina De La Marina", a term that Ray knew filled Kate's heart with pride. It was one thing to be the Queen of the marina, but quite another story to be "La Reina De La Marina."

There was a certain chemistry between Kate and the fellows at the marina. Kate referred to them as her Marine Animals, "Los Animales", so the feeling of respect that they had for each other was mutual. Their radar would perk up as soon as they heard Kate's familiar white station wagon crunch past the gravel in the parking lot. They followed her to the Sea Goose at a respectful distance, ostensibly to get a bag of ice from the bait house at the end of the dock. However, they were just out for a mid-morning stroll past slot #514 on their merry way to brownie-induced sugar high.

Remarks from Las Animales ranged from "Best dang cookie I've ever tasted", to "Man this is so smooth that it just melts in your mouth." Ray watched Kate's chest swell up with pride each time someone stopped by for one of her cookies. She knew they were just trying to finagle another cookie or brownie treat, but she never got tired of someone telling her how delicious they were.

"Those Dockyard Beezarks are going to get you so pumped up with their compliments that you are going to pop the sugar snap buttons on your shirt," Ray remarked.

"I'll bet you'd like to see that happen," Kate replied.

Ray bit into one of her brownies. "Damn these are good!" he said.

Kate smiled and took a deep breath, making sure one of her sugar snap buttons did in fact work itself free. She had a nice cleavage and knew exactly what effect it was going to have on Ray.

"Now get back to work or else you are going to have to sleep in the guest room all by yourself tonight."

"Yes boss!" Ray said.

* * *

There was a special extension to the Copano Bay Marina that was used for docking shrimp boats. This extended area had a separate entrance and parking lot. There were facilities for unloading their catch, and small workshops scattered around the parking lot to allow the shrimpers to perform repairs on their boats.

A small path connected the main docking area with the shrimpers extension to the dock. From time to time Kate noticed a few shrimpers coming over to the marina store for supplies, mostly beer and ice. Picking up her basket of cookies, Kate walked over to the Shrimpers Dock. She quickly recognized a few of the guys who had attended the Rhodes funeral.

She left them with the basket of cookies that she had brought with her. She assured them that they were welcome to stop by slot #514 any time they needed a pick-me-up snack. Even though she did not know the shrimpers personally, they were well acquainted with who she was and her relationship with Brenda and Robert Rhodes and the Sea Goose. During her short visit to the Shrimpers Dock she learned that Robert and Brenda had often visited the Shrimpers Dock for supplies and for advice.

The shrimpers confirmed what Kate already knew, that Robert and Brenda had both a little girl and an older son who liked to play with cars and trucks. Kate learned that Brenda used to call Allen 'Zoom' and that Myrtle and Zoom were always with Brenda whenever she had gone to visit the shrimpers. By the time she returned to the Sea Goose Kate was convinced that the shrimpers had not had anything to do with the tragic events that had transpired on board the PharmaSea.

Over the course of the next few weeks, Ray and Jerry continued to make progress on the repairs to the Sea Goose. Ray was determined to impress Kate with his handyman skills and he worked tirelessly on the repairs to the cabin. Between Los Animales at the marina and the shrimpers who came over to scarf up Kate's cookies Ray and Jerry were on a fast track to get the Sea Goose back on the ocean again.

One of the marina regulars, a fellow called O'Connor, offered to help with the installation of the new navigation system. O'Connor always wore an Australian Outback hat that set him apart from the other regulars at the marina. He had spent several tours of duty in the Navy and the hat was a souvenir from his days in the Pacific.

"How do we know this system will ever work properly if we allow you to do the installation, Mr. O'Conner?" Kate asked.

"Piece a cake, Ms. Houlihan," O'Conner replied. "I've been working on boats and doing my own repairs for years," he said reaching for the largest chocolate brownie that he could see on the table.

"Is that your third brownie today, Mr. O'Conner?" Kate asked, almost making the poor man choke on his first bite. "I would hate for you to get an upset stomach, you know."

"You don't need to worry about his stomach, Ms. Houlihan," said Jeff, one of the other regulars. "It's his kidneys that have taken a beating from the Jamieson spirits that he rewards himself with every time he catches a redfish." Everyone standing around the cookie table laughed.

One of the shrimpers stopped by the cookie table and set a basket down on one corner of the table. He motioned for Kate to come to the table and try one of cookies he had brought. The cookies had swirls of chocolate colored spirals that had a cinnamon flavor and tasted delicious.

"What are these called," Kate asked as she picked up one of the thin, crisp cookies and took a small bite.

"They are Tai Heo," the shrimper replied. "We call them Pigs-Ear cookies."

"Oh, they are delicious," Kate replied. "Do they have bacon in them?"

"No, no miss Kate. No bacon," replied the shrimper with a laugh. "You like?"

"Yes, thank you so much," Kate said.

"I'll bring some more tomorrow," said the shrimper. He stayed for a few minutes to chat with the marina regulars and then he retreated across the path to the other side of the marina.

Between the brownies and the Pigs-Ear cookies that went back and forth across the marina, there was an unexpected windfall of marine knowledge each time someone stopped by to visit the Sea Goose. Most of their advice was directed lovingly to Ray.

"No, no, no," remarked one of the Los Animales as he watched Ray cutting a sheet of plywood with a circular saw.

Ray wondered what he was doing wrong. As far as he could tell, the cut had been perfect until the time that he had been so rudely interrupted.

"You don't want to use plywood Ray," said his critic. "It won't hold up well with exposure to water. Better use a hardwood like oak, or spruce. Cedar is more water resistant and lighter too, so that might be the way to go.

"Thanks," Ray replied, not quite sure what to do with his freshly cut piece of plywood, now that it was completely useless. However, it was good advice. He could not help agreeing with the fellow who had offered this gem of wisdom. Plywood probably would not hold up in wet, humid and damp conditions.

* * *

A few days later Ray had completed the cabin and wheel house repairs using yellow cedar and oak throughout. He had stained varnished, and sanded and re-varnished all the surfaces with a finishing coat of an oil-based marine urethane varnish. The refinished surfaces gleamed and sparkled, and felt smooth to the touch. Shirley and Kate were admiring their handiwork. They had stopped by after work just when Jerry and Ray were finishing up for the day.

"What do you think about having Mr. O'Conner help us install the new navigation system?" Jerry asked the group.

"I think he knows what he's doing," Ray replied. We might be able to use his help with rewiring the electrical system.

Everybody agreed that it would do no harm to get his assistance. Jerry and Ray approached O'Connor to find out if he would be willing to give them a hand.

"My specialty, mate," O'Connor replied. "That's what we were trained to do in the Naval Academy."

Kate's attitude towards O'Connor softened when she learned about O'Connor's service background. Anyone who had graduated from the US Naval Academy was sure to do an excellent job.

Kate's father had served in the Armed Forces for his entire life and she had a healthy respect for anyone who was willing to put his life on the line for his country. Captain Houlihan was one of the unsung heroes who had served in Asia and the Pacific. He had made tremendous sacrifices that had gone virtually unnoticed except by his closest friends and family. He would turn over in his grave if he knew that his wife Cathleen had taken up with a loser like Walter after he had passed away.

"Can you bake us some cookies, Ms. Kate," Jerry said. "Let's see if we can find out how much Mr. O'Connor will charge to help us get this figured out."

"That shouldn't be too hard," Kate said.

"Speak of the Devil," Shirley said, as Mr. O'Connor walked past Slot#514.

"Hello Gorgeous," O'Connor said, giving Shirley a cheerful smile.

"Hey Handsome," Shirley replied. "We had a question for you."

"Shoot," replied O'Connor. "I'm free anytime you are sweetheart."

"How much would you charge to put in the navigation system?" Jerry said. He came right to the point. No need to beat around the bush.

"Well that depends!" O'Connor said.

"Okay," Ray said.

"On whether Ms. Kate's cookies are Chocolate Chip, or Oatmeal Raisin."

"Seriously O'Connor, how much to install the Navigation System."

"Seriously Ray, just a couple of cookies should do it," O'Connor said. "I'm an employee of Nueces County and they really frown on anyone moonlighting on the side. Maybe you can take me fishing with you sometime when you get everything working again."

"Deal," said Kate.

"Deal," said O'Connor.

They shook hands all around. O'Connor reached in his pocket and took out a small object wrapped in some tinfoil.

"I've got a small present for you, Ms. Kate," he said. "It's just my way of saying thanks for all the good stuff you have been bringing us every time you come to the dock." He handed her the object and waited for her response.

Kate unwrapped the object. It was a small carved wooden pelican. "It's beautiful. Thanks Mr. O'Connor."

"You're welcome," he said. "Now if you'll excuse me, I should be getting on back to the Harbor Master's office."

"I cannot wait to go fishing," Shirley remarked.

"If you want to go on a Fishing Charter, you may want to contact Brady Red's Fishing Service in Port Aransas," remarked a voice from the boardwalk. It was Larry, the Harbor Master drifting over to Slot#514 to see if there were any cookies left. The Seafood restaurant at the end of the dock buys a lot of Red Snapper from them. I hear that it comes from the El Sombrero area." Larry picked up a brownie and walked back to his office.

Kate's ears perked up when she heard the mention of the Oil Rig where Robert and Brenda had lost their lives. She waited till Larry had left to return to his office at the entrance to the marina.

"We'll have to look into doing a fishing trip," she said. "Good idea, Shirley. There's nothing like fresh Red Snapper, right off the grill."

"Sounds good," Shirley replied. "If you'll take care of the Red Snapper then I'll make up some fresh pasta salad to go with it."

* * *

Later that day Kate handed Ray the wooden pelican that O'Conner had given her as she was driving home with Ray. "It's very well made," Ray said. "It even has a crossbones 'X' followed by a date underneath."

"I know," Kate replied.

"It looks like a signature of some kind, but without any letters, except for the 'X'," Ray said. "No sign of any name or initials but it sure has a date, alright."

"I guess he uses the dates to keep track of his carving prowess, so he can tell if he is getting better over time" Kate said.

"Makes sense," Ray replied. "That way if he carves two little pelicans that look the same he can check the date to see which one is more recent and compare it with the one he likes more to see if his skills are improving."

"When Shirley and I were cleaning Robert and Brenda's personal effects from the Sea Goose we found a small hand carved duck, with a similar type of engraving underneath. The duck we found also has the crossbones 'X' followed by a date underneath. It is very similar to the engraving underneath the pelican and is dated in much the same manner. If I did not know any better, I'd have to say that they were both made by O'Connor."

"The 'X' underneath the pelican has a little detail on either end. It is actually a carving of a pair of cross-bones," Ray said. "It's definitely a signature of some kind. All that's missing is a skull between the bones of the 'X'. Do you think he was involved in the murders?" Ray asked. "He seems like a nice guy, but he could be one of the Drilling Rig Pirates."

"He sure does," Kate said. "However, what are the chances that he gave Baby Myrtle a wooden duck to play with and she never took the time to unwrap the aluminum foil that it was wrapped in? Most little children would unwrap a toy immediately. My guess is that it must have fallen out of his pocket accidentally when he was on board the Sea Goose and it must have rolled underneath the bed. That's where it must have remained until Shirley and I found it. The duck was dated just a few days before the tragedy occurred."

"Yes, I agree," Ray said. "That does seem to put him at the scene of the crime. O'Connor, or someone who received a wooden duck from him was on the PharmaSea on or before the time of the murders."

"We also know that Robert and Brenda often stayed on the Sea Goose all night to save the cost of mooring expenses at the marina, Kate replied. "Heck, they practically lived on the boat. They would have had to come to port after the duck was crafted."

"Right," Ray continued, picking up Kate's line of reasoning. "The duck was either left behind on the boat by O'Connor or someone who knew O'Connor. If it was someone else then that person would have had to have received it as a gift from O'Conner since he does not sell his carvings to people, he just gives them away. A gift to someone else would have to have been made shortly after it was carved and before the tragedy, in order for the duck to appear mysteriously on board the ship where you happened to find it."

"If we knew when the Rhodes family was in port, and whether they met O'Connor we might be able to narrow down exactly when he actually stepped foot on the boat" Kate said.

"Good thinking, Kate", Ray said.

Kate smiled. She had a beautiful smile. It went well with her hazel-brown eyes. Several weeks had passed by since the tragedy and Kate realized that she may have just found her first clue to solving the tragedy. The one thing that could connect the killer to the crime. Especially if it was O'Connor.

"We will need Troy's help to get marina records to see when the PharmaSea docked at Port Aransas," Ray said. "I wonder if O'Connor was helping Robert with repairs to the PharmaSea. He really seems like a nice guy. I hate to think someone like him would be able to commit such a heinous crime"

"A nice guy with an ice pick in his brain," Kate remarked.

"I'll try to find out if he knew Robert and Brenda Rhodes when he stops by to install the navigational system," Ray said.

"That's another thing," Kate said. "Is he really coming to help us install the navigational system or does he just want the opportunity to snoop around looking for something that he could not find the day Robert and Brenda were killed? Don't forget that he could be one of the Drilling Rig Pirates?"

"We will have to keep a close watch on him," Ray replied. "I think we should let Troy know about this so that he can update Jesse and Cindy. It's funny how things work out. Weeks go by and there is not a whiff of anything unusual and then suddenly something unexpected takes place and the trail gets a little hotter once again."

"I bet the Marine Animals at the dockyard are watching us like hawks," Kate said. "My guess is that some of them are probably mixed up in the murders, or they know who did it. They might be pretending to come over to sample cookies when in fact they are simply keeping tabs on us."

"It sure does sound like that might be the case," Ray said. "We need to keep our guard up. I'll let Jerry know that we need to keep a watch on O'Connor when he comes over to install the navigational system for the Sea Goose."

"What exactly does a navigational system do?" Kate inquired.

"Basically, it gives you the latest weather updates, tidal charts, and helps you plot your course. Most navigational systems have a depth finder to make sure you don't run aground by accident."

"That's nice," Kate said. "I like a man with a good depth finder."

"Are you serious," Ray said.

"Especially if he knows how to use it," Kate replied. "Hey, I might need some help with your depth finder, one of these days." She gave him a wink and smile."

Ray loved it when she talked smack with him. It takes two to tango and he needed an appropriate response because Kate had just thrown down the gauntlet.

"Sure," he said. "Anytime you're ready! Just let me know and I'll bring it on by your place. You're welcome to it as long as you promise to take good care of it!"

"Oh, trust me, I will." Kate replied. "I'll make sure it's well cared for at all times."

"In that case, I'm going to have to take you out for dinner," Ray said. "Let's head on over to the Swamp Shack for some crawfish and etouffee."

"Sounds like a plan," Kate said. "Thanks for staying with me, Ray. I love having you by my side."

"Ditto for me, Kate," Ray replied. "I can't think of a single thing I'd rather do, than the spend the rest of my life with you."

* * *

The navigational system arrived later that week. Jerry made sure that he read the installation manual from cover to cover several times before picking up the phone to ask O'Connor if the deal to install the navigational system was still a go. True to his word, O'Connor agreed to help Ray and Jerry install the new navigational system on the Sea Goose.

"It really shouldn't take more than an hour," O'Connor said. We should have time to take the boat out for a spin by the afternoon.

"Thanks O'Connor," Jerry said. "We will see you tomorrow. "

"Looking forward to it, Jerry," O'Connor replied. "See you then."

Jerry picked up Ray early the next morning, and they drove down to the Copano Bay Marina, bright-eyed and bushy-tailed, ready to get to work on the new navigational system. However, the project really did not get underway until mid-morning when Kate arrived with her basket of goodies. The usual retinue of Los Animales followed Kate to the Sea Goose at a respectable distance, curious to see what she had brought them.

Shirley had accompanied Kate to the marina. The girls whispered and giggled all the way from the parking lot to the Sea Goose. They knew intuitively that all the guys in the dockyard had stopped whatever they were doing to watch them walk across the boardwalk that led to slot#514. Kate heard a pair of footsteps behind them and realized that they were being followed by one of the Los Animales who was about twenty paces behind them. However, the girls never once turned back to look behind them. There was a Tee junction in the boardwalk where it made a jog to the left. Shirley stopped briefly to lean over a railing and look at the ducks. Kate gave her a withering glance. She knew exactly what was going through Shirley's devious, depraved mind. Anyone who was nearby got a good look at Shirley's creamy white thighs and her knickers. The marine animal behind them paused to light a cigarette.

"Hello ladies," he remarked as he approached Kate and Shirley. "Top of the morning to you." He tipped his hat as he walked past them.

"And the rest of the day to you," Kate replied.

The girls stayed to watch the ducks for another minute or two, and then continued their way to the Sea Goose. They set-up a folding table on the boardwalk and watched the Marine Animals converge towards the basket of goodies on the table. Kate had brought over an extra helping of cookies and brownies. She planned to replenish the basket as soon as it started to run a little low. It did not take long for that to happen.

The Marine Animals wasted no time in showing up to snack on the goodies and to commiserate the fate of the previous owners of the PharmaSea. They stayed until every remaining cookie crumb had been devoured. It felt good to get to know some of their neighbors at the dock. After all, these were the fellows who might come to their rescue if they happened to see their boat in distress on the open sea. After exchanging a few pleasantries with the Marine Animals, Kate and Shirley decided to return home. It was time to meet up with Charlotte and Myrtle and get ready for dinner. Shirley stopped to feed the ducks again on the return trip to the parking lot.

"You are so bad," Kate said as she watched Shirley lean over the railing once again.

"Say, what?" Shirley replied with a sideways glance at Kate. A raft of ducks floated towards her and she emptied her bag of duck food into the water.

"Oh nothing," Kate said.

Ralph let out a piercing wolf whistle and said "Hello, hello, hello." He hopped around excitedly in his bird cage.

"Hello Sweetie," Shirley said as they walked past his cage. She dropped a slice of apple in his bird-food dish before continuing along towards their car in the parking lot.

* * *

After Kate and Shirley left them alone to work on the navigational system the boys went through the rest of the goodies in no time at all. O'Connor didn't hardly do much of the installation. Ray did all the work. O'Connor leaned back on one of the chairs and read the instructions out to Ray who connected the cables and tied up loose ends to make sure everything was installed correctly.

The one-hour installation turned into two, and then into a four-hour project. Jerry corrected O'Connor repeatedly and forced him to read the installation manual to make sure that everything was wired correctly.

"This isn't anything like the navigational systems that I have installed before," O'Connor admitted finally.

"But you have installed navigational systems before, haven't you? Surely you can figure this out," Jerry said.

Ray took several mini-breaks walking out to the deck to stretch his legs while Jerry and O'Connor decided how to connect the blue wire to the green wire and the green wire to the yellow wire. At least that is what he felt he was doing.

After several hours of painstakingly following O'Connor's instructions and watching Jerry and O'Connor go through all the beer they had in the cooler everything was all wired up and good to go. However, Ray knew that was going to be a miracle if it worked at all.

"Anything else you think I need to do?" Ray asked.

"You did drain all the fluids, right?" O'Connor asked.

Ray looked surprised. Jerry laughed. He got up to relieve himself into a coffee can that he poured over the deck into the water that surrounded the marine.

"I'm serious," O'Connor said. "You have to drain all the fluids. The engines on this boat haven't been turned over since it arrived at the marina. All the fluids have been pulled down by gravity to the lowest point in the engine. It's been a hot summer and some of the fluids have evaporated so the particles in the fluids have started turning into shellac. The longer the engine sits the more condensation there is inside the engine which makes it start rusting from the inside out."

Ray listened carefully. O'Connor deserved an extra ration of Ms. Kate's cookies.

"If you start the engine without preparing it properly, you will end up pushing all the rust, sludge and everything else that has settled to the bottom through the system and contaminate the cooling systems and bearings and everything else."

"Makes sense," Ray said. "Let's get started on cleaning out the engine."

Jerry returned and helped himself to another beer. O'Connor was right behind him. Ray turned to the Cummins Diesel and began working on the drain plug with a wrench. The liquid that leaked out of the engine about ten minutes later was a dark, thick, viscous tar. Ray collected it in a drain pan and replaced the drain plug.

Kate and Shirley reappeared just when the boys were getting the last few loose ends tidied up. Kate drove Ray into town to purchase some fresh motor oil. She helped him pour the golden-brown motor oil into the engine when they returned. Ray emptied the drain pan into the container that had held the fresh motor oil. He sealed it off carefully, so it could be returned and recycled later.

It was now time for a test drive. However, there was just one small problem. In their haste to complete the repairs Jerry and Ray had neglected to purchase a key switch to start the motor. It was a minor obstacle that was solved by adding a jump wire across the terminals to the key switch. The engine came to life immediately. The boat started to vibrate in unison with the sound of the motor.

"Looks like you fellows know all the tricks of the trade," Kate remarked. She couldn't help noticing how Ray had started the engine.

"Aye aye, Captain," Ray replied. He turned the throttle up just a hair. He selected the controls to make the boat go forward and held his breath. Part of him expected the boat to go into reverse instead of going forward, and part of him prayed that it didn't just tear through the marine at top speed. He eased the boat away from the marina and into the broad expanse of Copano Bay. The Cummins diesel engine made a soft thwacka, thwacka, thwacka sound and they eased away gently from the marina.

They drove across the bay without incident. Ray's hands were white from holding the controls so tightly that he had hardly any circulation left. O'Connor and Jerry opened a fresh beer and were dancing a jig on the deck. Kate and Shirley joined in and clapped their hands excitedly.

"Would y'all keep it down out there," Ray requested. "I'm trying to concentrate here."

"Hey," Kate said. "It's my turn buddy. Why don't you take a break and go get me a beer?"

Ray handed the control of the Sea Goose over to Kate. Everything on-board the Sea Goose was working beautifully. Kate proceeded to commandeer the Sea Goose on her maiden voyage through Copano Bay. It was exhilarating. Kate could feel the wind at her back as she proceeded to handle the controls at the wheel house.

Kate drove clear to the other end of Copano Bay. Everyone on board waved excitedly at the other boats that they passed on their journey. They made a large wide circle across Copano Bay. Shirley and Jerry took turns driving the boat as well. O'Connor had a harmonica in his pocket and was playing 'Row, Row, Row your Boat' with gusto. He did not ask to do so and neither Jerry or Ray offered him a chance to take the controls. When it was time to return, Jerry took over the controls and they returned safely to slot #514 at the marina.

≈≈≈≈≈≈

12. Gone Fishing

Ray woke up early next morning and drove down to the Goose Island Bakery to pick up some blueberry muffins for the B&B, and some for Charlotte and Jerry. As usual, Troy's police car was parked outside the Bakery. Troy sat behind the wheel of his cruiser, listening to the chatter on his police radio.

"Good to see you keeping everybody in this town safe and sound," Ray said.

"Trying to," Troy replied.

"Anything new about the Drilling Rig Pirates?" Ray inquired.

"Not really," Troy said. "It's been pretty quiet lately. Just business as usual. If Baby Myrtle had not dropped into town like she did, it would almost be as if the murders on the boat had never happened."

"I know what you mean," Ray said. "Can I get you some coffee and a donut?"

"No thanks, Ray. Shirley has me all fixed up already," Troy replied. He reached down and held up a cup of coffee with the Goose Island Bakery logo on the side.

Ray gave Troy a "thumbs up" sign and entered the Bakery. Troy liked to park outside the Bakery and listen to the police radio in his car. This allowed him to keep an eye on Shirley and make sure she was safe, even if he couldn't go in to visit her.

"Top of the morning, Ray," Shirley said with a smile as Ray entered the Bakery.

"Likewise, Ms. Shirley," Ray replied. "How's the new baby? Is she doing okay?"

"She's a blast. Kate and I took her to the beach the other day. She had a lot of fun running through the surf and making sandcastles shaped like mermaids." Shirley packaged up some muffins for Ray. "I feel really bad about what happened to her parents. What do you think the pirates were doing out in the ocean on a stormy night like that? I guess they got away with murder. However, I have to believe they were there for some other nefarious reason."

"I agree," Ray said. "We have to figure out who did it and why. It's for the Baby!

Ray drove back to Marlin Ave and stopped by to drop off some of the muffins for his neighbor and to check up on the Baby. Charlottes living area had been transformed into a play room. There were stuffed animals everywhere. The interesting thing about them was that each animal had been paired up with a puppy. All the toy dolls had bears, and monkeys had a small dog next to them.

"I guess the baby likes puppies," Ray remarked.

"She sure does," Charlotte replied.

Ray had a quick cup of coffee with Charlotte, said hello to his favorite munchkin. He delivered the remaining muffins at the B&B, and left the house to continue working on the repairs to the Sea Goose. He had a couple of months of vacation remaining and he wanted to make sure everything was in order with the boat before he returned to Odessa. He had not really decided whether he was really going to return to Odessa. The temptation to stay on at Goose Island and spend his time helping Kate with the operational needs ot the B&B was very strong. He loved waking up each morning with her head upon his shoulder.

* * *

Kate slept in and woke up feeling well-rested, bright-eyed, and bushy-tailed. She found Ray's note pinned to the refrigerator underneath a mermaid magnet that held it in place. Ray's note said, 'Coffee Pot is ready to go, just press the 'start' button'. That was exactly what she needed.

After breakfast, Kate picked up the phone and began making inquiries from several of the Fishing Charter companies located near Port Aransas. She wanted to compare costs, and amenities, and find out just how friendly the staff was over the telephone. The cost of a full day excursion was roughly the same across the various Fishing Charters that she spoke with. Amenities varied depending on the size and the age of the vessel in use. On average the cost was roughly five hundred dollars.

When Kate asked the first Fishing Charter representative if they would take her out to El Sombrero she noticed a definite change of attitude. The tone at the other end of the telephone changed from being very open and helpful to one that was more reserved. Her request for a Fishing Charter was quickly declined. Evidently, they wanted to have nothing to do with her, and El Sombrero. She received the same reaction from the next two Fishing Charters that she spoke to. Brady Red's Blue Horizon Fishing Charter was the only outfit that welcomed her request. Their response was delivered without hesitation.

"Sure, we can do that," said the lady who was taking her call. We offer fishing trips to El Sombrero any time you would like."

Kate made reservations for herself and Ray for the following week. Shirley and Troy, and Charlotte and Jerry did the same. There was no charge for Baby Myrtle because she was under two years old.

* * *

"How very strange," Kate said when Ray came home that evening. "It's almost as if they all have their little piece of the ocean all divvied out. Brady Red seems to have dibs on all the fish near El Sombrero.

"That does seem a little unusual," Ray said.

"This is a free country," Kate said. "There's only two ways to get everybody to stay away from a particular place. Through intimidation, or by bribery. My guess is that it's the former. If Brady Red had bribed the other Charter companies, then that would eat into his profits because there is so many of them who operate from Port Aransas. He would not be able to stay in business for long. There is something strange going on here, Ray,"

"I agree," Ray replied. "Although, I guess that makes Brady Red's the expert for El Sombrero. If you want to go fishing there then he's definitely your guy."

"We'll have to let Troy know about this.," Kate added.

"Give me another month and we will have the navigational system in place and then we can go to El Sombrero any time we want," Ray said.

"Yes, but I do think it is strange that none of the other Fishing Charter companies I have contacted is willing to go there," Kate said. "And what is even more unusual is that none of them recommended Brady Red. They never volunteered his name by saying 'Sorry we don't go there but you might try to contact Brady Red'. I'm pretty sure they would have to know that he's the go to guy for El Sombrero."

Kate had that look in her eyes that Ray recognized. She was out for to hunt for bear, and she had her boots on, her rifle loaded, and her horse was saddled up and ready to go.

"You don't think Brady Red's real name is Elliott Bradenton, do you?" Kate said suddenly.

"No idea," Ray replied. "Honestly, I don't know who either of these people are."

"That could explain why the shrimpers seem to be avoiding him."

"Okay," Ray said. He had no idea what Kate was talking about.

"We need to keep an eye on Larry, too," Kate said.

"Larry?" Ray asked. "Larry who?"

"The harbor master at the Copano Bay marina," Kate replied. "He's the one who suggested I contact Brady Red. He could be tied into this as well. He's always walking around, checking up on us."

"That's his job, isn't it?" Ray asked.

"Exactly," Kate replied. "That's what I mean."

* * *

Time flies, whether you like it or not. Another week went by in a flash. Troy ran a background check on O'Connor who had easily installed the new Navigation System on the Sea Goose.

"It's nothing," he said, as he steadfastly refused to accept payment for his services. Kate wrapped a few goodies in cellophane, tied it with a bow, and put his name on it whenever she went down to the Copano Bay marina. The gang had taken the Sea Goose out for a spin in the bay a few times. Everything seemed to be in good working condition. There was some talk of cancelling the fishing trip and going out to El Sombrero on their own. However, they were still learning how to operate the boat and they decided to continue with their reservations for the Blue Horizon fishing charter.

"Wake up sleepy head," Kate nudged Ray. "We have a long drive to Port Aransas. Don't forget that we have to ride the ferry to get there." It was the day of the fishing trip and her alarm was getting increasingly louder with each passing moment. She reached over his motionless body and turned off the snooze button on her alarm.

"Can you do that again?" Ray asked. He loved it when her body brushed past him each time she did turned off the alarm in the morning.

"Pervert," Kate said. "It's the big day, Ray. Time to Rock and Roll. Let's go catch some fish."

Ray opened his eyes in time to see Kate getting dressed. He found himself staring unabashedly at her feet, ankles, calves, thighs, hips, behind, waist, torso, perfectly shaped breasts, a most kissable neckline, the raw beauty of her face, lips, nose, eyes, hair. He loved everything about her. She had the most perfect, stunning figure to go with her 'Wonder Woman' personality. He could just eat her up each time he saw her. Naked.

* * *

The drive from Goose Island to the Ferry at Aransas Pass had been uneventful. They boarded the ferry on the mainland side of the

Corpus Christ Ship Channel. It was still dark when Kate drove her station wagon on board the ferry. At that early hour of the day the wait time for the ferry was negligible. Kate looked out the window of her car hoping to see dolphins in the water, but the only sign of marine life was a long line of pelicans floating effortlessly over the water. A few minutes later the ferry had crossed over to the Port Aransas side of the water.

They drove off the ferry to the Port Aransas Jetty at the end of Highway 361. Kate and Ray parked their car next to a cluster of banana trees at the end of the parking lot of the Port Aransas Jetty. They walked down the boardwalk towards the Blue Horizon desk. They checked in and filled out all the legal forms and waivers. The charter did not leave for another half hour and so they wandered into a small outdoor patio to wait until it was time to leave. Pretty soon, Shirley and Troy and Charlotte, Jerry and Baby Myrtle showed up as well. Baby Myrtle was sleepy, and she had her head on Charlotte's shoulder. Jerry carried the baby bag with all the supplies that she needed for the day.

Shortly after they had all gathered in the area near the fishing charter, one of the crew appeared and directed them to the vessel, Blue Horizons. They walked down a small stairway to the boardwalk and then on to where Blue

Horizon was parked. Now this was a fishing boat to be proud of. It practically gleamed in the morning sunrise. Everything was neat and clean as a whistle. It must have cost a fortune.

A friendly looking man with a handlebar moustache helped them on board the vessel. It was Captain Brady. Charlotte and Kate recognized him instantly. He had attended the funeral for Robert and Brenda. He had spent a lot of time talking with Lola at the reception. Kate had also seen him talking to Kenneth Porter, but was not unusual. Kenneth did get around, and not just from a strictly physical sense. Like Ken, Captain Brady had a beer belly to match Ken's jelly filled donut figure. "To each his own," Kate thought to herself. She made a mental note to ask Ken if Captain Brady's first name was Elliott.

Captain Brady gave the group a warm welcome and took the fishing party on a tour of the boat. He made sure that Myrtle had a life jacket on from the minute she stepped on board the Blue Horizon.

After the tour the sat down on the bench seats along the front of the boat. One of the crew appeared beside them and passed out some cold beer and showed them the ice chest that contained the rest of the drinks. He showed them where they could stow their personal gear. Everyone was extremely friendly and there was some pleasant recorded music coming out of the speakers near the wheel house.

"You know, I could have sworn that Captain Brady has a twin brother called Charlie", Charlotte remarked as the fishing boat eased gently away from the dock.

"Why is that?" Kate asked.

"Well, I was speaking with a lady called Gail at the Hospital and her husband Charlie looks just like Captain Brady", Charlotte said.

"I don't remember either one of them," Kate replied.

"I'm probably just losing my mind," Charlotte said.

Captain Brady steered the boat carefully through the channel that led from the harbor at Aransas Pass out into the Gulf. He pointed out a few of the landmarks, including the Lydia Ann Lighthouse. Once they were out into the open sea, he handed the wheel to one of his crew and sat down to visit with the group. Kate had just put on some sun tan lotion, so her skin glistened in the sunlight. She could see Brady Red staring at her cleavage and felt that he was coming on to her. He kept looking at her swimsuit ravenously as if she was hiding a fresh pair of glazed Krispy Kreme doughnuts and couldn't wait till to take them to his cabin for a mid-morning sugar high.

The crew did not waste any time as they headed out into the Gulf. They made good time and passed several other vessels of varying shapes and sizes. Captain Brady seemed to have the most modern boat on the water. It must have cost a fortune. Kate could not help wondering how he could afford such a luxurious craft. The five hundred dollar per person fee did not seem as if it would be enough to cover the expenses of owning an operating a boat like the one she was on.

After they had been on the water for about an hour they chanced upon a shrimp boat making its way laboriously through the Gulf, its outrigger booms spread wide on either side of the boat.

"Those booms provide a shrimp boat with an added layer of stability," Jerry said. "A shrimp boat lowers its booms as soon as it gets out into open water because it can be a little top heavy to have large metal booms sticking up in the air."

"So, do they just drag those nets through the water to catch shrimp?" Charlotte inquired.

"Well the bottom part of the net has weights attached to it so that it sinks towards the bottom," Jerry replied. "In addition, the top part of the net has floats attached to it. It makes a conical shape under the water. As a shrimp boat trawls through the ocean the bottom of the net skims the ocean floor. Shrimp and other species are picked up from the ocean floor and they get trapped into the middle of the net."

"What about large fish and sea creatures?" Shirley asked. "Don't they also get caught up in shrimp nets?"

"Sure. They do," Jerry replied. "Larger fish go crazy when they get caught in a net and start tearing it up. About fifty years ago, when Shrimping was at its peak the shrimpers invented a turtle exclusion device and integrated it into the design of their shrimping nets. When a large fish that is feeding at the bottom of the ocean is scooped into a shrimp net, it has a natural tendency to swim upwards. The turtle exclusion device is akin to a large hatch or opening at the top of the shrimp net to release these creatures from the catch."

"That's nice," Shirley said. The thought of hauling a turtle off the sea floor in a shrimp net was very abhorrent. "I'm all for saving sea turtles."

"I agree," Jerry replied. The first turtle exclusion device was invented by a fellow from Georgia. It was actually called the 'Georgia Jumper' when it was first developed."

"How easy is it for another boat to approach a shrimp boat?" Kate asked. "Do the outrigger, or the shrimp nets get in the way?" Kate tried to picture the Drilling Rig Pirates pulling up alongside the PharmaSea, boarding it, and attaching Robert and Brenda. "Don't the nets get all tangled up if another boat gets too close to it?"

"Well, sure they do," Jerry replied. "You could never get too close to the stern of a shrimp boat. Proper etiquette on the water is essential. When Vietnamese shrimpers started fishing in the Gulf they made themselves very unpopular because they kept tangling up the nets of the other shrimpers. You see Texas shrimpers fish east to west, whereas the Vietnamese are used to going North to South. That caused all kinds of trouble until the Vietnamese made the adjustment."

"Yes, I recall that there were a lot of friction between them for years," Ray said.

"Shrimpers catch anything that happens to get trapped in their nets," Jerry added. "They just release anything that they don't want to keep. Some anglers like to follow shrimp boats and fish behind them. Shrimpers don't much care for that."

Captain Brady began following the shrimp boat from a safe distance. Troy was fishing on the port side of the boat and had a bite on his line almost immediately. At almost the same instant, so did Kate. Her rod dipped rapidly, and she felt a strong pull on the handle.

Kate had supported the rod against the railing of the boat and it was all she could do to hold the line steady. Everyone on the boat approached Troy and Kate. Kate felt a pair of strong husky arms wrap themselves around her and reach for the handle which was pressed tightly against her, between the railing and her body.

Captain Brady had been closest to her when she had caught the fish and she could feel him press up against her body. She could feel his belly pressed up against the small of her back. His hands reach below her waist to take the handle of the fishing rod from her. He could hardly get any closer to her. Kate found that she could hardly breathe.

As she struggled between the fish she was trying to reel in and her desire to get free, Kate recognized the ring he was wearing. It was one she had given Ray many years ago when they were madly in love with each other. She was now able to focus on landing the black fin tuna at the other end of the line. Ray handed the rod back to her when the fish began its death spiral. She reeled it in slowly, feeling its weight in the water. When a large shadow appeared beneath the waves she reached around and turned to Ray.

"No more beer for you," she said. "You need to lose some weight."

"Why sure, Kate," Ray replied. "Anything you say."

Kate was exhausted by the time the Black Fin Tuna was safely on board. Her knee-jerk remark to Ray was out of place. She knew he was in great shape and did not need to lose weight. The only person on board who needed to lose weight was Captain Brady, and possibly the black fin tuna she had just reeled in. The fish was huge, and Kate realized that she was going to have enough fresh fish to feed all her friends and neighbors on the island for a week. However, the whole process of spearing the fish and hauling it out of the water was a little messy. There was a customary photograph of her standing on the deck of the boat with her catch. Even though the heavy lifting had been done by the crew, Kate felt an urgent need to go downstairs to the washroom to clean up.

The washroom was just past the entrance to the engine room. As she passed by the engine room, she overheard a brief segment of conversation between two of the crew.

"Captain said we're on for night crawler duty tonight," said the first crew member. He had a neatly trimmed beard.

Kate wondered what that meant. Was it a new type of fishing bait?

"Oh man! Not again!" said the other crew member. "I had plans for tonight!"

"Well you know how it is," replied the bearded sailor.

"I wonder what that was all about," Kate wondered. She knew she could not tarry in the narrow hallway outside the engine room without being discovered. She continued her way back to the deck where the others were still fishing. As far as she was concerned she was done for the day.

She opened a Guinness and sipped it slowly. Myrtle was seated next to Shirley. She was wearing a floppy cloth hat with a wide brim to help protect her from the sunshine. Myrtle was holding on to the railing and jumping up and down with the waves. Charlotte had slipped her hand in Jerry's. Troy and Ray were having a conversation about the fish that Troy had just caught. Ray was sipping on a Diet Coke. There were several crew members milling around the deck.

Kate walked over to the other side of the boat to have a word with Ray. She handed him the Guinness and took the Diet Coke from him. As she passed the wheelhouse on the way back to her bench seat she saw a pair of small wooden ducks looking out the window of the wheel house. One of them was a little larger than the other. It looked like something O'Connor would have carved. She wondered if the date underneath the ducks would match the date underneath the duck she had found on the Sea Goose. If only she could sneak into the wheelhouse for a few minutes for a quick look at the ducks.

Captain Brady was standing behind the wheel when Kate tapped on the glass. He tapped back at her with a grin and motioned for her to come to the other side of the boat. Kate made her way across and stood at the entrance to the wheel-house. The ducks were within easy reach. However, Captain Brady and his beer belly were in her way.

Kate flashed her winning smile and Brady Red moved slightly within the wheel-house to make room for her. He gave her a tour of the wheel house and even let her operate the ship's horn. She could feel his breath on her neck and smell the cigar that he was smoking. She was torn between trying to distract him so that she could flip the ducks over and making a dash for the relative safety of the deck outside the wheel-house.

Kate was trying to get into position to reach for the ducks when Captain Brady reached around her to show her how to operate the wheel. Captain Brady took full advantage of his position and pushed himself as close as he could get to Kate. When Captain Brady grasped her twins with his big burly hands, Kate could tolerate his advances no longer. She tumbled forward against the wheel and knocked him out of the way. He fell to one side and one of the ducks to the floor. The duck disappeared as it fell to the left, away from the door. Captain Brady leaned down to pick it up, giving Kate a chance to extricate herself. Kate saw the signature carving beneath the duck that Brady had picked up. He set it back in position next to the other duck before Kate could read the date itself. The moment passed, and a few seconds later Kate stepped outside rather than endure another round of wheel-house fun with Captain Brady.

* * *

"That was a great trip," Ray remarked as he drove home with Kate.

"I know," Kate said pensively. Obviously, Ray had no idea what she had gone through in the wheel-house with Captain Brady.

"What's wrong?" Ray asked.

"I don't know, Ray. Something about the trip did not seem real. It was as if we had just been to Disneyland. We were waited on hand and foot. However, we never saw the underground tunnels that the cleaning staff uses to take out the garbage," she said.

"I'm not sure I see a problem with that," Ray said. "We were supposed to feel as if we were visiting Disneyland. The boat was impressive. Must have cost a fortune."

However, something was still bothering Kate. "It just feels as if were watching a movie," Kate said, giving him an icy stare. "There is something else going on, something very wrong and I just can't put my finger on it."

"One thing that seemed incongruous was the sheer size and luxury aboard the Blue Horizon," Ray said. "I'll bet that vessel burns so much fuel that I would have to call it the 'Hungry Hippo' if it was mine."

"Exactly," Kate remarked. "There is no way that he makes enough income from the fishing charters to cover his operating expenses. Brady Red has to have another source of income, or a lot of spare cash stashed away in a bank somewhere to afford his lavish lifestyle."

"Did someone on the crew say anything to you," Ray inquired.

Once Kate got a crazy notion in her head, it would take her a long time to get it out of her system. In the meantime, she was going to be as much fun as a Polar Bear on an Arctic glacier without its daily supply of Diet Coke. He was going to be living in purgatory on a survival diet of crackers and cheese with a Martian.

"Not really," Kate said. "I did not like Captain Brady. When you were helping me land the blackfin tuna, I did not know who it was and for a moment I thought it was Captain Brady.

"That explains a lot of things," Ray said with a laugh.

"However, I overheard a conversation that a couple of the crew members were having with each other. Something about night crawler duty for them after the fishing trip ended," Kate said. "I think the ship is going out again tonight."

"No way!" Ray replied. "They have to be exhausted. Those fellows worked hard all day. They reeled in the fish for us. They cleaned and packed them for us. That's messy, hard work. I have to believe they are out in a bar somewhere getting a beer."

"I'm pretty sure they said they were going out again tonight," Kate said. "I wonder what they are up to."

"Do you think they are going back out to fish for endangered species," Ray asked. "Turtles, maybe."

"That gets me really steamed," Kate said. There was something about Captain Brady that Kate despised. It was his sense of entitlement, that he could prey on unsuspecting young women with impunity. "Hey, did you notice the ducks in the wheelhouse of the fishing charter?"

"What ducks?" Ray asked.

"Little wooden ducks. There were two of them. Looked just like the one O'Connor likes to carve. I went into the wheelhouse to get a look at them but did not get a chance to see the date underneath."

"Oh, my!" Ray said. "That's just ducky! That could connect O'Connor with the PharmaSea and the Blue Horizon. He really seems to get around, doesn't he?"

"He sure does," Kate said.

"I spoke to him the other day," Ray said. "I told him that you had really liked the wooden pelican he had given you. He was delighted.

"We will have to keep an eye on him," Kate said. "I can't put my finger on it but I'm sure he's connected to the tragedy at the PharmaSea."

≈≈≈≈≈≈

13. Stakeout

Kate and Ray picked up some take-out food at Fulton, on their way back to Goose Island from Port Aransas. The fish they had caught earlier that day had been packed in a cooler full of ice and Kate did not want to open it that evening.

It was still warm when they sat down in the kitchen for dinner. The bottles of red wine that she had left out on the counter for the evening social were empty and ready to be disposed of in the recycle bin at the end of Kate's driveway. Kate had picked up a chicken salad dinner for Lola. She joined them in the kitchen and enjoyed listening to them recount the fishing experience. Karen and Kevin had already turned in for the night.

Kate had made her mind up that she had to learn more about what the night-crawlers planned to do that night. Ray tried to persuade her to leave it to Troy to figure out what it entailed, but Kate did not want to let it go. They had a long chat after dinner and Kate was convinced that the only way to find out what night-crawler duty entailed was to go back and stakeout the Blue Horizon that evening. She reasoned that it wouldn't hurt to return to Port Aransas that evening, just to see what was going on.

"We won't be gone very long. Maybe a couple of hours. We'll be back in time to share a bottle of wine with Charlotte and Jerry," Kate said.

Ray agreed to go along with the plan despite having some lingering reservations about the time that it would take to drive back to Port Aransas and return home later that evening. It was probably going to be too late to socialize with their friends by the time they returned. They picked up some supplies, including water, snacks, and some night vision binoculars. Later that evening, Kate drove her Buick station wagon back down to marina at Port Aransas with Ray. Kate picked up some pepper spray before leaving home. As an added precaution she put the Glock in the glove compartment of the station wagon. It was right after sundown and Kate was tired. Driving back and forth from Goose Island to Port Aransas had not helped.

They drove slowly past the marina restaurant and the party boats in the slips next to the marina restaurant. There was a small parking lot on one side of the marina and they found a parking spot facing the harbor where they could watch boats come and go through the narrow inlet that led to the marina.

Captain Brady's boat was clearly visible on the other side of the inlet. Kate and Ray trained their binoculars on the boat and observed little or no movement on the boat.

"What do you think night crawler duty is?" she asked Ray in a whisper.

"I'm not sure," Ray replied. "It must have something to do with fishing. A night crawler is a wiggly worm that is used to attract large, beautiful fish. Like you," he said. Ray leaned over towards her.

"Oh no you don't, Ray," Kate said. "This is serious. Can you stay focused for just one minute and keep your night crawler out of sight?"

He reached over to give Kate a small kiss on her cheek. She turned at exactly the right moment and kissed him back. Three short, small kisses that left no doubt in his mind. She was saving the last dance of the evening for him and him alone.

Kate took out a pair of night vision binoculars and was amazed at the clarity with which she could see every detail on Captain Brady's fishing boat. However, there was still no movement on the boat. None at all. It was like watching paint dry.

"I'm going to take a nap," Ray announced. He leaned his chair back and pulled his cap down over his eyes.

Kate's arm shot out and punched him rudely on the shoulder. "No, you don't buddy," she announced. "You need to commit to this or you can just pick yourself up and walk back home."

"But Kate," Ray protested. "This is so boring! There's nothing going on." He wanted to tell her that they could be sleeping in a nice warm bed, right this very minute. Safe and sound, snuggled against each other. His face resting gently against her skin.

"But nothing!" Kate whispered sternly. "You need to get with it, or else I'm going to kick you of the car. Butt first."

Ray was about to spend the next few nights sleeping on the outdoor sofa on the back porch when he noticed a slight movement in the distance. He trained his night vision binoculars on the Blue Horizon and did not see any activity. Refocusing his vision to the parking lot he saw a glimpse of movement once again. Someone was walking rapidly across the parking lot towards the boat.

"Look," Ray whispered. "There's someone getting on that boat now!" he said urgently.

Kate trained her binoculars on the boat and noticed a figure moving slowly around near the wheel house. He kept moving into and out of the wheel house. It looked as though he was stacking up a set of life jackets ang placing them on an ice chest on the deck. She snapped a photograph of him with her binoculars. It was a very handy device.

"There's a car driving into the parking lot on the other side of the water," Ray said.

Kate kept her binoculars trained on the boat. However, she shifted her field of vision slightly to the side so that could also look at the car that had just parked next to a couple of palm trees. It was a black sedan with a chrome plated Chevrolet emblem on the trunk. It was windy, and the leaves were blowing over to one side. She saw all the car doors open and recognized the crew member whom she had heard making the comment about 'night crawler duty' earlier in the day. He was wearing a hooded T shirt with a large set of numbers and some writing on the back.

"There's the night crawler dude," she said. "The fellow who was talking to his buddy about the special trip they are planning to go on tonight. He's got a dark blue hoody on with a star on the front that says 'Shut Up' on it in big bold letters. It has the number 75 on the back with some more writing on it. The letters in back are smaller so I cannot tell what it says."

"That's a Dallas Cowboys shirt," Ray replied. It says, 'Suit Up'. I think 75 is a reference to Mean Joe Greene. He's a legend from the seventies."

"Looks like an old shirt," Kate remarked. Probably a hand me down."

Three more cars pulled up and Kate did not recognize a couple of the individuals who parked their cars and walked up to the boat.

"Those fellows must have just learned about this trip. It was late in the afternoon when we got back from our fishing expedition to El Sombrero. I wonder if they received a message from someone while we were out fishing."

"Maybe so," Ray said. Maybe we should sic Troy on them. If he had a search warrant, he could probably get their telephone records. However, they have not done anything illegal yet."

A total of about six individuals boarded the boat. Captain Brady was not one of them. They fired up the engines and Kate and Ray could the sound of a boat moving slowly through the harbor. A few minutes later, they sailed out of the harbor without turning their lights on.

"That's a different boat," Kate said. "It's not the Blue Horizon."

"That's strange," Ray said. "It looks like they are stealing the boat. They didn't turn their lights on when they were leaving."

"I know," Kate replied. "I bet they are up to no good."

"Guess what," Ray said. "I can see the Blue Horizon is still parked on the other side of the dock. You're right. They did leave in a different boat when they left just now."

"You're right," Kate said. "This one looks more like a shrimp boat than the Blue Horizon.

* * *

It got really quiet after the shrimp boat left the harbor. Kate and Ray had no idea how long they would be gone or when they would return. Kate started to relax after they boat left the harbor. She reached into her purse and took out a small flask of brandy. She handed it to Ray.

"You came here quite well prepared," he said, taking a swig and handing it back to her.

"Do you want some moonshine," she asked with a wink. I think I have a case of something special in the back.

"You think of everything, Wonder Woman!" he replied. "Especially when there's a full moon."

Kate looked at the horizon and noticed that the moon had just come out from behind a cloud. The edges of the moon were still partially covered by the cloud. The moon looked larger than usual as the moonlight shone through the cloud.

"I love seeing a full moon," Kate remarked. She reached in her purse and took out a bag of pistachios. She handed the package to him and they proceeded to munch on pistachios with alternate swigs of whiskey.

"I like the twin moons you keep under your shirt," Ray said. "It's like being on Mars. When you breathe it's like watching the solar system at work."

"Pervert," Kate said. "The twin moons on Mars are called Phobos and Deimos for a reason. Panic and Terror. That's not very nice, you know Ray."

"Yes, but think of all the criminals you have brought to justice over the years, Ms. Bond," Ray said.

"I can't help wondering if the crew that just left is after some type of protected sea creature," Kate remarked. "A special type of fish, or possibly a sea turtle. Are turtles protected?" Kate asked.

"I'm sure they are. Turtles are valued for their meat and skin. Also, their eggs." Ray replied. "The urban myth about turtle eggs is that it is an aphrodisiac that helps restore erectile dysfunction."

"That's got to be a bunch of hooey." Kate replied.

"I know," Ray said. "However, it's rumored that turtle eggs produce incomparable sexual arousal."

"Better than this?" Kate asked as she pulled up the front of her T-shirt and Phobos and Deimos flashed brilliantly for an instant before they disappeared behind a cloud when her T-shirt came back down again.

'Oh my God," Ray said slowly, pausing to catch his breath after each word. "I don't think my life will ever be the same again."

"Don't get any ideas," Kate said. However, she moved closer to give him a long lingering kiss and to hold his hand, and he held on to it tightly not wanting the moment to end. She was very grateful for Ray's help and was just showing her appreciation in the only way he would understand. It was the least she could do.

* * *

At some time in the night, they drifted off to sleep. The windows of the car fogged up completely and the moon disappeared.

Kate awoke with a start. She could not see out of the fogged-up windows. Kate looked at her wristwatch. It had been more than an hour since the fishing boat had left the dock. "Ray," she said softly, giving him a nudge. "Wake up!"

"What's up?" he asked sleepily. "Are they back yet?"

"I'm not sure," she said. "I cannot see a thing."

Ray reached for his handkerchief and wiped the fog off the windshield. There was no sign of the fishing boat that had left the dock.

"I'm going to step out for a minute to take a look around," he said. "I'll go see if the fishing boat has returned to the dock. I'll be right back."

"Are you sure that's a good idea?" Kate asked. "Maybe we should call it a day and go back home?"

"We may not get another chance. There's no way to tell when the next night crawler trip is going to be planned. I just want to take a few photographs of fishing boat at the dock," Ray said. "Maybe they left one of the crew behind at the dock. We need some pictures to help identify the people who are involved in this activity. I'll be back in less than five or six minutes. Not any longer. Call for help if I'm gone more than that," he added, as he quickly stepped quickly out of the car.

"The interior car lights came on immediately as soon as Ray opened the car door. He closed it quickly behind himself and disappeared into the darkness. Kate felt totally exposed. It seemed to take forever for the lights inside the car to fade and turn themselves out. The windshield had fogged up again, and Kate used Ray's handkerchief to wipe it down once again.

She wondered if it would help to lower her car window. However, almost immediately she realized that she could not do that without putting the key in the ignition and hearing a beeping sound and seeing the flashing message lights on her dashboard. She missed Ray and wondered how long it would be before he returned.

"He's probably playing with his night crawler," she thought to herself with a smile. Just then, she heard the throbbing sound of a diesel engine in the distance. Could it be Captain Brady's fishing boat returning to the harbor?

* * *

The boat docked quietly on the other side of the inlet. One of the crew jumped ashore and tied the boat to the dock. The rest of the crew watched him from the deck. One of the crew was standing at the stern of the ship smoking a cigarette. Kate noticed another crew member walk up to him and have a short conversation with him and walk away. The fellow who was smoking tossed the burning cigarette into the water.

"That's odd", Kate thought to herself. "Why aren't they helping him dock the boat?

One of the crew appeared on the port side of the boat and helped the fellow on the shore to secure the gangplank. The crew disembarked slowly each carrying a small duffle bag full of whatever ocean contraband they had been hunting.

"At least they aren't stealing sea turtles," Kate whispered turning toward the empty seat next to her where Ray should have been. He had still not returned to the car. "I would have been really mad if they had come back carrying a stolen sea turtle under each of their arms.

The crew of the fishing boat shuffled off towards the parking lot and disappeared quickly into the darkness, Kate noticed that they had all gone off in one car. "I guess they are all going somewhere to celebrate. Or maybe just going out as group to IHOP for breakfast and pancakes," Kate whispered to herself. She was getting pretty hungry, herself.

"Where are you Ray!" Kate wondered. It had been about ten minutes since Ray had stepped outside the car. The marina was deserted. It had gotten very quiet and she was ready to call it a night. Something did not feel right. She reached for her cell phone and sent a text to Troy. If Ray had fallen somewhere she was going to need some help to look for him.

As she waited for Troy to reply, Kate noticed some movement on the fishing boat. The crew who she had seen leaving just five minutes earlier had magically reappeared on the deck of the boat. Kate looked around the parking lot and noticed that there were several other vehicles still parked in the darkness under the palm trees. The second group of crew members disembarked quickly and drove off in one of the other vehicles in the parking lot.

"That's weird,' Kate thought to herself as the same thing happened two more times. Each returning crew member carried a small duffel bag. Kate counted the cars in the parking lot. There were now two more cars left. She stared intently at the boat, as the same thing happened two more times until the parking lot was empty. She took pictures of it all with her binoculars.

Suddenly it all made sense. Only six crew members had left for the outbound trip.

However at least twenty-five people had returned from the trip. They had split up into four groups on their return and made it look as if it was just business as usual. The fishing boat that had left Port Aransas several hours earlier must have had a rendezvous with another boat somewhere in the gulf. The human cargo they had returned with had blended in with the crew of Blue Horizon on the return.

* * *

Ray had been gone a long time. Kate was starting to get a little concerned. She sent him a text message on her cell phone. "Where are you? Let's go home!" Kate said in her message. She pushed the send button and waited for his response. There was nothing. She sent him another text that she was sure would elicit a response, "Where are you? I can't wait to go home alone with you, Sting-Ray!"

A few seconds later Kate heard a few short chirps from the car seat next to her. Ray must have dropped his cell phone on the seat when he had stepped out of the station wagon. She looked in the mirrors on either side of the vehicle, and in the rear-view mirror. There was no sign of Ray. She waited patiently and reached in her purse for the small bottle of perfume she kept in it for special occasions. It had been a long night and it was now time for some soft sweet spices with a hint of orange flowers. She could see a neon sign in the distance and wondered if he had walked all the way to it to use the restroom.

Kate decided that she would drive out to towards the restaurant to pick him up. She started the engine and put the station wagon in reverse. She backed up a few feet to turn towards the restaurant. There was still no sign of Ray. The restaurant was about two hundred yards away, at the other end of the parking lot. If Ray came back and found her gone, he should easily be able to spot the car at the other end of the parking lot.

Kate was just about to head forward in the direction of the restaurant when she heard a sound behind her. It had to be Ray returning to the car. He sure had been gone a long time. Perhaps he had decided to stay in hiding when the fishing charter returned with their human cargo.

"Did you see that?" she said to Ray as the car door next to her opened slowly. However, even before she turned around, Kate knew there was someone else in the car with her. It was not Ray. She heard the fog-horn of the Port Aransas Ferry in the distance. Then suddenly she felt an intense pain as something whacked her on the back of her head and everything went dark.

She dropped the binoculars on the floor of the car and slumped down over the steering wheel of her station wagon. The driver's side door to her was opened. Kate felt herself being pulled out of the car and being dragged on the ground.

"Hey Rusty," she heard someone say. "I'm going to need some help. Go get me that ice chest that we use to store the fish. You know. The one with wheels on it."

"Sure thing, Mongo" Rusty replied.

Kate lay prone in the parking lot for several minutes, waiting for Rusty to return with the ice box. She moaned softly. Her head hurt like crazy.

"You're that broad who was asking all those questions," she heard someone say. "You've got some nerve! Sneaking around like you're Jane Bond."

She felt Mongo's thick rough hands reach into her shirt and heard the sound as the fabric tear when he ripped her shirt off. That was unacceptable. It was her souvenir shirt from her trip to Ireland. The one that had the letters IRE on the left side of her shirt and LAND on her right.

Mongo straddled her as she lay on the ground and began manhandling her. Her arms were trapped underneath his thighs and she felt him pulling on her jeans. It wasn't easy. She had gained a few pounds since her last birthday and her jeans fit so tightly that she already knew he would never be able to get them off. He started to choke her. Kate was starting to feel very violated and irate. She leaned forward and bit him as hard as she could.

He screamed and fell backwards. Rusty returned with the ice chest and said something about keeping quiet.

"Help," Kate screamed. "Somebody! Please help!"

Mongo recovered and whacked her on the head again and she passed out completely.

≈≈≈≈≈≈

14. Fumigation

Kate awoke in the darkness of engine room of the fishing boat. Kate had no memory of being hauled around the parking lot in an ice chest, but it was obvious that was how they had transported her across the parking lot.

She was lying on the floor with her hands tied behind her back. Her shirt was torn but she still had her jeans on. Her feet had been tied together and the cord that went around her legs had been pulled tight so that it was attached to her hands. Her knees ached at the joints from being hog tied and bent over backwards. It was hot, dark, and uncomfortable. Each passing minute seemed to last for an eternity.

She could feel beads of sweat dripping down her face. The room was engulfed with the smell of diesel fuel and fish. It was nauseating, and she felt sick to her stomach. There were some muffled sounds in the room above her, but she could not tell what was going on. At least they had not thrown her in the fish holds located next to the engine room.

Kate wondered if Ray had also been captured. Was he also lying in pain and agony somewhere on the boat. "Is this how it ends?" Kate wondered. All they had to do is go out to El Sombrero, slit her wrists and throw her overboard. Ray too. She wondered if Ray was being tortured in the next room. If the sharks did not eat them, they would just bleed to death in the ocean. It was only a matter of time before they came to interrogate her as well.

Her head was throbbing with pain. What could she possibly tell them about herself? Would they even care? She had been caught red handed watching them with her binoculars and taking pictures of them conducting their illegal human trafficking activities. Something told her that they probably would not believe her if she told them that she was just there because she was an avid birdwatcher.

She rolled over and moved closer to the wall. Then she raised her feet and kicked the paneling of the wall with her feet. Three short, three long, and three short kicks. She waited to see if there was any response? If Ray was on the boat, he would surely reply with a message of his own.

Kate looked around the engine room trying to get her bearings. The aging Cummins

Diesel across the room made a steady hum. It looked familiar. From all appearances, it was an in-line, six-cylinder engine. It was very similar to the engine that was used to operate the Sea Goose. The boat was perfectly still so they were probably still docked in the harbor. She wondered how long she had been unconscious. It had been around 10 pm when they had captured her.

Her body ached from having been thrown into an ice chest and transported across the parking lot of the Port Aransas Jetty to the engine room of this dirty, filthy, stinking fishing boat. They had ripped her shirt in the process. However, at least she still had her clothes on. That could change. She was sure that Brady Red was behind the operation. He would probably want to rape her before he threw her into the ocean. The thought that she might have to be his sex slave until he got tired of her company made her sick to her stomach. How could she possibly get out of this crisis?

Kate tried to do a quick assessment of her dilemma. The dock was generally deserted after midnight and remained that way until the wee hours of the morning. She would have to do something to escape before the boat left the harbor in the morning or else she would probably be sleeping with Captain Brady or the fishes. Not that there was much difference between the two. Whatever she did it would have to be done immediately so that she could escape before they came back for her. If she was still there in the morning she wondered if she could make enough noise to attract some attention. Once the engines were at full throttle no one would be able to hear her above the sound of the Cummins diesel. Where were all the little people when you needed them most! A short visit from King Brian of the Leprechauns, or one of his trusted assistants who could grant her a wish could really make a difference for her.

* * *

Ray opened his eyes slowly and with difficulty. The last thing he remembered was stepping out of Kate's car and walking over to hide behind a palm tree in the harbor. He had taken a few pictures of the harbor with his binoculars when he heard a sound behind him in the darkness. "It's probably just an animal," Ray thought. He didn't think anything of it. The parking lot had been deserted.

"Is that you Kate?" Ray whispered.

However, before he could turn he felt something hard hit him on the back of his head. Even before he fell to the ground his first thought was "Wow, that girl sure does pack a punch". It felt as if a tree branch had fallen on his head. That was a little strange because palm trees do not have branches. He hit the ground and saw his assailant standing over him getting ready to strike him again. That was when he passed out.

And now this! He woke up and there was a bright white light in his eyes. He had a distinct floating on air feeling one that left him feeling completely dis-oriented.

"Kate," he whispered. "Where are you.

He looked around expecting to see the harbor and Kate's car. He tried to get up but felt as if he was pinned to the ground. He had to get up. He had to find Kate. What had happened to the fellow who was trying to bludgeon him to death? He must have left him for dead in the parking lot. Ray tried to reach down and zip up his pants, but he couldn't move his hands.

He must have hurt his shoulder because he had a fierce pain in his side. Surely it was not a recurrence of a nagging rotator cuff injury that he had lived with for years. It couldn't be his rotator cuff. That would take months to recover from.

The ground felt soft. He closed his eyes and opened them again. Slowly. He was lying in bed, not moving his arm at all and it still felt as if it was on fire. Perhaps he had raised his arm to protect his head when the tree branch had fallen on him. There was a screeching sound in the distance. It came closer as it approached him, and then it receded. It sounded like a wounded animal.

As he came to his senses, Ray realized that he was waking up in a hospital bed and there were restraints on his arms that prevented him from making any sudden movements. The screeching sound that he heard in the distance approached him again, and he recognized is as a cart with a squeaky wheel going down the hallway outside his room. He had no idea what had happened to him. He closed his eyes, and everything went dark once again.

Between alternating spells of wakefulness and sleep he tried desperately to grasp what had happened to him. He quickly realized that it was not going to be possible to bounce out of bed and rush to Kate's assistance. He was filled with panic and worry. The maniac who had attacked him had probably done the same thing to Kate. For all he knew she too was lying somewhere in the same helpless state that he was in.

Ray's heart sank. He had failed to protect Kate when she had needed him the most. He had let her down in the worst possible way and could never forgive himself. Ray was distraught over the possibility that he may have lost Kate forever. He felt totally and utterly worthless, as if he had just lost the most important thing in his life. The one thing that mattered more than anything else. The one person who made his life worthwhile.

He would never again hear her laughter, feel the gentle touch of her hand, or watch her peel off her jeans when she was getting ready for bed. He would never smell her fragrance next to him, the whispered "I love you" that rocketed him to the pinnacle of passion each time she was near.

The pain in his shoulder refused to leave. If Kate was okay he expected to see some sign that she had visited him in the hospital. He looked around the room for evidence that she had stopped by to see him, but there was none. Somewhere in the room he expected to see a book she was reading, a bag of groceries, some crackers and cheese, some fruit perhaps, a sweater, a scarf, her purse or something that let him know she had just stepped out and would be back soon. However, there was no sign that Kate had ever been in the room with him at all. He closed his eyes with a deep sense of foreboding. The readings on instrument panel cluster next to his bed started to fluctuate wildly as he passed out.

* * *

Kate heard a key turn in the door. She could not see who had entered but it was evident that they had come for her. She could hear their movements behind her and was pretty sure there were at least two people in the engine room with her. She felt her legs being freed and tried to kick the person behind her.

"Aren't you a feisty little witch," said the voice behind her. A couple of rough hands grabbed her chest and flipped her over to face the other direction.

"Hey," she yelled. "That hurts!"

Brady was standing in the doorway. He turned to the fellow who had just mauled Kate's breasts. "Do be careful with her, Mongo. She's not like all the other girls you hang out with."

"Sorry Captain," Mongo replied. "I was just trying to see if the twins on her chest were real."

"Oh, they are real all right, Mongo," Brady Red replied. "I was standing right next to them today morning and you have no idea how much heat they generate. It's like standing next to a radiator."

"Pervert," Kate said.

"It's nice to see you again. I am so sorry, Ms. Houlihan. Our accommodations are a little more rustic than what you are accustomed to." said Brady Red. "But don't worry, you won't be with us very long."

"What's going on here?" Kate demanded. "What do you guys want from me? I was just sitting in the parking lot minding my own business. You don't think you can pull a stunt like this and get away with it? You're going to have every police office in the state of Texas after you if you don't release me immediately."

"Oh, we'll release you soon enough, Ms. Bond," said Mongo.

"We have a very special surprise planned for you, my dear," Brady said. "I hope you like strawberries with whipping cream."

Mongo smiled.

Kate shuddered. It was obvious that she was not going to be able to talk her way out of her predicament."

Brady Red walked closer to her and took out a switchblade from his pocket. He placed his hand against her flesh and flicked the blade hard against the strap of her black lace bra. It fell away and exposed a wide expanse of flesh. A few drops of blood trickled down her left breast. Brady leaned forward. He wiped the blood with his finger and tasted it. Then he leaned forward, exposed her breast and licked it hungrily.

"Oh my," Brady remarked. "You, my dear, are a feast for sore eyes. I cannot wait to see the rest of you. Up close and personal."

"Me too," Kate said fiercely. "We are just going to have to get it on, aren't we?" Her eyes flashed with rage. She was going to kick him in his privates, the first chance she had.

"I'll be back for you dear," Brady Red replied. He reached down with his right hand and squeezed her crotch.

Kate grimaced. "I can hardly wait, big boy" she said. She winked at Mongo.

Mongo laughed.

"Come on Mongo," Brady said. "Tie her up. Let's get this boat cleaned up. We still have work to do."

Mongo tied Kates legs again. This time he was as careful as he could be.

"You have no right to do this to me," Kate protested.

"We'll let you swim back to shore when we return," Mongo said.

"Yeah, with a bag of chum," Brady laughed. "You like you're in pretty good shape. If you can outswim the sharks that come after the chum you should have no problem getting back home in time for supper."

"Is that what you did to Virginia?" Kate said. Her eyes flashed daggers at Brady. They found their mark. In an instant Kate knew what all the shrimpers must have known all along. That Brady's first name was Elliott, and that he had killed his wife Virginia about twenty years ago.

Brady Red did not say another word. He reached over and slapped her. Hard. Kate felt a few drops of blood trickle down her chin. Her lips were bleeding and there was nothing she could do about it. Why did she have to stick her foot in her mouth whenever she opened it? Was it so terribly important to know what had happened to Virginia twenty years ago? The answer was simple. Yes, it was!

Kate knew that she had now crossed the red line and could expect no mercy from Brady Red. Not that there had ever been any chance that were going to let her leave under any circumstances. Even before she made the comment that had reduced her life expectancy to about 24 hours. Brady moved closer to slap her again. Kate snapped her leg up sharply to knee him in the groin. He screamed and fell backward grasping himself in pain.

Mongo finished tying her up as Brady groaned in pain. Then he helped his boss up off the ground. Brady got up slowly and stumbled outside. Mongo locked the door and left. Kate stared at the Cummins Diesel. It hummed silently in the darkness. She had not had time to assess her situation until then. However, now that she had met her captors, Kate knew that she was going to have to escape before they came back for her.

"If that scumbag comes anywhere near me," Kate thought to herself, "I'm going to take that knife of his and stick it up his rear end. I'll sleep with him if I have to, just to stay alive, but he's going to end up deader than a door nail if he lays a finger on me."

She lay on the floor of the engine room in the darkness without moving. For several minutes she could hear muffled sounds of people talking and moving around in the hallway outside the engine room. Thanks to the steady thwacka, thwacka, thwacka, hum of the Cummins Diesel engine next to her, Kate could not determine what was being said.

The amount of activity seemed unusual, considering the late hour and the fact there were just a handful of people on board the fishing vessel. Kate heard something metallic falling to the ground. It had a silvery sound as if a bag of coins had fallen and broken loose. The sound was accompanied by a shout from Brady Red. "Be Careful," Kate heard him say. Then everything went quiet.

* * *

Had they left? Kate had fallen asleep and it was deathly quiet when she awoke. The sleep left her feeling refreshed even though the room was hot and seemed to have no air circulation at all.

Kate jerked her body back and forth until she was able to flip around and face the other side of the room. The view of the other side of the room was a little better. At lease she wasn't face to face with the Cummins Diesel. She was sweating profusely from the heat and the exertion that this small, useless, maneuver entailed. It was still quiet outside and if there was anyone else on the boat then they must be sleeping soundly in a nice warm comfortable bed somewhere. Kate flexed her legs and pulled the rope as hard as she could. Perhaps she could work it loose and get the cords that bound her hands to slip over her wrists so that she could free herself. It was no use. No use at all.

There was a small workbench about two feet from her and Kate turned her body some more until she was able to get into a position directly underneath the table. She raised herself up on her knees and push up as hard as she could. Now that's called using your head for a change. The rope that bound her legs and wrists continued to hold tight throughout. It had barely loosened at all. The knots that held the rope in place had tightened and there was just a little more slack, that was all.

When she finally toppled the table over it fell to the floor with a huge crash. Kate waited fearfully expecting the door to the engine room to fly open any minute, and for the inevitable verbal tongue lashing that she was due to receive from whomever had been assigned to watch her. Nothing happened. Did they think so little of her that they had simply locked her up for the night and left her alone on the boat?

When the table fell over a few papers fell to the floor together with some writing pens. There was also a screwdriver on the floor. Kate's eyes lit up. Now that's something to work with. She wriggled over towards the screwdriver. Maybe she could cut through the rope with the screwdriver. After a few failed attempts to use the screwdriver as a knife Kate quickly realized that this was an exercise in futility. The rope that bound her wrists had chafed them till they were raw. "You really needed to keep a switchblade in a secret compartment in your shoes, Ms. Bond," Kate thought to herself.

* * *

It was almost two o'clock in the morning. Ray awoke with an agonizing pain in his left shoulder. Someone entered the room and placed a hand upon his shoulder. It did not feel good at all. He opened his eyes. It was Troy.

"Ray, Ray, wake up Ray," he heard Troy say repeatedly. "Kate is missing. We need your help to find her."

"What happened?" Ray asked groggily.

"Kate is missing," Troy said. His voice conveyed the urgency that he was feeling. "You need to tell me what happened. We need to find her right away."

"Oh no," Ray moaned. His worst fears had been realized.

"Kate sent you a text message tonight at around 10:54 PM," Troy said. "We traced the message to the parking lot of the Jetty at Port Aransas."

"How did you know, we were missing?" Ray asked.

"Well, we were expecting you for dinner last night," Troy said. "At the very least, we thought the two of you would come over to Charlotte's place to visit the baby. Shirley and I had dinner with Charlotte and Jerry. We left Charlotte's house shortly after nine. We figured that Kate and you were out on a date night, or something. However, when the two of you did not return to Goose Island at all, Charlotte got worried and contacted me.

I had to get a court order to get permission to check your cell phone records. Once we had that we were able to trace the last message you received from Kate. GPS data showed us that both Kate and you were in a parking lot near the Port Aransas Jetty. I came to Port Aransas to look for you immediately. I found you just before midnight, bleeding half to death under a palm tree in the harbor," Troy said. "You had multiple stab wounds in your shoulder. I brought you to the Emergency Room at the Hospital."

"Wow," Ray said. That explained why his shoulder was in so much pain. Kate's message had saved his life. "And Kate?" he asked Troy. "Is she okay?"

"That's the problem," Troy said. The urgency in his voice was very apparent. "Kate is still missing and so is her station wagon. We need your help to find her. Can you tell me exactly what you were doing at the Port Aransas Jetty?"

Ray recounted the details of the stakeout at the harbor. Troy listened carefully. Mid-way through his narrative one of the nurses entered the room and did her best to get Troy to leave. Ray assured her he was fine and insisted that she let Troy stay until he was finished.

"So, you were together with Kate in her vehicle," Troy inquired

"Yes" Ray said.

"And you saw a human trafficking operation in action?" Troy asked.

"Yes," Ray replied. "Both Kate and I saw it with our own eyes. We think Brady Red is mixed up in all this."

"Why is that?" Troy wanted to know.

Ray explained the connection between the toy duck that Kate had found on the Sea Goose, and the toy ducks in the wheel house of the Blue Horizon. Troy listened intently.

"So, you were both in the parking lot of the Port Aransas Jetty when Kate disappeared?" Troy asked.

"That's right," Ray said.

"I see," Troy replied. "Thanks Ray, you have helped me more than you can imagine. There's no time to lose since both Kate and her car are missing. We are going to have to put out an alert to all local law-enforcement units in the area near Port Aransas immediately. She must have been kidnapped."

* * *

Kate was about to give up when she saw a small hacksaw lying on the floor of the engine room. It was wedged up against the wall where the table had been before she had knocked it over. From a distance it looked like a hidden picture in a child's coloring book. Kate wiggled herself slowly back into a different position.

With her back to the wall she snagged the hacksaw blade with her hands.

She began working the hacksaw by moving it back and forth against the rope. It was slow going. Her wrists ached with each chafing movement of the rope that bound her wrists together. One strand at a time she was able to cut through the rope that tied her feet to her hands. Boy that felt good. She was finally able straighten her knees.

It was only a matter of time before she was able to free herself. She was finally able to wriggle free and slip her hands through the rope. Kate found a huge marine spanner. Good. She did not feel nearly as defenseless as she had felt just a short time earlier.

She tried the door to the engine room. It was locked. She used the screwdriver that she had found earlier and removed the bolts that held the door handle in place. Then she jammed the screwdriver between the door and the door jamb right where the lock would have been and kicked the door as hard as she could. It flew open and she was free. She held the spanner firmly in her right hand. At the first sign of trouble she would not hesitate to use it on anyone who got in her way.

Kate crawled cautiously up to the deck. There was no one on board the ship. A couple of seamen were standing on the boardwalk next to the boat smoking cigarettes. The short stubby guy with the big belly was probably Mongo. The other guy was probably Rusty. There was no sign of Brady. She could still feel his hands against her skin and smell his breath in her face.

In the silence that surrounded the boat, their words were clearly audible. They had picked up nineteen illegal individuals that night. Each crew member received a thousand dollars for each illegal who was transported safely into the United States. Not a bad haul for a nights' work. Nineteen thousand dollars apiece.

"It's like taking candy from a baby," Mongo remarked.

"Yeah," Rusty replied. "All we do is go over to the drop site, pick up the floaters, reel them in and then drop them off at the warehouse."

"We keep doing this for a few more years and we should be able to buy our own boat." Mongo said.

"Yeah, count me in," Rusty said. "I'll bet Brady makes a killing running his tourist business."

Mongo guffawed, as if that was the funniest thing he had heard all day. "I'll say," Mongo remarked. "He sure does make a killing!"

Kate had heard enough. She tried to gauge the distance from the boat to the parking lot. There was no way for her to get past them undetected. She really did not want to get captured and tied up again. She crawled into the wheelhouse and studied the controls. They seemed very similar to the controls of the Sea Goose.

She was prepared to yank the starter wires and hot wire the motor if she needed to. However, the key was still in the ignition. They had not expected her to be able to free herself. Kate flipped the lever to throttle the engines and the boat started moving slowly away from the shore. She pushed the throttle down and the boat started to advance more rapidly.

"Hey," yelled one of the seamen. It looked like Rusty, the taller of the two fellows she had seen from the deck. He threw his cigarette in the water and raced unsteadily down the boardwalk. He had probably had a few drinks with his shipmate while they were talking about their financial windfall from their efforts earlier that evening.

"Hey, you! What are you doing?" yelled the other seaman. It was definitely Mongo. He raced after Rusty but couldn't keep up because his beer belly kept getting in his way. He would have been better off if he had let Rusty chase after the boat alone. Mongo tripped on a loose board and went down like a ton of bricks. It looked like a rerun of the Laurel and Hardy show. The only reason these idiots had captured her in the first place is because they had had the element of surprise. They had snuck up on Kate in the parking lot and knocked her out when she wasn't looking. Under any other circumstances she would have hog tied them and fed them to the wolves.

It was too late for either of them to board the fishing vessel. The boat was at least twenty feet away from the shore. Kate heard a muffled pop and saw a flash from the shore. She heard the sound of breaking glass on the boat. Seriously! Were they shooting at her?

Kate opened the throttle and the boat lurched forward. The line that tied it to the boardwalk grew taut and then a piece of the boardwalk disappeared as it broke free. Kate resisted the temptation to give them the finger. "Let's not get ahead of ourselves Ms. Bond," she said to herself. "Let's get away from here first."

Kate steered the boat into the open water. When it was a safe distance from the shore she killed the engines. The progress of the boat slowed immediately. She took the spanner that she had in her hand and jammed it against the steering wheel. The boat would go in circles forever.

Kate recalled seeing an assortment of tools in the engine room where she had been held captive. She ran back down to the engine room and returned with an acetylene blowtorch and whatever remained of the cords that had be used to bind her hands and feet. She pulled the trigger on the blowtorch and it burst into flame immediately. Kate tied down the trigger to the blowtorch so that it would continue to burn until it ran out of fuel. She placed it carefully on the floor of the wheel house. Then she stepped out on the deck and walked over to the railing on the port side of the ship.

Kate took off her jeans. She tied a knot at one end to trap some air in the legs and jumped into the water.

The first thing she noticed when she hit the water was how cold, black, and deep it was. The waves were huge. It was all very disorienting. Fortunately for her the lights on the shore at Port Aransas were bright enough and close enough to guide her back towards the shore. If she had not been a good swimmer she would have never survived. It took her more than half an hour to cover the short distance to the shore. She was exhausted. It was hard work even though the tide was coming in.

When she finally reached Port Aransas she crawled thankfully out of the water and lay down on the beach just out of the reach of the surf. She was exhausted. She was dressed in a T-shirt and her underclothes. Good thing she had chosen to wear her black bra and panties that day. She took off her bra and adjusted the shoulder strap that Brady Red had sliced with his pocket knife. She tied a knot so that it would stay in place and put it back on again. A casual passerby would probably assume she had been out for a midnight swim.

Kate looked out over the water. In the distance she could see flames shooting up from the fishing boat that she had abandoned a short time earlier. That was one fishing vessel that would not be going out to sea on any more night-crawler runs.

She put on her jeans and walked towards the shore. She was barefoot and stepped carefully across the sand towards a small street that ran parallel to the beach. There was an abandoned flipflop in the sand and she put it on her left foot. Now she just had to watch where she stepped with her right foot.

Kate looked around and tried to get her bearings. A sign in the parking lot told her she was at the Port Aransas Beach Park. It was deserted. As she strode away from the beach she turned left on Cotter Avenue in the opposite direction from the Port Aransas Marina. She had no desire to meet up with Mongo and Rusty again that night. It wasn't long before Cotter intersected with Beach St.

There was a hotel nearby, just a short distance down the road. You could hardly miss it with all its bright lights and neon signs. Man, what an eyesore. The best part of living on Goose Island was that at least the beach was as natural and pristine today as it had been when it had been created by its Maker.

Kate walked over to the entrance to the hotel. She looked like hell and felt even worse. The door was locked and the clerk behind the desk took one look at her and steadfastly refused to let her into the lobby. She looked around the parking lot to see if there was any kind of security detail on duty, but there was nobody around. Kate punched the button on the intercom and asked the surly receptionist if he would please call the police.

"If you can let me inside for just one minute, all I need to do is to make a simple phone call," Kate said.

"Sorry Ma'am, our policy does not allow us to admit you after midnight."

"I understand," Kate said, as she leaned on the button on the intercom. "Normally I would not bother you, but this is an emergency.

"Sorry Ma'am," the desk clerk insisted. "If you don't leave right now I will have to call the authorities."

"Please," Kate said. "Please, please, please call the police."

"Let me check with my manager," replied the receptionist over the intercom.

Kate stood outside the glass door shivering in her damp clothes. Through the glass door that separated Kate from the lobby, she could see him talking agitatedly on the telephone. Any Texan worth his salt would have opened the door immediately to help a damsel in distress. It was such an insult to have just escaped from the clutches of Brady Red and his night-crawlers only to be treated as if she was a blot on the face of humanity.

There was a cast iron bench next to the hotel entrance. Kate sat down and waited patiently in the parking lot for the police to arrive. What a night it had been. She had barely escaped being shark bait so that a couple of young kids could go on night crawler duty to rake in nineteen thousand dollars a night transporting illegal immigrants into the country. Maybe they would have to find themselves a real job now that their fishing boat was headed straight to Davy Jones' Locker.

≈≈≈≈≈≈

15. Hurricane Harbor

Kate heard the signature sound of police sirens in the distance. The sound grew louder as the vehicle approached from Highway 361 South and then seemed to veer off in the direction of the Dolphin Docks. That was odd. They were going the wrong way. The police car had just gone past the hotel where she was at. They must have gotten lost. Kate listened for the sounds of the sirens, expecting them to turn around and return. Instead she heard the sirens of a second emergency vehicle approaching from Highway 361 South as well. Boy they had really sent the cavalry out to meet her.

However, when the second vehicle veered off in the direction of the Dolphin Docks Kate knew that something unusual was going on, elsewhere on Mustang Island. Then she heard a third and a fourth police car so that darkness of the night sky was lit up with flashing red and blue lights, and the air was filled with a cacophony of police sirens. It was music to her hears. Someone was finally going after Brady Red and his gang of common criminals.

Kate realized that they were too busy to come to her rescue. She had pretty much rescued herself. She walked back down the road from the hotel towards Port Aransas. Good thing she had kept her jeans with her when she had jumped off the fishing boat or she would be walking down main street in Port Aransas in her black lace underwear. She walked along purposefully as if she knew exactly what she was doing. No telling what would happen if the bar flies who were just getting ready to go home saw her beautiful, bodacious, body bouncing along the side of the road. She would probably get kidnapped again. She noticed a nice rounded rock in the shrubbery outside a restaurant that she was passing. She picked it up on the spur of the moment since she had just decided that she would feel better with it in her hand to defend herself from any 'wanna-be' kidnappers.

It was a fair distance to the Dolphin Docks and there was always a chance that she might run into the two thugs who had chased after her when she had stolen their boat. The sirens and flashing lights appeared to be coming from the direction of the Port Aransas Ferry. Picking up her pace she walked past several half-deserted streets for what seemed like an eternity until she could see the Ferry. All the restaurants that she passed were closed. It had to be way past midnight. Her path to the Ferry had just taken her across the narrow strip of the peninsula that shelters the Port Aransas Jetty from the Gulf Intracoastal Water Way.

The flashing red and blue lights at the Ferry were coming from the police cars and emergency vehicles parked on the shore. A quick glance around confirmed her worst fears and suspicions. The distinctively sleek silhouette of Captain Brady's Blue Horizon fishing charter could be seen cruising rapidly out of the harbor. Despite the late hour, a crowd of onlookers had gathered at the Ferry. A police office could be seen at the edge of the ferry with a megaphone.

"Blue Horizon. Heave to Port Immediately," said the officer. His voice could be heard loud and clear. "Blue Horizon. Heave to Port Immediately," the officer repeated. However, Blue Horizon continued its steady escape from the harbor unabated.

The sound of the sirens and the megaphone had woken up the people who lived near the Ferry. In no time at all Kate was surrounded by folks who wanted to see what the commotion was all about. Kate felt safer immediately.

The Coast Guard Cutter fired a flare. It arched into the sky and lit up the water. Everyone could now see the Blue Horizon churning up the water as it travelled rapidly down and out of Aransas Pass. It was headed to the blackness of the Gulf. The Coast Guard Cutter was following in the wake of the Blue Horizon.

Kate found herself standing next to a couple of middle-aged girls. They were wearing pajamas and flip-flops. They must have just woken up and must have just emerged from one of the hotels nearby. They seemed like a pair of honest, law-abiding individuals.

The lady standing next to her, wearing white pajamas with small red polka dots struck up a casual conversation with Kate.

"My names Donna," she said. "Are you okay? You must have banged your lip on something. It's all swollen."

"I'll be fine," Kate replied. "Thanks for asking."

"Are you sure?" Donna said. "We can call the cops for you if you're having trouble with someone."

"Thanks, Kate said. "Do y'all know what in the world is going on? Are we witnessing a real-life drug bust?" Kate asked.

"Not sure," replied Donna's friend. "We just heard all the noise and came to see what all the excitement was about."

"Looks like a boat called the Blue Horizon is making a run for it," Kate said.

They introduced themselves. Donna and her sister Susan were spending the week in Port Aransas.

"I'm sorry, I seem to have left my cell phone in my car," Kate said. "Do you think it would be if I borrow your phone to make a quick phone call to my husband?" Kate did not mention that she had left her phone in her station wagon the night before and that she had no earthly idea where her station wagon was at that moment.

Donna Oliver was kind enough to let Kate use her cell phone.

The first phone call Kate made was to Ray. He did not answer his phone and so Kate left a message on his voice mail to let him know where she was. Kate wondered what had happened to Ray. She had left the fishing boat in a hurry and had not had the time to check and make sure that he was not on board. There was always the possibility that he was lying unconscious somewhere else on the boat. If he was still on board the fishing vessel that would not be good. In that case then he was almost surely floating slowly across the Gulf. He would not be happy if he woke up and found himself in Cuba or Mexico. Perhaps she could contact the Coast Guard to organize a rescue for him.

He second phone call was to her best friend Shirley. Shirley answered on the first ring and Kate wanted to hug her for always being there for her.

"Shirley, it's me, Kate," she said.

"I know," Shirley replied. "Where are you? We have been looking every for you. We even have the Coast Guard looking for you this very minute."

"I'm near the Ferry in Port Aransas," Kate replied. "It's a long story. Do you think you can come out and give me a ride home? I'm afraid I don't have any money on me, and I've lost my shoes."

"Please stay right where you are Kate," Shirley said. "I'll be there right away."

"Thanks Shirley," Kate said. "Don't worry, I'm not going anywhere else tonight. I'll wait for you on the mainland side of the Ferry."

"Hang in there Kate," Shirley said. "I'm on my way."

"Thanks Shirley. Bring me some dry clothes if you can. I'll be more than happy to wear one of your T-shirts, and jeans if you don't mind. I just need something dry to put on. It doesn't matter if it does not fit properly."

"You got it, Kate," Shirley said. "Be there in a jiffy."

"I'll be here, Shirley," Kate said.

Kate returned the cell phone to the lady standing next to her. She turned her attention to the harbor. There was now a Coast Guard Cutter chasing after the Blue Horizon. The Coast Guard Cutter had its siren blaring and lights flashing. From a distance it was hard to tell if the Coast Guard Cutter was travelling faster or slower than Blue Horizon. Kate wondered what Brady Red was hoping to accomplish. Was he trying to make a run for Mexico? If he could get there before the authorities could arrest him, he might be able to hide out in Mexico forever. Maybe even continue going South to Brazil or Argentina. No doubt he had a fair number of connections, and probably a secret bank account or two. Maybe even a mistress to help him with his finances.

The Coast Guard Cutter was practically bouncing on the water and occasionally getting airborne. With the wind coming in off the water in the gulf, it made for choppy seas. The Cutter bounced along the five-foot swells in the water, keeping a close watch on the Captain Brady's fishing boat. The gap between them closed rapidly. There was no way Brady could outrun the Cutter. The spectators on the shore saw a shadowy figure on the deck of the Blue Horizon and a couple of brilliant flashes of light.

"Is he shooting at the Coast Guard?" Kate's neighbor Donna asked.

"It sure looks like it," Kate replied. "He's got to be pretty desperate to try a stunt like that."

"Either that, or he's a complete moron," Donna said. "He just added ten years to his prison sentence, and I doubt they'll give him time off for good behavior when they are reviewing his case a decade from now!"

"Probably both," Kate said. "Some guys just have a big ego and never get used to reality." Kate licked her lips. Brady was about to get his just desserts in a hurry. This was way better than kicking him below the waist.

"I've known a few whose brains were located below their waist," Donna's friend remarked.

The girls laughed. It was good to be alive and to be able to share some laughter and joy again. Kate felt a fresh surge of energy. She wanted to reach out and kiss Donna and her friend for being there.

"Where are you girls from," she asked.

"We are down here from Canada," Donna replied.

"I'm glad you're here," Kate said. "Stop by the Goose Island B&B next time you are here. I run the B&B and will be happy to give you a discount on your stay." Canadians were a close second towards being her favorite people in the world. As far as Kate could tell Canadians liked Country and Western music and Blues almost as much as she did. Shania Twain, and Diana Krall were just few of the artists whose music she enjoyed.

The Coast Guard Cutter was impervious to the steady stream of bullets that bounced off its bullet proof hull. It changed directions ever so slightly every few minutes throwing the Blue Horizon off course. The gunman on the deck of the Blue Horizon did not see the abandoned fishing charter that was drifting lazily in the water in front of him. He sprayed the Coast Guard Cutter with bullets and ran straight into the fishing trawler. The resulting explosion was a fireball that blew a hole in the side of the fishing trawler. It obliterated the bow of the Blue Horizon.

"Wow," Donna said.

"Yep!" Kate replied. "Hope he knows how to swim. It's a long way to Tipperary from where he's at right now."

"Well he definitely took the low road," Donna said. The girls laughed again.

Kate heard the steady chop, chop, chop, in the air behind her as the coast guard helicopter approached. She waved at the coast guard chopper. A roar when up from the spectators who all cheered the coast guard vessel that was now approaching from the shore.

Kate said goodbye to the Canadians and walked over the Ferry with a heavy heart. It was time to cross over to the mainland side of the Ferry and meet up with Shirley. The elation that she had felt when the Coast Guard had cornered Brady Red gave way to an immense feeling of loss. There was still the slim possibility that Ray could have been on the fishing vessel that had just been obliterated by the Blue Horizon. Even though she had not seen him on the fishing vessel there was a chance that Rusty and Mongo had captured him and locked him up somewhere else on the fishing vessel.

"I sure hope Ray was not on board that fishing ship when the Blue Horizon crashed into it," Kate repeated to herself over and over again, as she boarded the Ferry. It was a miserable feeling. Kate was wracked with guilt because she could not be certain that Ray had not been present on the fishing boat when the Blue Horizon had crashed into it a short time ago.

Why hadn't she taken the time to check the boat thoroughly before she had jumped off to save her own sorry skin. "I'll never forgive myself," Kate said softly to herself. "If Ray was on that ship, I'll never forgive myself." She wiped away a silent tear, and then another and finally placed her head in her hands and sobbed uncontrollably as she leaned over the railing on the Ferry. She looked out into the black darkness of the water that swirled around the Ferry. "This must be what it feels like to win the battle and lose the war," Kate thought. Every bone in her body ached with fatigue and she was overcome with a deep feeling of melancholy.

The lights from Port Aransas twinkled in the night and cast their reflection on the water as the Ferry travelled quickly over to the mainland side of Aransas Pass. The coast guard chopper could be seen leaving the scene as he returned to base. Some of the emergency vehicles that had been parked at the Ferry Terminal on Mustang island had turned off their emergency lights. She could see them start to leave the area.

Kate stepped off the Ferry in a daze. The aches and pains from having been bound and gagged for most of the night now made her ache from head to toe. It was almost dawn and there was a clear blue sky overhead. Kate looked down at the water next to the ferry and saw some dark circular shapes floating lazily within it. A couple of turtles had stopped by to say "Hello."

"Where were you there when I needed you," she said to them softly. "I would have felt a lot safer swimming ashore if I had had you to keep me company."

She found Shirley waiting for her with Troy on the mainland side of the Ferry. They were parked a short distance away in a Visitor's Parking area. Shirley ran up to her and gave her a hug.

"You're wet!" Shirley exclaimed. "What just happened?"

"Just another train wreck," Kate replied.

"Are you okay?" Troy asked. "Is all that commotion on the other side of the Ferry what I think it is?"

"That's right," Kate replied. "I think the Coast Guard just caught up with Brady Red."

"That figures," Troy said. "We sent the Coast Guard a distress call when we learned that you might have been kidnapped at the dockyard. They were planning to scour the seas and look everywhere for you. They had just started checking all the boats in Port Aransas to search for you. "

"Brady must have made a dash for the open sea when he saw them checking all the boats coming and going through the harbor," Kate surmised.

"In that case Brady Red chose the worst possible time to make a run for it," Troy said. "From all appearances, the Coast Guard was on his tail in a flash."

Troy's phone rang and he stepped to one side to take the call. It was Jesse from the Coast Guard.

"Did they catch up with Captain Brady?" she asked Troy.

"Not exactly, Kate," replied Troy. "There's nothing left of him. It seems that Captain Brady is no more. He died in the explosion when his boat crashed into the fishing vessel that was floating in the Gulf.

"Good," Kate said. She felt a wave of relief course through her body. "Has anyone seen Ray?" Kate inquired. She was almost afraid to ask.

"Ray's in the hospital," Troy replied. "He's a little beat up but I think he's going to be fine."

"Oh, my goodness, Troy," Kate said. "Thank you so much. I'm so relieved. I was afraid something terrible might have happened to him. Thank You, Lord."

"You can thank him for getting the Coast Guard out here tonight," Troy said. "Ray gave us the information we needed to piece together the information we needed to start looking for you. He's worried sick that he's never going to see you again."

"Nice swimsuit you have on, 'Wonder Woman'" Shirley said. She handed Kate a towel and looked at her black lace bra.

"It's my 'miracle' underwear swimsuit," Kate replied with a laugh. "You should see the boy-shorts that go with it."

"I'm going to have to get one just like that," Shirley said. "You're lucky you didn't get kidnapped before we found you."

Kate smiled. When she was seated comfortably in the back of Shirley's car, wrapped in a dry towel, Kate felt a huge sigh of relief. She took off her wet 'Wonder Woman' bra. Even though it was mostly dry by now, it was still damp and uncomfortable. She put on Shirley's extra-large sleep shirt. It felt nice and dry.

Thank Heavens for the Coast Guard. She opened the thermos that Shirley had brought with her. The only thing missing in the coffee her was some Irish Cream.

≈≈≈≈≈≈

16. Across the Bay

Shirley and Troy drove Kate home to Goose Island. She was fast asleep by the time they crossed the Copano Bay Bridge at daybreak. If you hadn't been there when it happened, you might never know that it had occurred.

Kate struggled to wake up and stumbled out of the car when they reached her house on Marlin Ave. Charlotte ran out to meet her as soon as she arrived. It had been a long night and Shirley and Troy dropped Kate outside her house before continuing to the Bakery. Kate and Charlotte walked around the side of the house and went in the back entrance.

"I'm so glad you're okay, Kate," Charlotte said.

"Thanks Charlotte," Kate said.

"I want to hear everything that happened, Kate," Charlotte said. "I have been worried sick about you."

"Yes, Mother," Kate said.

"I'm going back to my house for a minute to pick up Baby Myrtle," Charlotte said. "Then I'll be right back to keep you company."

"Sounds good," Kate replied. "I'll leave the door open. I'm going to go up and change into some clean clothes. I should be back down shortly."

"You should lock the door, Kate," Charlotte said. "I have a key to your house, remember. You gave me one a long time ago and I still have it with me."

Kate locked the back door. She went upstairs to her room. There was no sign of anyone playing in the hallway or on the stairs. She lit the candle with the Virgin Mary on her bedside table and said a silent prayer. Then she went into the bath to take a shower. It felt good to stand naked in the shower and rinse off all traces of seaweed, slime, engine room grime and fish scales from her body. She put on some fresh underclothes, a clean white T-shirt and blue jeans.

"Better?" Charlotte asked, when Kate returned to the kitchen. She placed a steaming cup of coffee in front of Kate. Despite the early hour, Myrtle was wide awake. She gave Kate a big hug.

"Much better, thanks Charlotte," Kate replied. Myrtle rested her head comfortably on Kate's shoulder. "Thanks for coming over, and thanks for bring over this cute little baby girl." Kate wrapped her arms around Myrtle.

The baby giggled and tried to wiggle out of Kate's arms. Kate gave Myrtle a kiss. She had avenged the death of Myrtle's parents. It was a good feeling to know that henceforth, the baby was completely safe from Brady Red and the Drilling Rig Pirates he had commanded.

"I don't know how you do it, Kate," Charlotte replied. "When I saw you earlier today you looked terrible, but now you look as fresh as a daisy."

Thanks." Kate smiled. "It feels good to be home."

"What happened," Charlotte said. She had started mixing up some pancake batter in the kitchen.

"A lot," Kate replied. "I think we found out who killed Robert and Brenda."

"Was it Brady?" Charlotte asked. She held up the saucepan that she had just taken out of the kitchen cabinet. If Brady Red had been anywhere near her she would have given him a sound whack on the head with it.

"Yes," Kate said. "I'm not sure if he's the one who pulled the trigger, but he might as well have. How did you know?"

"Woman's intuition," Charlotte smiled, placing the saucepan on the stove.

Charlotte stayed on at the B&B and prepared some pancakes and eggs and placed them in front of Kate and Myrtle. Baby Myrtle loved Charlotte's pancakes. She nodded her head excitedly and attacked her pancakes with a vengeance. The girls loved watching the baby eat. Kate was famished and immediately devoured the meal that Charlotte placed before her.

Charlotte helped Kate get coffee and breakfast ready for the guests at the B&B. After breakfast, Kate excused herself and went up to her bedroom to catch some shut-eye. She drew the curtains and lit the candle of the Virgin Mary next to her bed. She said a silent prayer to thank the Lord for having protected her and Ray through the terrible night that she had lived through. Then she lay down on the bed and closed her eyes. She fell asleep immediately.

Charlotte cleared away what remained of the breakfast buffet. Before returning to her house with Myrtle, she went upstairs to check on Kate. She blew out the candle on the table next to Kate. Charlotte closed the door silently behind herself when she left.

* * *

Kate slept through the day. When she awoke, Kate went over to Charlotte and Jerry's house. Kate's station wagon was still missing and so she borrowed Jerry's truck to visit Ray in the hospital. Visiting hours were still open until seven in the evening. She tapped gently on the door to his room and walked softly into the room. It was a huge surprise for Ray. He broke down and cried when she entered the room.

"Oh Kate," Ray said "I'm so glad you're okay. I missed you so much."

"I missed you too, Ray," Kate said. "You have no idea how glad I am to see you."

She sat down beside him and held his hand. Ray whispered her name repeatedly and caressed her hand. He grasped it tightly, kissed it and placed it against his heart. They sat there like that for several minutes, just looking into each other's eyes, not saying a word.

"I love you, Kate," Ray said.

"I love you too," Kate replied.

Ray smiled. The room stopped spinning and he could hear the birds outside his window chirping in the sunshine. His world had been restored.

"I can't bear to think of living without you, Kate," Ray said. "Wherever you are, my heart is right beside you. Wherever you go, my heart goes too. Please don't leave me, Kate," he pleaded. I could not live with myself if anything bad had happened to you.

"I love you, Ray," Kate whispered. I'll never leave you. Never." She crossed her heart and bent down to kiss his lips. "Now settle down and get some rest. I need your help to finish the repairs on the Sea Goose."

They held hands for a long time. Kate sat down and made herself comfortable in the chair beside him. She had brought a few books to read and she stayed next to him until he fell asleep. She kissed him gently when she left his room. It was long after visiting hours and one of the nurses got up from the Nurses Station to unlock the door to let her out. She walked over to Jerry's white pick-up truck in the parking lot and drove home to Marlin Ave.

* * *

Lola returned to Goose Island in time to pick up a copy of the local newspaper describing the events that had transpired at Port Aransas. It did not take her long to deduce that Brady Red was involved with the death of her son and daughter in law.

"It says here that he just drove into his own fishing boat," Lola remarked. "That doesn't sound like a really smart thing to do."

"I know," Kate replied. "I don't think he had any idea where he was going."

"He probably had a little too much to drink, I would imagine," Lola said.

"Drunk as a skunk," Kate replied. "You know how those grizzly old seafaring pirates are. Just an accident waiting to happen."

"Well, I'm so glad he got his just desserts. I think his past caught up with him. Everything happens for a reason," Lola said.

"Yes," Kate said. "I think his past was halfway to Cuba when the Coast Guard yanked him back to Texas by his suspenders!"

Grandma Lola smiled. After reading the article from cover to cover a few times she went over to Charlotte's house. Grandma Lola had put her house in North Caroline up for sale and was planning to purchase a small house in Goose Island as soon as the sale was completed.

Before leaving Raleigh, Lola had visited her family attorney in North Carolina and drawn up the legal paper-work to nominate Charlotte and Jerry as Myrtle's legal guardians. There was a clause in the documents putting Kate in charge of Myrtle if anything should happen to Myrtle. Myrtle's trust fund would cover all her expenses until she was eighteen.

* * *

Ray was released from the hospital a few days later. He had been under observation at the hospital for a mild concussion following his injury. The doctors had been more concerned about the concussion than the shoulder injury. For the first days he was not eating properly and did not seem to be getting better. However, he had perked up so remarkably when Kate had stopped by to see him that there was no reason to keep him in the Ward any longer. Besides, he could not wait to finish the work on the wheelhouse of the Sea Goose, even though he would need help doing anything physical for the next few months.

Ray's shoulder injury was coming along nicely. It was heavily bandaged, and the bandages had to be changed periodically. It bothered him that he could not change the bandages himself.

They celebrated Ray's return with a sunset cruise around Copano Bay in the Sea Goose. Ralph greeted Ray with a wolf whistle and said "Hello, hello, hello," as he walked past the marina office. Kate and Ray, Shirley and Troy, Charlotte and Jerry, and Myrtle. Kate invited O'Connor to join them on the cruise. Kate had invited her house guests at the Goose Island B&B, Kevin and Karen Casey for the sunset cruise. It was a real treat for the couple from Minnesota, the Star of the North. Even though Minnesota is widely known as the land of ten thousand lakes, Kevin and Karen had never been on a sunset cruise before.

In a magnanimous gesture the owners of the Sea Goose thought fit to invite some of the Islanders, Don and Francesca Giordano, some of the staff at Giordano's, and Kenneth Porter. Kate had also invited O'Connor from the marina.

The wine flowed freely. It was not an expensive brand. One that was readily available for about few dollars a liter. Everybody had a great time. O'Connor had a blues harp in his pocket and he played a few tunes. Some of the guests danced on the deck. There was a pleasant breeze, good conversation, and the sunset was beautiful with several shades of amber that lingered on the horizon until the sky turned dark.

Shirley and Troy had a special announcement to make for the group. "Me and Troy," Shirley began tipsily, her face flushed with excitement. "Troy and Moi. We have decided to get married just as soon as we can make all the arrangements. You are all invited to the wedding."

Everybody on board on the Sea Goose applauded. Troy beamed.

Bridget, his future mother in law, blew him a kiss. She had wanted her daughter to marry this man for a long time. He was quite unlike some of the other fellows Shirley had dated while she was growing up. He didn't have any tattoos on his arms or legs, or anywhere else that she could see. He didn't drive a motorcycle. He was not a musician trying to tempt Shirley with anything stronger than an occasional beer or a glass of wine, and he looked cute in his police uniform and dark reflective glasses. The ones she had gotten him for Christmas.

Shirley's Dad, Sean walked up to Troy and shook his hand. They had had a little father son chat the previous day and Sean liked what he saw in Troy. A hard working, down to earth, honest man who would lay down his life for his daughter.

Ray squeezed Kate's hand. "We're already married, aren't we?" he asked her.

"Always have been and always will be," she replied. "However, I'm not taking any birth control pills. I'm not sure what the kids will say when they find out why their last name is different from yours."

"We might need to fix that," Ray said. "Any child of yours is a child of mine." Ray walked over to the wheel-house to take the controls from Jerry. It was time to bring the Sea Goose back to the marina.

* * *

Kate was standing next to Kenneth Porter after Ray left. His ears perked up when he heard Ray's remark.

"Sounds like you might have something in the oven, Sis", Ken said.

"I'm not pregnant, Ken" Kate said. "Not yet."

"Well let me know if you need any help," Ken said. "I think I know where we can find a father for your baby."

"I'm sure you're just the man for the job, Ken" Kate replied. "I'll be sure to call you as soon I need a donation."

Ken beamed. "I'll share my flounder with you," he said.

"I'm sure you would like to do that," Kate replied. "I guess you must have heard about Brady?" Kate asked.

"Yes, I heard he died in an accident near Port Aransas. He always paid his rent on time. It's, too bad," Ken replied.

"I guess so," Kate said. "I didn't really know him very well." If the newspapers had not reported the truth about Brady's demise, then she did not want to be the one to start spreading rumors about the cause of his death.

"He used to rent a warehouse from me," Ken replied. "I opened it up after he died. There was nothing in it. I thought that was strange. He must have just emptied it out the day before he passed away.

"Yes, that does sound strange," Kate said. "Is that the warehouse that has a new ramp? The one where you can back up a large van all the way up to the dock to load and unload your cargo?

Kate didn't have the heart to tell Ken that it really did not sound strange to her at all. Especially, if Brady was using the warehouse to hide a bunch of illegal immigrants. The warehouse would surely be empty as soon as the last illegal immigrant departed.

"Exactly," Ken replied. "That's the one. We had a nice ramp put in just last year to make it easier for the shippers to come and go. We even put in a small office in back with a nice restroom for the office staff to use. It even has a shower in it so that you can wash off if there's any kind of chemical spill or other mess in the warehouse."

"I bet that cost quite a bit?" Kate said.

"Oh, it cost a fortune," Ken replied. "However, it didn't cost me anything. Brady picked up all the expenses. I'm going to miss him," Ken said. "He always paid his rent on time."

"Your honor, I rest my case," Kate thought to herself. Flocks of pelicans coasted along the Copano Bay causeway. Myrtle clapped her hands excitedly when she spotted a dolphin swimming alongside the boat. Kevin and Karen took a photograph of themselves with the dolphin clearly visible in the water behind them.

Myrtle ran along the length of the boat screaming at the dolphins. Shirley chased after her to make sure she did not fall into the water by accident. When she picked Myrtle up the baby continued to point to the dolphins who were still swimming rhythmically alongside the boat. Myrtle started blowing bubbles. Shirley tickled her and asked her if she was a dolphin. Myrtle nodded.

Kate had baked some cookies for all the guests and she handed each person a goody bag with the treats as they stepped off the boat. She had packed a few extra in a special bag that she had saved for O'Connor. He was more than grateful with the goody bag she handed him when he stepped off the boat at the end of the cruise.

"You're the best, Ms. Kate," O'Connor said.

"Thanks," Kate said.

Less than a minute later Kate heard a loud wolf whistle and Ralph's familiar voice said "Hello, Sweetie," to O'Connor as he walked past the Marina office. Kate smiled. Ralph had just doubled his vocabulary. There was no telling what Ralph was capable of with an extra ration of apple slices and grapes.

Kate placed the little wooden duck she had recovered from the Sea Goose on the dashboard in the wheel-house. Kate smiled to herself. It was funny how her cookies had helped to hold Brady Red accountable for his actions.

≈≈≈≈≈≈

17. Just Ducky

Shirley and Troy's wedding was long overdue. Everyone on Goose Island knew that Troy was madly in love with Shirley. He had been love-struck from his first day on the police force when he had pulled Shirley over for having a burned-out tail light at the Goose Island Town Square. Shirley had just parked outside the Goose Island Bakery early one morning. She had turned off her car keys and was about to step out of the driver's seat when she was met with a rude surprise.

Troy flashed his police lights for a moment, parked next to her, and appeared beside her just as she had placed one foot on the pavement and was about to get out of her car. Shirley's dress had ridden up her thigh and she didn't need to be a rocket scientist to know that he was staring at her white lace petticoat underneath her dress while he wrote out a citation for the tail light.

Troy's first words to Shirley were "Did you know you have beautiful tail lights?"

"I do?" Shirley giggled. "Why thank you officer!" She had no earthly idea what he was talking about. He was obviously a very handsome fellow, but she was a little uncomfortable with the intense way they he was looking at her. Besides, what was all this foolishness about her tail lights.

"I mean you have a beautiful tail," Troy continued.

Shirley laughed. "You do too," she said cheerfully. She was still devoid of any clue as to what the problem was.

"Please sign here," Troy added, handing her the citation. "It's not an admission of guilt, but you will have to get a new light bulb. Your left tail light is burned out."

When Shirley had found out that she was being issued a citation that she could ill afford to pay she had given him a good piece of her mind. No doubt she would continue to do so for many years to come. The sound of her voice berating him for pulling her over when he could be looking for hardened criminals still echoed like a soft sweet melody that had continued to whirl around his head like sound of the surf, or a pair of dickey birds going tweet-tweet-tweet.

Shirley had called him a Dimwit, and rumor has it that this information found its way to the local Sherriff's Department because his peers called him DW behind his back for years.

The incident was resolved when Troy appeared at the Bakery at the end of the day with a toolbox and a fresh light bulb and offered to change the light bulb at no charge.

The wedding was held late in the afternoon the day before Mother's Day, the second Sunday in May, on Shipwreck Beach. The wedding invitation specified "Hawaiian" attire, and everyone present wore bright, festive shirts. Guests were given a brightly colored lei necklace to wear. When it was time for the wedding, the guests took their seats in front of the altar. Shirley's mother Bridget began playing "Can't Help Falling in Love" on a portable keyboard that had been placed beside the altar. Bridget face was aglow with pleasure. She was beaming. She sang the chorus to the song as she played it and hummed the rest of the tune.

There was a red carpet leading up to the altar. Baby Myrtle was the flower girl. She walked along slowly reaching in her basket to toss out a few petals after every few steps. She tripped on her dress as she approached the altar. The flowers tumbled out of her basket and spilled out on the sand. Myrtle proceeded to pick up the petals and put them back in her basket. Myrtle got a huge hand of applause when she continued down the aisle and finally made it up to the altar. Kate scooped her up and gave her a kiss. Myrtle wrinkled her nose, narrowed her lips, scrunched up her cheeks, and made a stink face at Kate and everybody smiled.

Lola had returned from North Carolina in time for the wedding. During her trip to the East Coast she had met with an attorney, changed her will, and created a trust fund to help pay for Myrtle's expenses until she turned twenty-five. Lola was seated in the row behind Kate and she leaned forward to say hello to her granddaughter. Myrtle rewarded her the same cross-eyed stink face that she had shared with Kate. Lola leaned back happily in her seat and smiled at Baby Myrtle.

Bridget started playing "Here comes the bride" and the guests stood up and turned to look behind them. Shirley came down the aisle with her Dad, Sean. Her flowing peach outfit looked magnificent. Sean looked remarkable in the blue suit he had borrowed from Jerry. He could have passed for a banker, except for the pony tail that held his thin grey hair together.

Shirley decided against wearing a white dress. She had picked out a Corpus Christi coral colored wedding dress. Troy wore a blue suit, a white shirt and a striped blue and peach regimental tie that matched the colors in Shirley's dress. It was the perfect complement to Shirley's coral colored dress.

"Nice tie," Shirley said when she saw him for the first time that evening.

"Just for you, my love," Troy replied.

They exchanged wedding vows. Troy added a few more 'evers' when he said he would love her forever and ever and ever and ever and ever and ever and ever and ever.

"I know," Shirley said. "That's why we are getting married, silly boy."

The audience laughed as Shirley leaned forward and gave him a peck on the cheek. She also reached over surreptitiously and squeezed his behind. "And because you are always as hard as a rock," Shirley added.

That brought the house down. It was a very special moment. One that was captured on camera and which would live on forever in their wedding videos.

The marriage ceremony was performed by Jesse, the Coast Guard Captain. Jesse went about his business very efficiently and ended the wedding with a blessing for the married couple. Pretty soon Troy heard him say "You may kiss the bride," and Troy wasted no time in doing just that.

* * *

After the wedding the guests headed over to the Goose Island Town Square. Shirley had planned a small reception in the small park in the Town Square, just outside city hall. Wedding guests were encouraged to bring beach umbrellas and lawn chairs to the event. The main seating area consisted of rows of picnic benches with Hawaiian themed tablecloths held in place by river rocks. Tiki torches and patio lights provided a festive touch to the occasion. Olga, the county clerk had taken the time do decorate each of the tables with small placards with witty sayings and conversation starters.

One of the tables had a sign that said, 'You Stole a Pizza My Heart'. Another one read 'I'm Muffin Without You'. A third read, 'Nacho Average Bride'. All the cards had a culinary theme, and each one brought a chuckle from the guests who sat down at the table.

Wedding guests meandered over to the park in ones and twos from Shipwreck Beach. Before long the Square was overflowing with a large happy crowd. There was plenty of parking for everyone and no one needed to worry about getting towed away from the Goose Island Town Square since Troy was too busy to be out writing parking tickets. Troy had delegated the responsibility to Olga, and she was too busy serving Mango Margaritas to bother with her administrative responsibilities.

Olga had become an expert in the fine art of making Mango Margaritas in just one short evening. She added just enough mangos and ice to the blender to make sure that the margaritas were nicely creamy and frosty. This was followed with tequila and a sweet orange liquor to give it the tangy taste that she liked. And, yes, she had to taste each batch several times to make sure it was done to perfection. She poured the drinks into disposable glasses and placed them on a table in front of her. She made sure that kids got the non-alcoholic version.

Shirley had hired the house band from the Swamp Shack to play at the reception. They had set up their musical gear at the top of the steps leading to City Hall. They had been given strict instructions not to play any sad songs and for the moment they were content to play "Donde Estas Yolanda."

The lead singer, Michelle, was an attractive woman with a lot of energy. She had a beautiful set of pearly white teeth to go with the brilliant smile that she flashed at the audience each time she opened her mouth. She made sure everyone had a great time and provided announcements and updates on the dinner menu and reception arrangements between songs.

The band seemed to come together around her and the guitar player was playing musical riffs with an energy that seemed to flow between them. Each time he jerked his body she moved her hips with a rhythm that was infectious. The accordion player, Carmine was Don Giordano's son and he added a blues touch to the music that infused the Goose Island Town Square with joy and laughter.

Myrtle, the flower girl, followed Shirley around the venue. Myrtle was wearing a peach dress that matched Shirley's wedding dress. If there was one person at the reception who looked more beautiful than the bride, it had to be Baby Myrtle. She was as cute as a button. Shirley had her in her arms as she greeted the guests.

The reception included a mixer for the guests to mingle with drinks and appetizers, to be followed by wedding cake, and a wedding dance. Food at the reception was catered by Don Giordano and his wife Francesca. Francesca served a fresh garden salad with greens and Roma tomatoes that she had harvested from her own vegetable garden. Dinner was a delicious lasagna with several layers of paper-thin pasta filled with ricotta cheese, onions, peppers, and sausage. There was even a table with baked chocolate drop cookies and even a large basket full of Pig-Ears.

*   *   *

Kate and Ray caught up with Shirley and Troy at the reception after the wedding.

"Congratulations," Kate said.

"Yes, indeed," Ray added. "You make a beautiful couple."

"You're next, buddy," Troy said.

"You're dead meat!" Shirley said.

"Thanks." Ray smiled. "Anytime she's ready, I'll be at her beck and call. I'm looking forward to it." He could think of nothing better than to spend the rest of his life with Kate.

Troy knew exactly what Ray meant. He gave Shirley a little squeeze.

"Hey, watch it buster," Shirley said. "Just because we're married doesn't mean you can move into my space any time you want." She gave him a friendly shove and pushed him back to a safe distance.

Troy looked disappointed.

"You need to wait till we get home and then you can come as close to me as you want," Shirley said.

Kate smiled. It might be fun to spend the rest of her life with Ray, but she had not mentioned this to him. They had both agreed that there was no need to change their relationship or rock the boat in any way. However, it had been nice to wake up in the morning and find him sleeping in her bed every morning for the last few months.

Kate spotted Jesse at the end of the room. She gave him a big wave and he came over to join the small group at one end of the reception area. Jesse brought Cindy with him. She had on a sparkling, sequined outfit and looked more like a movie star than a DEA agent.

"Thanks for sending the Coast Guard out to rescue me the other day," she said.

"You're welcome," Jesse said. He handed her a small package. "This is a small gift for you."

Kate opened the package that she received from Jesse. It contained two small wooden ducks. One of the ducks was a little larger than the other. She examined them carefully and turned them over. The signature crossbones shaped 'X' followed by a date was clearly visible. The date was the same as the one on the duck that Kate had found on the PharmaSea. "

We found these in the wreckage that was floating around near the Blue Horizon," Jesse said.

"I guess Robert and Brenda just happened to be at the wrong place at the wrong time," Kate said.

"That's pretty much what happened," Cindy replied. "Very unfortunate. The Mexican vessel who dropped off the human cargo mistook the PharmaSea for Captain Brady's fishing boat. The Mexicans dropped their human cargo off on some rubber rafts similar to the one that we found Baby Myrtle on and left to go home."

"Sounds like they just tossed everybody overboard and left almost immediately," Kate said.

"Exactly", Jesse replied. "I think the bad weather had something to do with it. I don't think they could get too terribly close to the PharmaSea. Just close enough to latch on to the bow with a hook and then they throw everybody over with instructions to pull themselves aboard the shrimp boat."

"Wow," Kate said. "That could be a challenge in good weather. I can't imagine anyone doing it in a storm. "

"The storm did not reach El Sombrero until a few hours later. We think the attack took place around 11:00 pm. Rough seas, no doubt, but no storm. It's not easy to transfer people from one ship to the other at sea," Jesse said. "Just hard work."

"I hate to think what happened next," Kate said.

"I know," Jesse replied. "Very tragic. After the Mexican vessel left the area there were several unsavory individuals floating on inflatable tubes in the water. The tubes were linked to each other with ropes, and one of the individuals tossed a line over to the PharmaSea. After that all the illegals hauled themselves over to the PharmaSea and clambered aboard before they realized they were on the wrong boat."

"Robert and Brenda were probably asleep at the time," Kate said.

"Exactly. Otherwise they would have noticed what was taking place and would have had a better chance to defend themselves. What happened next is not surprising. The pirates attacked Robert and Brenda and commandeered the PharmaSea."

"Couldn't they have worked out some type of deal with Robert and Brenda?" Kate asked.

"I'm not sure why they killed Robert and Brenda," Cindy replied. "I think some people delight in violence. It seems to give them power over others. We tracked down several hundred individuals who had entered the country illegally with Brady Red's assistance. The photographs you had taken at the Port Aransas Marina helped tremendously. We were able to locate everyone who entered Texas the night you and Ray were at the Port Aransas Marina. They led us to many of the other individuals who Brady had shipped into Texas on earlier night-crawler trips. All the individuals whom we could find were just the dregs of society. The worst type of human being you could hope to meet. When someone enters the US illegally they are usually running away from the past."

"I know," Kate said. "If they could enter the US legally there would be no reason for them to pay huge sums of money to a smuggler to come in through the back door. It's too bad."

"Yes, it is," Cindy continued. "We also found your station wagon."

"Oh really," Kate said. She had just bought a herself a nice new Jeep with the money she had received from the Insurance Company for the loss of her station wagon. It would be very inconvenient if she had to give it back. "Where was the station wagon?"

"It was literally in the bottom of the ocean," Jesse replied. "Rusty, or Mongo, whoever drove it into the Gulf wasn't very smart. At low tide we could see the rear end sticking out of the ocean."

"I agree. That wasn't very smart," Kate replied. "I would have driven it over the Dolphin Dock. The water is deeper there."

"Good thing you're not a criminal," Cindy said. "We would never catch you."

"Thanks." Kate smiled. It was always nice to receive a compliment.

"We also found the binoculars that fell out of your hands when you were attacked. The memory stick was still in it. You took some great pictures. They gave us enough information to lead us to the people who had been involved in the tragedy on the PharmaSea. What happened on the PharmaSea was not pretty."

"Oh," Kate said.

"Here is what we learned from the illegals," Cindy continued. "One of them was a gang leader called Paco who was running from the Federales in Mexico. He would kill his own mother if she got in his way. Paco found Robert and Brenda asleep on the PharmaSea. He attacked them because he wanted to rape Brenda. Robert died trying to protect her. After Paco shot Robert, Brenda tried to defend herself with a knife and cut him several times during the attack. However, he ended up overpowering her. He was in a rage, and he stabbed her repeatedly. She managed to get away from him and he shot her as she was trying to jump overboard to escape. The baby fell into the ocean and landed on one of the inflatable tubes that the illegals had used to board the PharmaSea. Baby Myrtle floated away into the darkness and ended up on Goose Island where she was rescued by Shirley and yourself."

"Oh, my," Kate said quietly. "That is so very sad. I am so very sorry."

"Me too," Cindy said. "It is indeed, most unfortunate. Everything happens for a reason. Perhaps Robert and Brenda lost their lives so that we could catch these criminals and prevent them from causing more harm to others. In any case, when Blue Horizon showed up some time later they set the PharmaSea on fire to attract attention to themselves and then everyone on the PharmaSea transferred across to the Blue Horizon."

"You were also right about Virginia Bradenton," Jesse said. "We went back and interviewed some of the shrimpers about Brady Red and they confirmed our suspicions. His real name was Elliott Bradenton. He was forced to leave the Shrimping business because the shrimpers ostracized him after Virginia disappeared.

The shrimpers knew he had had something to do with Virginia's death. When she disappeared, they refused to have anything to do with him. He could not get anyone to help him man the Shrimp Boat. Nobody came forward to alert the authorities of their suspicions about Brady. Some of the shrimpers were new immigrants from Vietnam. It must be a cultural thing. When Virginia went missing they did not feel comfortable going to the authorities."

"I guess he used the Blue Horizon for his Fishing Charters and kept the old Shrimping vessel for the night-crawler stuff," Troy said. "The money from the night-crawler runs probably helped finance the purchase of the Blue Horizon and his lavish lifestyle."

"We didn't actually catch him with any narcotics," Cindy replied. "However, there's no reason that he could not have been involved in drug smuggling on the side. We'll have to keep a close watch on things for a few months to see if anyone else steps up to fill the human trafficking vacuum Brady left behind when he died."

"How did Brady gain possession of the wooden ducks that O'Connor had carved?" Kate inquired. "Was O'Conner mixed up in the human trafficking network in some way?"

"Funny you should mention that. We talked to O'Connor about the ducks," Troy said. "The set of three ducks was a gift from O'Conner to Robert Rhodes. He gave the ducks to Robert Rhodes for helping him jump-start his car in the marina. It was late one evening when he was about to go home for the day. He had been at work since the early hours of the morning and had accidentally left his lights on. He has an old Dodge Plymouth and the lights don't turn off automatically. When Robert helped him out he had no money to pay Robert for his services, so he gave him a set of three wooden ducks."

"One of the illegals found two of the ducks on the PharmaSea," Jesse continued. "He took them with him when the illegals transferred across to Brady's fishing boat. The illegal probably did not know there was a third duck. When they reached Port Aransas the illegal was so excited to be in Texas that he hopped off the fishing boat without the ducks. Captain Brady found the ducks on his fishing boat the next day. He liked them a lot and took them with him. Later, he put them up on the dashboard of the control room of the Blue Horizon. Captain Brady had no idea where they had come from or how we were able to use the ducks to connect the Blue Horizon in the vicinity of the PharmaSea on the day of the murders."

"I would never have suspected Captain Brady if I had not seen the ducks in the wheel house of the Blue Horizon," Kate said.

"It's a really nice carving," Jesse replied. "However, O'Connor had nothing to do with the tragedy. The ducks just helped us piece together the tragic events that transpired on the PharmaSea."

"There is one other thing," Cindy said. "You were right. There was another child in the boat. It was Robert and Brenda's son Allen. He is about three years old."

"Oh my goodness," Kate replied. "Are you serious? What happened to Allen?"

"Completely serious," Cindy said. "Allen was kidnapped by the illegals. Brady auctioned the child off to a family in California.

They paid him six figures for the boy. Allen was rescued a few days ago and we are in the process of reuniting him with Grandma Rhodes."

"That's amazing," Kate said. "Grandma Rhodes was expecting to meet her grandson Allen when she first came to Goose Island. I'm sure she's going to be delighted to see him."

"Allen should be here within a few days," Cindy added. "I hope it's okay if he comes here to live with you for the foreseeable future."

"Well of course," Kate replied. "It's more than okay. We'd love to have him." In an instant, Kate could picture Allen playing with little yellow cars, and red pick-up trucks in her hallway at the Goose Island B&B. Her house would never be the same again. She couldn't wait to take Allen and Ellen to the beach! Her life would never be the same again.

"Once we had the illegals in our custody we were able to discern what had happened to Allen," Cindy continued. "Finding Allen helped us locate several additional children who had been separated from their families. You have no idea, what a difference you have made in their lives."

"Thanks," Kate replied. She was overwhelmed at the thought of reuniting Allen and Myrtle.

"It's too bad about the PharmaSea and all that happened to Robert and Brenda Rhodes. It might take us awhile to find a cure for cancer without their research," Troy added.

"I know," Kate said. "However, it sure feels good to be able to serve up a heaping helping of some good old Texas Medicine!"

"That old buzzard had it coming," Jesse said.

"He sure did," Kate said.

"It was a lucky break when he drove right into his own fishing boat," Jesse said. "I guess he got careless and forgot to secure it. It was just drifting around in the Gulf when he drove into it. We would have had to chase him for hours if he had not crashed into it. It was very foggy later that night when we caught up with him. I think that he might even have been able to get away in the darkness. Even with instruments it's hard to chase someone down on the open sea in a dense fog.

"Did you know that Charlotte saw him at the Emergency Room of the Hospital the day we found Myrtle," Kate said. "I wonder if he had to take someone in for treatment. I would have mentioned it sooner, but only found out about it recently."

"Makes sense," Jesse replied. "Someone could have been injured in the altercation on the PharmaSea. We'll be sure to look into it."

Kate smiled. She had not told anyone how she had escaped the fishing boat. Some things are better left unsaid. Her friends would only worry about her if she left them know what she had been through. For the moment her secret was safe with Mongo who was going to spend the next ten years swabbing floors in the Huntsville State Penitentiary.

There is something about a near-death experience that changes you forever. Kate felt very fortunate to be alive. She did not want to mar the celebratory spirit of the occasion with the details of her escapade on board the fishing vessel or her encounter with Brady Red and Mongo and their veiled threats involving whipping cream.

For the moment she simply wanted to enjoy her best friend's wedding and make it a memorable occasion for Shirley and Troy. Later she had plans for Ray. Plans that could involve whipping cream if the sun moon and stars lined up for the two of them when they returned home after the wedding.

* * *

Shirley's mother, Bridget had baked the wedding cake. As the original owner of the Goose Island Bakery, Bridget proved that she had not lost her touch. She had baked a passionfruit, mango wedding cake that had been beautifully decorated with soft white swirls of creamy coconut buttercream.

Kate and Charlotte took turns holding Myrtle through the cake cutting ceremony. Myrtle went to great pains to eat her cake with a spoon. She wanted to do it all by herself but eventually gave in and let Kate feed her. Charlotte took lots of pictures of the wedded couple and Baby Myrtle.

Just then the house band from the Swamp Shack started playing the Hawaiian Wedding Song. Troy turned to Shirley and led her to the dance floor.

The audience gave them a big hand when they began their first dance together as a couple. Shirley picked up the end of her peach wedding dress with her left hand, so she would not trip over it. She looked as beautiful as a flower in May and her body seemed to flow out of the fabric. Everybody applauded as the song ended. Troy and Shirley made a wonderful couple and it showed with every step that they took across the dance floor.

After Troy and Shirley's dance ended, the next dance was the father-daughter dance with Shirley and Sean. They danced to 'Hawaiian Country Roads' version first performed by Iz Kamakawiwo'ole. Finally, Troy danced with Charlotte. His parents had passed away a few years ago. Charlotte had offered to be his Mom for the evening. They danced to a tune by Waylon Jennings called 'Good Hearted Woman'.

* * *

The next song was a C&W Blues tune called 'Millionaire'. Several couples in the audience drifted on over to the dance floor. Ray took Kate's arm in his hand and led her to the dance floor.

He placed his hand around Kate's waist as they danced the Texas two-step across the dance floor. Just like the lyrics in the song, Ray could not help feeling that he had to be the luckiest man in the world. She was the four-leaf clover that he had found, or was it the other way around? The four-leaf clover who had found him! Being with Kate made him feel that he was a millionaire, with a love more precious than diamonds or gold.

Kate had made a huge difference in his life. She had inspired him to succeed beyond his wildest imagination and was his only true friend and companion. They had shared so many incredible experiences together that he treasured her company more than anything else in the world. She was so unpredictable that he could never take her for granted. He looked forward to every next moment with anticipation, never knowing what lay ahead, only that it would be infinitely more exciting because he was able to share it with her.

"I love you Kate," he whispered in her ear as they made their way across the floor.

"Love you too," Kate replied. She pulled him close and kissed him. Just like their first date. Three short kisses that left no doubt in his mind that she loved him as much today as the very first time they had met.

Kate felt as though she was floating on air as the lyrics and the music wafted the air. She held his hand and twirled around the dance floor happy and content in the knowledge that his love was more precious than all the gold in the California.

* * *

The music and the dancing continued for the next few hours. Several people in the wedding reception were on the dance floor gyrating to the rhythm of the music and everybody seemed to have a smile on their face. The fellows from the Swamp Band had shifted to a Cajun-Reggae-Island rhythm and even Grandma Lola could not help tapping her feet to the beat of the music.

Kate saw Kenneth Porter making his way around the dance floor with Wanda Gleeson. They seemed to be having a grand old time. Wanda seemed to be hanging on to every word Ken whispered in her ear. "Oh well!" Kate thought. "You never can tell. She's too good for him, but I guess there's nothing wrong with it as long as he treats her with respect."

Myrtle was the star of the show as she showed off the dance moves that she had learned from Shirley. She danced until she could dance no more and then she curled up in Charlotte's lap and fell sound asleep.

"Now that's what I call being plumb tuckered out," said Grandma Lola when stopped by Charlotte's table and looked at Myrtle sleeping contentedly on Charlotte's shoulder. "Sleeping like a Baby!"

"I know," Charlotte said. "It's a wonderful feeling when a little baby falls asleep on your shoulder. There's nothing like it in the world."

Mango margaritas were served with a side of Jumbo, batter fried bioluminescent shrimp appetizers.

"I've heard some of the shrimpers at the marina say that bioluminescent shrimp are known in local circles to have some pretty powerful properties as an aphrodisiac," Kate said.

"You're the best aphrodisiac in the world, Kate" Ray said. "There's more magic in your smile, than in all the bioluminescent shrimp in Texas." He reached for one of the shrimps and bit into it slowly. "Taste's pretty good," he remarked. "Let's go home for some dessert soon."

Kate's eyes twinkled back at him in the glow of the party lights that had been strung through the trees of the Goose Island Square. She moved closer to Ray and entwined her hand in his and placed it on her thigh under the table. Kate squeezed his hand and turned to give him three short kisses. One short kiss followed by two more in quick succession. The touch of her lips against his never failed to rekindle the spirit of togetherness they had shared since their very first date. Three tender kisses. The first that said "I love you", and two more that said "I can't wait to see you again." This was Kate's signature move, the promise of the precious moments they would always share together.

And yet, he had almost lost her forever just a few short days earlier. Things change, and Ray knew the day would come when one of them would have to learn to live without the other. "Just let me die the day before you go," Ray thought as he held her hand and breathed the fragrance that she exuded.

* * *

The wedding ended with the departure of the bride and groom. Troy had rented a bright red pickup for the occasion and Ray drove it to the front of the circular driveway of the Goose Island courthouse. It had freshly scribbled 'Just Married' lettering on the rear window, and a few empty beer cans strung out behind it.

The guests left the reception area ahead of the bride and groom and stood on either side of the garden path leading to their truck. A basket of rose petals was passed around and everyone took a handful of petals to throw at the newly married couple as they were leaving. The Swamp Shack Band started playing 'She'll be Coming Around the Mountain' and the wedding guests started to chant along to the melody.

The bride and groom were held in check until everyone was ready for them to leave. They made a dash down the path to the truck parked in the driveway. Rose petals rained on them from both sides of the path and a few of the petal stayed on Shirley's dress as she hiked it up to hop in the cab of the pickup truck next to Troy. When the doors were closed, Shirley and Ray waved goodbye through the open windows and drove off into the moonlit night for their very first night together as a couple.

When it was all over Kate and Ray stayed to help with the clean-up. Flower arrangements that had been used to adorn the reception area were handed out to departing guests to take home with them. Don Giordano and Francesca supervised their staff to help clear away any food that remained. The Swamp Shack Band packed up their gear and returned to the Swamp Shack. The night was still young and there was a full moon. There was still time for one more set of music to continue the party at the Swamp Shack.

Ray persuaded Kate to stop by the Swamp Shack for a night cap. When the band started up again they began with a Blues tune called 'Lady in Red'. Ray took Kate's hand and took her out to the dance floor.

"This song describes exactly how perfect you are, Kate," Ray said. "I cannot believe that I'm standing beside you tonight."

"Thanks," Kare smiled. "It is my favorite color."

"We should get married, Kate," Ray whispered.

"Now why would we do that when you already have everything you could ever desire from me?" Kate asked.

"I don't know, Kate," Ray said. "We just should."

"All right then," she said. "The truth is that I'd love to be your bride. Any time, any day, anywhere. However, you do know that this indirect, weak-kneed, insouciant proposal doesn't count!"

So, Ray got down on one knee and asked Kate, the love of his life, for her hand in holy matrimony.

Everyone at the Swamp Shack stopped what they were doing when they saw what was going on in the middle of the dance floor. They formed a small circle around the couple and started to chant, "Yes, yes, yes!" softly, barely mouthing the words in a whisper. The expressions of the group surrounding Kate and Ray grew increasingly more emphatic until she accepted his proposal and lifted his spirit with her three short kisses. The group applauded, and a cheer broke out when Ray slipped a ring on her middle finger. It could have been a mood ring from a box of Crackerjack popcorn, and Kate would have liked it no less than the beautiful hand-crafted gold ring that she now wore engraved with the letters 'Je t'aime' on the inside.

Kate and Ray left the Swamp Shack a short time later. The stars twinkled in the night sky as they walked towards their car in the parking lot. The moon shone with a silvery light and the swish of the palm trees in the sea breeze seemed to whisper a blessing, as if to say, "Enjoy this perfect moment together. Especially tonight, and every night that you have each other. Here is another chance to make lasting memories to cherish forever."

≈≈≈≈≈≈

www.ingramcontent.com/pod-product-compliance
Lightning Source LLC
LaVergne TN
LVHW020657110826
845149LV00012B/2024
9780991321315